Godcountry
A Star Brothers Adventure

Colleen Drippé

Proxima Centauri

ST MARY'S, KS

Proxima Centauri
St Mary's, KS

Publisher's Note: This is a work of fiction. Names, characters, places, and incidents are a product of the author's imagination. Locales and public names are sometimes used for atmospheric purposes. Any resemblance to actual people, living or dead, or to businesses, companies, events, institutions, or locales is completely coincidental.

Book Layout © 2017 BookDesignTemplates.com
Cover art by Joseph Drippé

Godcountry/ Colleen Drippé. –2nd ed.
ISBN 9798323509706

Dedication

I never seem to run out of special people and the occasion of issuing this new edition of Godcountry is no exception. I would like to dedicate this book to a few of the most valiant people I know. First, Allen Shoff, writer, website builder, father and teacher to his multiple and growing family of children. To Matthew P Schmidt, author of The City and the Dungeon, who just keeps on overcoming obstacle after obstacle. And finally to my artist son Joseph Drippé who does my covers when he isn't working to support his wife and four children.

CONTENTS

CHAPTER ONE

I have been told my name is Eduardo Sabat, and certainly that is the name I have used for all of my life. But who I truly am, only God can say.

Years ago, I saw my face reflected in a pool of deathwater on a world far from here. That water was perfectly clear, bluer than the skies of earth, as though both light and color had been imprisoned unwillingly within that otherwise innocent element. And for those few moments, so was I.

There I beheld my own dark features, eyes shadowed, nose hooked like that of an Arab. My hair is black and curly with a tiny bit of grey, but I could not see it because I was wearing a protective helmet at the time. I needed a shave, I noted. I did not stay long in that place.

The seas of Sachsen are a different blue, warmer and more turquoise-hued, and they give no reflection at all. The water seems milky compared to the seas of earth, and I used to wonder if it would stay like that if I dipped some up in a cup. Once I borrowed a bucket from one of the children on the beach and tried it. To our mutual surprise, the water was perfectly clear and we rejoiced together in our discovery.

Sachsen is a pleasant world. I have often wished I might spend more time in Bloomhadn, that sprawling, vaguely Teutonic city where the sea and the flowers, the beggars and bricks and the soaring metalplast towers all come together in such loveliness that you hardly notice the sadness in the city's depths. It is as though the darkness that takes the streets each night is no more than a dream, that violence and sorrow pass away each morning at the rising of the suns.

I kept an apartment there, in the Crescent Tower, a privilege of membership in the Crescent Club. To my regret, I had not been completely honest with the committee when they accepted me, but there was no choice. Though my permanent Sachsen visa was bona fide, my citizenship papers were not. I claimed to be an earthman, which I truly was, but I was not a citizen of that world. My homeland, if I had any, was the now defunct Feullier Corporation, my badge of membership, the slave band that still encircled one wrist.

Feullier. I smile grimly at the memory of that deadly pool and wonder even now at the folly of the pilgrimage I made to see it. When Net Central struck—or whichever enemy of the corporation it was—my freedom flared for all to see, brighter than the triple suns of Sachsen. My bondage dissipated with the dust that slowly rained to the ground, blowing death to half a continent. Because Feullier had never entrusted its codes to the starnet, all its records were vaporized along with the main computer. I was free.

That had happened six years ago subtime and, even though I now had no legal existence anywhere, I soon found myself doing almost exactly the same sorts of things I had done as a slave. I was a professional looter of archeological sites and, along with a few other jobs here and there, I was making a good living.

"Search and rescue," Otto Zeller said to me one evening. This was the sort of thing we sometimes did together and I waited for him to go on.

We sat in the open air, though rainclouds threatened, and I drank wine while he had beer. There were other tables and lots of flowering shrubs and before us, a long terrace that led down to the sea. Otto did not live in Bloomhadn and he did not like the city much.

"On Quele," he added and suddenly the wine lost its savor. Quele was where I had mostly worked as a slave, looting the extensive—and forbidden—burial grounds. One of my friends had died there and I had no wish to return.

"It's a special job," Otto said, seeing me stiffen. "Otherwise I would not have asked you, Herr Sabat."

Otto was always very formal with me. He thought I needed to be called Herr Sabat to make up for all the times my human dignity was violated in the past. He was one of the few people who knew I used to belong to Feullier and I considered him as a friend. However, I called him Otto.

"I see," I said slowly, remembering.

There had only been one team of us on Quele, the elite, if I might use such a word to describe slaves. Six slaves, to be precise, and two free contractors. The last I heard, another of the former slaves was dead and one of the contractors was in prison.

"Godcountry," I said and my voice came out all wrong.

"Godcountry," Otto confirmed. "Can you get us in?"

I told him I could. "How many?"

"Three—including you."

I drained my glass and refilled it. Bloomhadn's skies are always misty, but tonight a heavy bank of cloud reflected the lights of the city. We almost never saw the stars here. "It's been a while, Otto," I said. "There will be changes."

"Political?"

I snorted. "Quele's politics never change. But Godcountry— that's different."

Zeller scowled at the pier lights. "This is going to be rather difficult, Herr Sabat. The rescue, I mean. The search will be unnecessary."

I watched as a few drops of rain spattered onto my hand. At nearby tables, umbrellas unfurled, but we did not activate ours immediately.

"He'll be in the temple complex by now. And almost certainly a prisoner."

"Ah." I turned my face up to the rain, but after a few seconds, I decided I'd had enough and flipped the umbrella stud. "Looter?" I asked, though I knew very well no looter would be worth Otto's fee, or mine. Looters were expendable. Feullier had taught me that and it was a lesson so deeply instilled that I would sooner have forgotten my name.

"It is an interesting story, Herr Sabat. I hesitated to believe it at first, but certain things have led me to take the job."

"I'm listening," I told him. The rain was cool and pleasant all around us, and the smell of wet stone and the perfume of the flowers soothed me. It was good to smell the smell of Sachsen and to know that for now at least, I was not on Quele.

"I was asked by a particular friend," Otto began. "You have not met him. His name is Father Liu—of the Star Brothers."

I looked up in surprise. "The Star Brothers? Is it one of theirs?"

"No, no. Nothing like that. His name is Hermradon Pelanot and he's a net engineer. From Hithia Colony, though he was educated on earth."

The name Pelanot meant nothing to me, but everyone had heard of the Star Brothers. They could be found on most colonies and it was said they went places where even Conpol dared not go. And when one considered that Conpol, Net Central's own intelligence division, was more likely to generate dread than to feel it, that really meant something.

"Go on," I prompted, sitting back, glass in hand. I knew that Otto himself was a Christian, but aside from certain scruples and an occasional intrusion of customs that were part of his ethnic heritage, the matter had never come up between us. Certainly I had not known he had any connection with the Star Brothers.

Otto went on. "Hermradon is the son of Hithia's colony autarch," he said. "He was lost about a month ago subtime while examining tendrils along the Quele nexus. Hithia," he added, "is contiguous to Quele."

I snorted in disgust. "Tendrils? Come on, Otto. The net is the net and it opens a quarter of a million miles above the planet. If he got lost, he's still in there."

"The Star Brothers say not and I am quite sure they made a thorough investigation. They still have a few starships of their own, you know, and they keep expert technicians on call."

I shrugged. "Alright, Otto. Forgive the interruption."

"Tendrils," he went on as he watched a beggar make the rounds of the tables, "are breakups of the net. They are not readily navigable and regular starships neither use them nor register their existence. But pilots say—"

Forgetting my apology, I interrupted him again. "I've never met a pilot I could trust. They live on drugs, Otto."

Meanwhile, I, too, was watching the beggar, a child of undetermined sex, wrapped in some dark stuff down to the ankles. A shock of wiry hair protruded at the top, apparently unaffected by the rain.

"I will not argue that," Otto said mildly. "However you must know there are private ships—not many because the Net Central cruisers are safer. Few of the old sort are built these days."

"So this Pelanot—"

"Prince Hermradon," Otto corrected me. "Hithians insist on proper titles."

"Prince, then," I said in exasperation. "He took a private ship and—Did he have a pilot?"

"He had one," Otto said. "For backup."

"So he set off from Hithia to explore these tendrils?"

The beggar had arrived at our table and Otto, who is a family man despite his dangerous profession, invited the child to sit with us. A pair of glittering black eyes met mine and I knew we were dealing with a loop addict, pretty far gone—male, I thought. I asked him if he were hungry.

There came a nod and bony hands clutched at the table edge. I was reminded of a wolf cub.

Otto punched in the sort of things he would have fed his own children, buns and sausages and the oranges which grow profusely near Bloomhadn. He hesitated on a beverage since few people on this part of the planet drank milk. I reached over and selected beer. One might as well be realistic.

"Now young man," Otto said when the food arrived, "help yourself and we will give you something when you have finished."

Our guest needed no urging and it soon became apparent he would require seconds. I ordered everything again while Otto resumed his tale.

"As you know, Herr Sabat," he said, "physical contiguity and net contiguity are two different things. Netwise we are nearer to Earth here than on many other worlds whose stars are spatially more proximate."

I nodded. Sachsen was often called Earth's suburb and had been the first world reached when net travel was originally developed. The discovery of a ready-made highway to the stars had been a heady thing. Whether or not the net was an artifact or a natural phenomenon—or even an organic construct as some suggested—the fact remained that every opening led to a habitable world. But this business of tendrils was new to me and I said so.

"According to theory," Otto said, pouring himself and the beggar more beer, "these tendrils come and go in cycles of thousands of years. They may reach the actual surface of a planet and they probably account for the fact that so many flora and fauna are the same from world to world. And some colonies seem to have been settled from Earth before the advent of star travel. Fenn for instance, or Lost Rythar. It's the only explanation—tendrils or something like that."

I pondered this, drawing some rapid conclusions. "Godcountry," I said slowly, "is a very strange place. Things change. Lots of things. It has always been sacred to the Quele because of that." I looked a question.

"Yes, Herr Sabat. The Star Brothers tell us the net touches down in Godcountry Preserve."

"So why don't they fly in and get him?"

"The prince did not leave behind his calculations."

"But they are sure he landed?"

"That they know," Otto told me. "He is no longer in the net."

"And they are sure the Quele have him?"

"Father Liu says the probability of that is very high. He also told me what they do to nonbelievers caught in Godcountry."

I had been watching the boy, who was busily stuffing the remains of his meal into his pockets. I looked up into Otto's face and I felt my own features harden. "I already know," I told him evenly, "what they do."

I had never told Otto about Kiel, the man we lost on Quele. I had never told anyone not concerned in the matter. After all, Kiel was only a corporate slave, a nonperson like myself. When the Quele caught him, our orders were to leave him to his fate.

Two of us disobeyed. The other one was named Maureen Kavanaugh. Unfortunately we failed and Kiel was sentenced to be buried alive, which sentence was duly carried out. When the company found out we had disobeyed orders, one of the contractors tried to intercede for us but we were punished anyway. Maureen changed after that; she changed a lot.

Otto had lit a cigar and the aroma of it wafted outward, mixing with the smell of the rain and the sea and the young beggar who sorely needed a bath. "Well then," he said, "you know the risks if you guide us in. As always my fees are very high and Hithia will pay."

"Mine are high too," I said.

Otto only looked at me.

The boy was growing restless, so I gave him some scrip and told him to go to a hostel. I knew he wouldn't, that he would spend the money on loop, but what could I do? Without it he would die. There was no cure. After a moment's thought, I gave him some extra money.

Without thanks, he left us and Otto heaved a sigh. "It is a shame to us, this city," he said. "So many like that child."

"You've travelled, Otto. It is the same everywhere."

"But it should not be." He puffed on his cigar, no doubt thinking about his own children.

I had no answer to this. Otto's faith made demands on him and on reality itself that mine did not. Virtue, in my eyes, meant to accept things as they are and I always tried to do so.

"Otto," I said now, pouring another glass of wine, "why are you taking this particular job? It isn't just the money—there are plenty of less dangerous places you could go than Quele."

He sat back in his chair. "I told you," he said. "I was asked."

"By the Star Brothers."

He nodded. "You must have wondered, Herr Sabat, why I pursue the trade I do. My home village is far to the north of Bloomhadn and I am one of the few burghers who is not a farmer or a guide or an innkeeper living off the tourists."

I had wondered, but Otto was not usually very communicative.

"I am a native of this Colony," he went on. "I have many kindred here, but not in the district where I now live. In my youth, I had the misfortune to quarrel with a very powerful man, to kill him in fact. And the law being what it was in my district—in all of the north, actually—I preferred to ship out on the first mercenary ship that would have me."

"You'd have been involved in a vendetta?"

"Probably. Or hanged. Neither prospect appealed to me."

I smiled slightly. Sachsen's north country was like that. So long as no one harmed a tourist, the villagers could be as colorful as they liked. Otto would have grown up in a house with a tiled roof and carved gables and I was willing to bet he had once worn lederhosen.

"My career with the first outfit was rather short," he went on.

"I could kill in self-defense, Herr Sabat, but not otherwise. That is a failing in a mercenary."

"I'll bet."

"And then I met the Star Brothers. Their lives were fully as exciting as mine. But where I and my companions made chaos, they made order. They were hard, tough men, and when they reminded me of certain things—for we were all Christians in the north, you know—well I took that reminder seriously."

"But you still couldn't go back home."'

Otto thought about this. "Home to me is not a place," he said at last. "When I am with my wife and children, then I am home. And when I am away, I think of them and I am still at home."

I could not repress a smile. "You have a comforting outlook, Otto," I said.

He took this at face value. "Yes, Herr Sabat, I do."

I considered. "So the Star Brothers asked you to bring out Hermradon. Why?"

"Why me? Or why him?"

"Both, Otto. Start with you. Why can't they rescue him themselves? They have a lot of political clout these days."

"Not on Quele," Otto said around his cigar. "It's death for a Star Brother to set foot anywhere on the planet. You must know about the Quele religion."

"Of course I do. But they've got so many gods it seems strange they can't make room for another one."

Otto was shocked, a condition I had seen before. "Herr Sabat!" he said sternly. "No Star Brother—no decent man would even consider such a thing! The Quele worship idols!"

"Alright, Otto. I understand. So the Star Brothers can't get in?"

"Not officially. And in an affair like this, they dare not risk attracting notice."

"Notice of what? You're not trying to tell me they've got spies down there, are you?" My respect for the organization went up a notch at the very idea.

"They don't discuss such things," Otto said primly.

"So you took the job."

"Father Liu wanted to go along but his superiors refused." Otto pushed retract on our umbrella as the rain had ceased for the time being. A moon or two gleamed through the tattered clouds. "Now as to the other question," he went on, "I will tell you about Hithia."

Hithia, Otto proceeded to inform me, was a recently recontacted colony, barbaric in the extreme and of little interest to Net Central. Only the Star Brothers paid much attention to the colony, but they at least tried to fend off the usual pack of sharpsters who always moved in on a newly opened world.

The autarch was grateful and had given them a sort of diplomatic status. He even considered becoming a Christian himself, though his understanding of the faith was not very deep and his enthusiasm stemmed mostly from his friendship with Father Liu, the current envoy.

"Now about the autarch's son," Otto added in a louder voice, as a boisterous party had just descended on a nearby table, throwing wine bottles in the general direction of the sea. "Hermradon was educated on Earth at the University of Asia. He's become a leading authority on Net Theory and has cut a lot of ties with his past."

"So when Hermradon disappeared, the autarch turned to Father Liu?"

"Exactly. He promised to let the Star Brothers establish missions among the common people and that the nobility would convert *en masse*. But that was only if God and the Star Brothers succeeded in the rescue, of course."

I thought about this. "It's a roundabout way to make converts," I said at last. "But probably not very sincere ones."

"Gratitude makes a good enough foundation," Otto said. "It has happened before."

"Alright. So we go in—you said three people? If Father Liu can't come, who is the third?"

"A Lost Rythan. I don't know his name."

I had had no experience with Lost Rythans, but I knew their ties with the Star Brothers were very close and that they were excellent fighters. They were not, however, known for the kind of finesse our mission would require, having a reputed tendency to bash and hack their way out of trouble with a fine disregard for—and perhaps a total ignorance of—discretion.

By now the party at the next table had grown so loud that we decided to move on. On the way back up the quay, Otto told me he had arranged a meeting out on one of the islands next morning. "Father Liu will be there and someone from Hithia," he added. "We'll finish the contract then."

"Why not here in Bloomhadn?"

"The Hithians want privacy."

He told me which island and it was one I knew. We'd go to the tavern on the beach and—there being only one of each, beaches and taverns—the whole thing seemed pretty simple. After that, he suggested a robocab.

I shook my head. "I like to walk," I told him. "It's a different city at night."

Otto snorted. We were passing through the great park that paralleled the ocean front and ahead were the shops. Otto was staying at an inn near the shuttleport so we turned in that direction.

A lot of squatters lived in the park, but they mostly didn't bother anyone. The ones who did were periodically rounded up and slapped with corporate contracts—as I had been when my mother sold me at birth.

We passed a couple of campsites where ragged tents glowed like curtained windows. There was music and somewhere a baby cried. We saw dancers further on. Then we crossed a brick street and keyed on our personal shields. This was not, after all, Otto's village we were traversing.

Past the park, we kept to the lighted ways but there weren't very many people. Most of the traffic was on the slidewalks up among the towers. Aircars drifted almost noiselessly above us in the canyons of the streets.

From ahead, there came the sound of a scuffle and as we came abreast of an alley, someone ran away. I smelled the rich reek of fresh blood—heartsblood. "Uh-oh," I said.

Otto played a light over the corpse of a child, such another as the one who had eaten at our table earlier. "Lieber Gott," he said. "I hate this city." He bent down to make sure the victim was dead.

I peered into the alley, saw movement and sprinted after the killer. My first owners had had me trained as a tutor-bodyguard and my earlier conditioning had been very deep. I could not let this pass. Before I even realized what I was doing, I had tackled a tall, bony youth and had my knife at his throat.

He wriggled in my grip, felt the point dig in above his jugular and began to weep hoarsely. He smelled of loop.

With an effort, I overrode the imperative and released my hold. He knelt on the greasy bricks, gasping as he reached up to feel the tiny wound I had made. No doubt he had a knife of his own and when he reached into his belt, I produced the stunner which, according to my forged papers, I am legally allowed to carry.

But he wasn't going for a weapon. Instead, he pulled out a wad of scrip and flung it at my feet before he began to back away on all fours, his face twisted up with fear. Probably this was what he had taken from the dead boy.

Otto came up just as the youth turned and fled.

"You got him?"

"A kid."

"He should be arrested, Herr Sabat. He has broken the law." "He's been punished," I said, kicking aside the mound of scrip. "Life is punishment enough."

We came back out into the street. Otto was not serious about calling the patrollers, but this time when he suggested a cab, I did not argue. I felt as though I were responsible for both boys, the one who was dead and the other one who would die later from loop.

It was my conditioning that made me feel this, I told myself. I was not responsible. I had never actually been a tutor; my contract was sold to Feullier before I graduated. And Feullier had long since beaten all capacity for nurturing out of me.

So I told myself, but I was lying in my teeth.

"Tomorrow," Otto reminded me as he left me at the Crescent Club. He spoke coldly as one professional to another and by this I knew that what we had witnessed that night hurt him as much as it had hurt me.

"Tomorrow," I told him at the upper plat and went inside. There was a little blood on my knees and I tried not to look at it as I rose in the grav well. I decided to do some more drinking before I tried to sleep.

CHAPTER TWO

The call light was on when I let myself into the apartment. I must have stared at it a full thirty seconds before I crossed the foyer and thumbed a key, only to start back like a vampire confronted by the noonday sun.

For that is what I saw on the screen. It was as though someone had taken the light of Sachsen's islands and spread it lavishly onto a canvas. Sunlight melted and ran down the sides of stone houses, sand gleamed whitely and the dancing sea and the orange trees threw back that light in gleams of pure color.

"Like it?" a voice cut in.

"Beautiful," I said aloud. "It looks like happiness distilled."

I heard a high, light laugh. "I have always enjoyed that about you, Eduardo," she said. "You use words as I use paint." I waited, still gazing at the painting. "Recent?" I asked.

"Very. Shall I leave it on?"

I sighed. If I told her not, her own features would confront me and I was not sure I wanted that right now. On the other hand, she saw me. As always she had me at a disadvantage.

"Leave it on," I decided, mentally noting my cowardice.

"You look tired," she told me. "Something is bothering you."

"But now I will gaze at your picture and before you know it, the sunshine will be in my heart."

She laughed again and this almost brought her before me. She was after all, my wife, though we had not lived together for nearly five years.

"Do you want to tell me about it?" she asked.

"Certainly not." I was lying, because I wanted very much to tell someone about the boy in the alley. I thought about fetching a drink but decided against it. She might do likewise on her end and that would not be good.

"I've been gone," she said. "Down at Corin Bay. I needed a break."

"I really do like it, Susanna. The painting."

"Too bad you're not a critic—or a patron. Then I wouldn't be hacking out portraits of rich tourists."

The galaxy was full of rich tourists, I wanted to tell her, and she might as well make her living from them as I did. But I kept quiet. "I'd be glad to become a patron," I said instead. "Your talent shouldn't go to waste."

"We've been over that before," she said and I was sorry I had spoken. "I'm not for sale."

She was hitting below the belt. I barely resisted a glance at the slave band. She did not apologize, however, and I got up and found another bottle of wine and a glass.

"Have you ever been on a world," she asked me then, "where the suns are separated? Where they each make their own set of shadows?"

"Yes, I have seen that," I told her. "There are some worlds like that."

"But don't they lose something? I mean, here we have a tight cluster and all the light comes together—"

"Your painting," I said, "might have been done on Earth. A single sun closer than our three would have the same effect."

"No wonder you like it," she said. "I keep forgetting you're an earthman."

"Yes," I agreed calmly, "I am an earthman."

"And you even lived there."

"I was born there," I said. "As you well know. And I went to school in North Africa until I was twenty."

"You still don't look too good, Eduardo. Tell me what's wrong."

By then I had made some progress on the bottle and so I told her about the boy in the alley. Both boys.

"Ah, poor thing," she said and her voice had gone soft.

I tried to remember how she had looked, those few times I had seen her pensive, vulnerable. Her untidy hair was a dark, gypsy brown, her face over-pale for it. Her eyes would keep changing color as she played about with pigment drops, but my favorite shade was a warm brown. More often she chose an orange that was almost feral.

Those eyes would grow wide—I tried to think of them as brown tonight—and her lips would come together in a short, quivering line. But that mood was as ephemeral as all the others. I might as well have tried to hold the sunlight in my hands.

I poured again and drank, letting my eyes rest on her painting.

"You could not kill the murderer?" she asked.

"I could easily have killed the murderer," I said. "Until I saw him."

"You and your fatherly heart."

By this I knew that she, too, had been drinking. She had never forgiven me for trying to make of us a family. She knew I was sterile, mutated from having been conceived too near a hot zone. I had suggested quite early in our marriage that we adopt a child, and the resulting fight led to our separation soon afterward.

"You didn't even ask for a clone," she had said bitterly. "You just thought you'd buy a ready-made product—an urchin sold on the street!"

I know now that I erred badly with her. I was quite ignorant in those days and a little giddy with freedom. To me, having a woman meant marriage and marriage meant that there should be children. It was all quite simple, from Susanna's reluctant agreement to a ten-year contract which was the longest I could get, to my request that she become an adoptive mother. It was a long time before I understood how deeply I had insulted her.

She told me I thought like a slave, that I only wanted to secure my fragile claim on stability, that I did not and could not love her.

She was probably right about all but the last part, but by then it was too late to tell her so.

Also, as I knew now, she was an alcoholic, a destructive, talented and somewhat shallow-minded woman. Though she was older than I had thought her, she had never matured much beyond adolescence and never would. Still, neither of us had ever suggested breaking the contract.

"Want to see the others?" she asked suddenly and I started, looking up at the screen in confusion.

"Others?"

"Paintings. What did you think I meant?"

I shrugged. "It's been a long day. And," I added, glancing at the board, "I have another call."

We were both silent for a few seconds.

"Can I buy this one?" I asked at last.

She thought for a moment and named a rather large sum. I told her that would be fine. She did not know the details of what I did for a living, only that I went away from time to time and that I made plenty of money. I suppose she suspected that my work was somewhat outside the law, but we had never discussed the matter. Which goes to show what sort of relationship we had had.

I made arrangements for delivery of the painting and signed off. But when I cut on the screen again, wondering who would call me at—I glanced at the clock—three AM, there was nothing except a swatch of improbably starry sky. A sprawling nebula lay on the horizon, trailing smears of light.

"Feullier," a male voice said softly, "has been bought out. All assets were taken up by Tokot Limited, twelve hours ago subtime."

My throat went dry and whatever peace the wine and Susanna's painting had given me dissolved into tingling clarity. "Who are you?" I breathed.

"A friend."

"But the codes are lost." I laid one hand on the slave band as though to hide it from this new threat. "There are no assets," I said.

The line transmission went dead, the nebula no more than a negative image burned into my retina.

I set the half empty bottle carefully aside. If my caller spoke the truth, I now belonged to a puppet subsidiary of Net Central itself. But it still remained to be seen whether they could take possession.

I held up my right wrist, considering options. There weren't many and they were all bad. I could arrange an illegal and probably fatal operation. The band was built directly into my nervous system. At the very least I would lose the use of my right arm, and more likely I would go into a coma and die.

I could turn myself in, of course, and have my brain milked of my small share of Feullier's secrets. Who knows, I might even be tried as a criminal, though it was more likely I would be set to doing even worse things for Net Central.

Or, I could wait and see if any of the codes turned up. There were three—one to call, one to punish and one to deactivate the band. I had only experienced the first two.

The empty screen stared back at me as I got up and went to the window. I cut the room lights, cleared the glass field and leaned out into the night. A bracing wind blew in from the sea and I saw the clouds race by above the city.

There was another choice, of course, if things got really bad. But they were not, I told myself firmly, so bad as that. Not yet, anyway.

With a sigh, I shut and opaqued the window.

And then another thought struck me. This person who called— and I was sure that no one of my acquaintance, not even Susanna, knew which company had owned me—might have been lying. I would have to wait and see what developed.

I had enemies; after all, I was a criminal. But my foes were far from here and wouldn't go after me in this way. They were mostly archeological societies and small colonial governments who might want back what I had looted. But as for myself, I was nobody, just one thief among many.

At last, I set an alarm and lay down for a few hours' dream-riddled sleep. I would not have had even that if I hadn't taken something that made my dreams even worse than waking.

Susanna's painting haunted me. The golden sunshine on the water seemed but a thin disguise for her own elusive and sorrowing soul. She hung over all like the edge of a storm far out to sea.

Then I dreamed I was back on earth at the classical academy. An old teacher of mine, another slave who drowned later, probably by accident, was trying to instill in us some appreciation for the Roman Empire.

We did not mock his sincerity; with our wristbands in place, we were a well-behaved group, but more than one of us cast an eye northward to where the Mediterranean washed against the Libyan shore. Europe was still hot after almost half a millennium, its glories on indefinite hold. Where led those fabled roads now save to a lingering, radioactive death?

Yet in my dream, I thought the sea had shrunk. They said my mother came from Malta, though she had sold me on the other side of the Atlantic, and it seemed now that my mysterious homeland lay but a short swim away. Only for some reason, I could not make myself enter the water.

"Home," my dead teacher told me solemnly, "is a way of life." The words repeated themselves over and over to the tune of the surf. *Way of life—way of life—life, life, life—*

And then I turned around and saw that the corporate enclave and the school outside of Tripoli had vanished. In its place a jumble of Roman architecture rose haphazardly among olive trees and blooming vines.

"Where have you been, my son?" an old man called and I ran toward him. "Must you always yearn for the other shore? Shall you not remain at your post until you are called? What worth has a man save that he can choose?"

I smiled at him because he loved me and wished me well. "Look, Epictetus," I said. "The slave band has come off. It wasn't as tight as I thought it was!"

He took it from me and cast it on the nearest dung heap. "You were always free," he told me.

And then the dream changed again and I was the old stoic, living in exile. I took one of Bloomhadn's beggar children by the hand. "Not even a sheep or a wolf," I said, "deserts its young. And shall man?"

"No, Father," the boy said and looked up at me trustingly even as the alarm began dragging me to consciousness once more. First I lost the ancient village and then I lost the sun and the olive trees. At the last, I parted reluctantly from my son and struggled to a sitting position on the edge of the bed. I had to hurry if I meant to pick up Otto and catch a skimmer to the islands in time for our appointment.

We set out in heavy fog, though the robopilot was unaffected. The skimmer was full of families with beach gear and hampers of food. A few fishermen stared wisely at the dancing sea less than a man's height below us. Only Otto and I seemed out of place in this holiday atmosphere. I saw at once that his night had been no better than mine.

He had told me to meet him outside a church where he had been to Mass and said that we would take a robocab to the quay. Neither of us wanted any breakfast, nor did we have anything much to say to one another.

But now in the skimmer with its rafts and balls, shovels and buckets and all the children running about, I began to feel a little better. The sun peeped out from a crack in the fog and our glassite dome darkened a notch to compensate.

I was still worried about last night's call—the second one—and my arm itched above the band. The itch was purely psychological, but I scratched it anyway. Otto saw me.

Not for the first time, I was sorry about the things I would never be able to tell him—not that I didn't want to but because only someone who had lived as I had lived would understand. Though maybe he did understand a little after all—as much as he was able. Who could say?

The sun patches grew larger until suddenly we burst out over the softly gleaming sea. You can't distinguish the individual suns of Sachsen, but together, they make an irregular blotch, smaller than, but just as bright as the lone sun of Earth. To the west of us, the coastline was still covered in a fog bank, but ahead, clear water stretched as far as I could see.

"You ever meet a Lost Rythan, Otto?" I asked as the first of the islands appeared on the horizon. "I mean, how do they operate?"

"I've met them," Otto said slowly, "but I have not worked closely with them. They are somewhat uncompromising."

I glanced at him sidewise. "Are they good in a pinch?"

"Very, Herr Sabat, from all I've heard. But they take getting used to."

Already I was making plans. As I saw the problem, we had to shuttle down to Quele's colony port, make our way from there into Godcountry, extract Pelanot and come back the same way. I could handle Godcountry if it hadn't made too many changes since I'd been there last, and if I had the extra manpower of the Lost Rythan. But it was up to Otto to do the rest. I said something to this effect.

"Quite right, Herr Sabat. You are hired for your own expertise as I am for mine. I have already arranged papers for three as representatives of an agricultural systems firm. We bypass certain difficulties that way and have a legitimate reason for visiting the colony."

"Sounds good enough. But do we have a reason for visiting the pilgrim villages?"

"That is being arranged," he said, but did not elaborate.

An hour later, we were on Brabant, the largest of the islands, where most of the tourists got off. From there we took a ferry to Kite Island and found the inn. Two boats were tied up at the pier, one obviously rented and the other an expensive job with a couple of expensive looking men on the deck. They eyed us suspiciously as we walked up the strand from the ferry dock.

"Hithians," Otto said and I gave them a closer scrutiny.

There was an odd cast to their faces, an air of wildness almost. Their skin was golden, their tied-back hair thick and dark. Short beards and gold earrings added an exotic note. They went on watching us as we walked to the inn. I had a feeling they were armed.

The sun was warm and I had long since taken off my jacket. The stunner was in an inner pocket and I swung the garment casually over one shoulder to bring this within reach.

"It's alright," Otto said quietly. "They always act like that."

I grunted. "Let's get some breakfast. The least we can do is keep them waiting."

We entered the inn which was nearly empty at this hour. Only a couple fishermen sat at one table and they rose to leave as we came in. A broad-faced girl with golden braids came up at once, her smile more than a little strained.

"In the back," she said in a low voice. "You are expected."

I waved a dismissive hand at her. "Feed us first," I said and this seemed to upset her even more.

"It is alright Fräulein," Otto told her quickly. "You may bring the food into us."

This did not suit me, but by now I was pretty hungry, so I let him order his usual sausages and buns, adding my own request for eggs and something to put on the buns. "Jam," I said, "and coffee."

Reluctantly I left the pleasant front room and accompanied Otto to an alcove where a plank door opened onto a screened porch. The screen shimmered with some sort of protective field. I paused in the doorway and took stock.

There was the priest, a tallish man of oriental descent, wearing the black cassock of the Star Brothers. Beside him, taking up the rest of the bench, sat two very big men with shoulder length hair and the sort of clothing usually associated with battle axes and crossbows, though as it happened, both wore stunners instead. No doubt these would be the Lost Rythans.

My gaze travelled on around the room but there was only one other person—a veiled woman who stared back at me fiercely out of eyes so dark they were nearly black. There were crow's feet at the corners of those eyes and her much-tattooed and ringed hands were bony and calloused.

The Star Brother rose politely as we came in, followed by the other two men. Otto made introductions. Father Liu, Heth Andrew Wolfbane, and Gaed Stephen Bloodbear. The lady proved to be a Hithian, Klavia Pelanot, the autarch's sister and consequently, Hermradon's aunt.

She went on studying my face after we had acknowledged one another, leaving me to wonder what she looked like beneath that veil. Not so young, I guessed, but probably rather handsome.

Then I saw her eyes move down to the slave band. I had worn a short-sleeved shirt and the metalplast was plain enough for those who knew what it represented.

We were given seats on her side of the table but I made sure Otto took the middle. I had had this problem before when negotiating for a job—the sudden downgrading of my status when it became evident that I was a slave—and I was in no mood for the explanations that must follow.

"I was led to believe this man was a free contractor," she said almost at once. I turned to face her.

"That is so, Lady."

"Then why do you wear that band?"

I bit back a sarcastic reply and let Otto speak for me.

"I can vouch for Herr Sabat," he said quickly. "It is as he says."

"We are fortunate to have Mr. Sabat's services, Lady Pelanot," Father Liu interposed. "He has worked in Godcountry itself and knows the ways of the sacred compound."

I raised one eyebrow slightly. Apparently the Star Brothers knew more about me than I knew about them.

"Worked?" Lady Pelanot inquired. "What sort of work?"

"Grave robbing," I told her before Father Liu could say anything.

She made a dismissive sound as my breakfast arrived and I turned my attention to the buns. "At least I'm not a hit man," I told her as I spread jam. "That was my only other option at the time."

Father Liu cleared his throat. "I think," he said, "I'll order tea. Lady Pelanot?"

She gave a slight shrug. "Make that beer," she told him and Wolfbane nodding approvingly.

"I'll fetch a pitcher," he offered.

Meanwhile Otto and I tucked in, though not before he said grace, which was his custom. For some reason, being rude to my future employer had cleared away the last of my depression and when, between bites, I looked up at her veiled face, it was almost with gratitude.

"Now," Father Liu said, when Wolfbane had returned with the beer and a pot of tea, "we'll get down to business. Otto, have you told Mr. Sabat the situation?" Otto said he had.

Meanwhile, I was staring at the Star Brother who had put a small piece of butter into his tea and was letting it melt. I was wondering just what colony had produced him.

"Then you must know, Sabat," Lady Pelanot said abruptly, "that we are going to Godcountry to rescue my nephew. I'm very fond of the boy though only the gods know what a royal pain in the—" She glanced at Father Liu and shrugged.

"Her ladyship refers to the fact that Hermradon has chosen a field of study not quite in keeping with his father's expectations," the Star Brother told us. "He has caused some concern before this."

Otto looked up, his expression neutral. "Did I hear Lady Pelanot use the word 'we'?"

"Yes, Otto."

"I see." He glanced at me and I shook my head.

"Unfortunately," I said out loud, "there are only three sets of papers."

"That is so," Otto said as though he had only just thought of it. "And I am afraid that Herr—" He cocked his head in the direction of the Lost Rythans.

"Andrew Wolfbane is to accompany you," Father Liu said hastily.

"Well then," Otto said. "Herr Wolfbane cannot be spared."

"I'm coming along," Pelanot said flatly. "Father Liu, tell them how things are on Hithia."

The priest sat back, dwarfed as most people seemed to be, by the Lost Rythans. "Hithia's customs are somewhat unusual," he began but was not allowed to continue.

Pelanot snorted. "Our national pastime," she snapped, "is assassination."

Otto wiped his mouth carefully and gave the beer a speculative glance. "You need have no fears of that sort in Godcountry," he said. "Herr Sabat is one of a very few offworlders who even know how to get in."

"Exactly," she said. "One of a few."

I leaned in front of Otto, trying to pierce that veil of hers. "You were surprised to learn that I had been a slave," I said slowly. "But you know something of the operation on Quele?"

The Star Brother gave me an apologetic look. "Some research was necessary," he said. "What Lady Pelanot knows, she got from us. That you were one of a team and that a teammate of yours was captured and executed on Quele. Of the others, at least three are still alive, working in trades similar to your own. There were also two contractors."

"One at large," I finished for him, "and one in prison the last I heard, on Earth. Amid Steed."

"Who is it," Otto asked Pelanot, "that wishes the death of your nephew?"

She shrugged and her bony hands came together in a sort of language we did not know. "Rival branches of the family," she said evasively.

"I see," Otto said again. "And you fear that this rescue may be made more difficult than we anticipated?"

"Money has gone out from certain accounts," Wolfbane put in. "But we're not sure yet where it went."

I thought of last night's call. It didn't take long to put two and two together, but my answer was still not four. Certainly one of my former colleagues could have been the caller—but why? Was he trying to frighten me off the job? If so, his approach lacked something. It was having the opposite psychological effect.

Meanwhile, Otto was off on a different tack. "This seems all the more reason why you should not accompany us, Lady Pelanot," he said. 'We are professionals and—"

"My father," she remarked almost conversationally, "died on the library floor. I was quite young when it happened, but later I witnessed the execution of his killer. I still have the knife he used. He was a cousin of mine."

Wolfbane and Bloodbear perked up at this, as though they would have liked to examine the weapon. She had struck a chord of sympathy, it was plain, and I foresaw that Otto and I would be outvoted.

"Later," she went on, sure of her audience, "my husband and children fell to assassins. Hermradon has been very lucky. So far."

"You've helped his luck along, haven't you?" Bloodbear prompted.

She acknowledged this with a slight nod.

The conversation gave me a strange feeling, as though I could see the boy Hermradon moving warily about his home—it would be something along the lines of the stone fortresses I had seen on other worlds—his aunt watching over him like his good demon. Indeed there was something spiritlike about this veiled woman, almost as though nothing lay behind the veil but eyes and will.

Otto brought me back to the present. "You are telling us you will not be an impediment out in the wilderness?" She nodded.

Father Liu took things up at this point. "Her brother does not approve, of course. But he has given his consent reluctantly. And of course Andrew Wolfbane will be there too. There is only one difficulty."

I looked up. Otto could take Pelanot as a secretary or something, I supposed. She didn't really have to have guild papers.

"The laws of Quele," the Star Brother said distinctly, "require certain things of visitors. Formal submission to the, ah, gods. And Lady Pelanot is a catechumen."

I swallowed my coffee wrong and tried not to sputter. Lady Pelanot did not strike me as a likely candidate for Otto's religion.

The others seemed to take the problem seriously, however, and I tried to do likewise. I had almost forgotten about Quele's pervasive idolatry, having had much more pressing things to worry about whenever I was there. Yet the fact remained that you could not do business anywhere in the colony without tripping over a member of their extensive pantheon. Unless you had legal immunity, Quele's gods became your own gods the moment you got off the shuttle.

"I could try to obtain another set of papers," Otto said, thinking hard. "But it will take time."

"Time we don't have," Pelanot snapped. "Your god will have to wait, Father Liu. He can have me after we complete this mission."

The Star Brother shook his head. "There would always be another surrender to make, Lady Pelanot. And another. You must make your act of faith now because now is the only time there is."

I set my cup down carefully, watching the Lady's eyes. I saw no faith there. Indeed, I could not read what it was that I did see, but it gave me the chills. This business of veiling women, perhaps—

"Give the papers to Lady Pelanot," I said aloud. "And I'll go as a company slave. You may list me as your interpreter if you like." "Mr. Sabat," Father Liu began but I cut him off.

"I wouldn't have to do much. At the port of entry they just take you to an altar and you say some words. Most people don't even know what they mean."

Otto did not meet my eyes. "You would know, Herr Sabat," he said in a low voice.

"And I've said them many times."

"That was before you became a freeman."

How could I tell him, I wondered, about that inner citadel—that part of a man which only he could deliver away from his own will? That I had guarded it always and that it was still mine no matter whether I were slave or free?

I shrugged. "Take it or leave it. I, at least, am not a catechumen." To my surprise, I found myself trembling with anger that those who had always been free should quibble over such a small concession made out of their abundance.

Otto would have spoken, but I got up and went out, not pausing until I stood once more in the clean sunlight. I wondered if it was true what Susanna had said—did I still think like a slave after all?

Only then did I look up, and I saw at once that something was wrong. The Hithians were gone from the deck of their boat and a strange craft was tied up at the pier. Its crew were looking at me and I did not like that look at all.

CHAPTER THREE

I was nearly off the porch—say two meters from the entrance. But even as I spun about, diving for cover, I knew I would not make it. I heard the flat crack of a projectile gun and wood splintered next to my head. At the same moment, a heat beam caught me neatly in the back and I stumbled, my coat sliding to the decking as I tried clumsily to retrieve the stunner.

Through a darkening haze, I saw people on the beach, running toward the inn. At last my questing fingers found the metalplast handle and I drew out the weapon, aiming unsteadily as someone pointed a rifle in my direction. I fired off a charge, rolled over and was caught under the arms by a pair of strong hands which lifted me bodily through the door.

Suddenly I felt a lot worse than I had before.

"Get him onto a bench," I heard Otto say and I realized that my rescuer was Father Liu. Wolfbane and Bloodbear were firing from the door and Klavia Pelanot was at the window. Our waitress had disappeared. I didn't blame her.

Otto helped carry me away from the door but what happened afterward is pretty confused. I started coughing when Father Liu put on a pressure bandage and that cough was both painful and difficult. And then, I remember, I found some solace staring at the beams of the ceiling. Was the roof thatched, I wondered? Or was it tiled or shingled? This puzzled me greatly.

Things were getting noisy. At one point the building was rocked by an explosion which was, as I found out later, a grenade. Someone had tossed the thing in the window and Otto, with remarkable coolness even for him, had scooped it up again and thrown it back out the door. It took out a mercenary and part of the porch.

The attack ended as abruptly as it began. Our besiegers ran back to their boat, all but the one who caught the grenade, and the Lost Rythans gave chase in the Hithian craft. Lady Pelanot's guards lay stunned on the deck, which was just as well for them, Wolfbane told me later, because Bloodbear's piloting was headlong in the extreme. But the strange craft turned out to be a skimmer and, leaving the water, it was soon lost to view.

All this I heard later. At the moment, I was occupied mainly in trying to breathe, a feat which became more difficult by the moment. Otto wanted to call the patrollers but Lady Pelanot refused. Her boat had a life support unit, she said, and surely I would last until we got back to Bloomhadn.

At the time, said boat was in use chasing our attackers—and not even the autarch's sister could ignore the blown-up porch and dead body in the yard. Me, she obviously considered expendable.

Those difficulties belonged to Otto however, for just as the innkeeper came out of the cellar and started yelling, I lost track of things entirely.

I woke back in Bloomhadn, in the infirmary of the Lost Rythan embassy, or the Enclave as they call it. An image of Otto's crucified god hung on the wall and I stared at this for some time before I managed to turn my head.

Heth Andrew Wolfbane sat on a chair beside the cot reading. In my semi-delirious state—for my impressions could only be called surreal for the first few minutes—the sight of this great, shaggy barbarian bent over a copy of The Imitation of Christ struck me as hysterically funny. But when I tried to laugh, I started coughing instead.

He got up and fetched me some water. "Careful. We gave you a lot of speed heal and you really need to take it easy."

After that he told me where I was and how I'd gotten there. Otto and Father Liu had gone to make official statements about yesterday's fracas and Pelanot, who refused to testify, had already left the colony.

"She'll meet us on Ponia, at Quele Station," he added. "She didn't want to go to the Hithian embassy for fear of assassins, and after she insulted the patrollers, there was talk of deporting her anyway."

"What was she so angry about?" I asked, speaking with an effort.

Wolfbane shrugged. "Secrecy, I suppose. But it's late to worry about that, isn't it?"

I sighed. "Secrecy from whom?"

Wolfbane sat back down in the chair, carefully marking his place in his book. "She wasn't too specific on that. Her relatives I think, but now there seem to be others involved."

"These people yesterday. Hithians?"

He gave me a troubled look. "I don't think so," he said. "And they left one behind, you know."

"Ah."

Wolfbane reached into his belt pouch and drew out a warped piece of metal which he laid in my hand. To my horror, I recognized the twisted remains of a slave bracelet.

I gazed at it, wondering what had become of the arm it had once encircled. "I see," I murmured, seeing more than I liked.

"Lady Pelanot retrieved it," Wolfbane told me, "before the patrollers came. She didn't want to complicate things."

"She's quite a woman," I said. Closing my eyes, I clutched the cold metalplast to me while a row of faces danced across my vision. There were four of them, after Kiel who was dead on Quele. Trevorr, a thin, brown woman with eyes that never met mine; Shane Res and Boris, both of the stocky, red-faced variety, one of them bearded and also, I had heard, deceased; and last of all Kavanaugh. Maureen Kavanaugh.

I could not remember a time before Maureen, for we had grown together like two vines there on the Mediterranean shore, unfolding ourselves beneath the ancient sun of earth. And when we were sold away from that place, we were still together, carrying what we were and would be within us so tightly bound that neither had yet seen that we were two separate people.

That knowledge came later.

Wolfbane took the band back from me. He must have seen something in my face but he waited quietly, not questioning.

I shook my head. "It's alright, Mr. Wolfbane," I said.

"Call me Heth Andrew. It is the usage of my people, the first name in honor of our ancient heritage and the second is the Christian name."

"I'll remember that, Heth Andrew," I replied. "And you may call me Eduardo, though I do not think any honor was intended when they named me."

He did not reply to this, though he raised on eyebrow slightly as he put the slave band away.

"Well," I said into his silence, "the question now is how many of my former teammates are we up against." Still, he waited.

"And which ones," I added. I fingered the band on my own wrist, wondering at the effort it took to keep my voice steady. I could not make myself believe it was Maureen who caught that grenade. I think that in some way I would have known—though my conviction stemmed from nothing more than a sort of morbid romanticism. It was a failing of tomb robbers.

Meanwhile I had other things to think about. A man had called me last night—no, it was two nights ago, now. I must have been unconscious since yesterday morning.

Should I tell Heth Andrew about that caller who claimed to be a friend? If he was another slave—but that got me nowhere. I had lost touch with all of them and none, that I could think of, would have tried to befriend me now.

I looked up. "What do we do after this?" I asked. "Are we still going to Quele?"

Wolfbane nodded. "We will meet Lady Pelanot at Quele Station. Not Net Central Territory, you see."

"When?"

"As soon as possible. First your breakfast and then—" He paused half out the door. "You can't stay here at the Enclave, I'm afraid. The Lost Rythan ambassador won't allow it."

I stared up at him wondering what new complication had come up.

Wolfbane gave me a small, somewhat rueful smile. "I am a Faring Guard, Eduardo," he said. "Gaed Stephen and I have no official ties with the embassy."

"I'm sorry, Heth Andrew," I told him. "I still don't understand. I have never worked with your people before and I have never heard of a Faring Guard."

He shrugged. "No time to explain it all now. Too complex. But we must be gone soon, somewhere, and Otto Zeller says you have an apartment. Is that so?"

I nodded slowly. "How long until I'm able to leave for Ponia?" I asked.

"We'll make it two days on speed heal." He disappeared, returning with a hearty meal in keeping with what I came to think of as Lost Rythan cuisine.

"Why my place?" I asked around a mouthful of brown bread and venison. I did not sound as casual as I meant to.

Heth Andrew, who had poured himself a beer from the pitcher on the tray, looked up. "We were hoping," he said carefully, "that you might have a visitor or two."

Looking up into his keen eyes as he said this, I found myself reassessing my first impression of Heth Andrew. A primitive he may have been, though I began to doubt even that, but he was no fool. For the first time, I began to feel hopeful about our mission.

"I hadn't thought of that," I said, "but it is possible." After a few moments' thought and another bite or two, I decided to tell him about the call I had already received.

But he was as puzzled as I, trying to fit things together and failing to spot any apparent link with our current situation. "No warnings?" he asked. "To avoid Hithian affairs, I mean? No threats of any kind?"

"No offers either," I pointed out, reaching for the beer. Lost Rythans did not go in for orange juice.

"But now," Heth Andrew said, thinking, "there has been an encounter. They have lost someone."

"If that was a Feullier bracelet, yes." I set down the beer, amazed at my coolness. "Someone has lost someone."

Heth Andrew frowned. "It was all fused inside. We could not be sure."

"You're sure," I said and he did not deny it.

Before I finished eating, Otto and Father Liu walked in, followed by Bloodbear. I welcomed them with the gratitude natural in the case especially since Father Liu had risked his life dragging me off the porch.

"How did things go?" I asked Otto.

"The Island Authority is only interested in indemnity, Herr Sabat. Between my insurance company and the Hithian government, there shouldn't be any problem."

"But it wasn't your fault!"

He shrugged. "My mercenary's license says it is. Otherwise I would not be allowed to live on Sachsen."

"What about the dead body?"

"Technically—" He gave me an apologetic look. "Technically a non-person. Anyway, it was impossible to establish her identity."

I started at this, dropping the glass. Fortunately it was almost empty and everything went on the tray. "What did she look like?" I got out in a low voice.

There was a moment's silence and I wished I had not asked. Then Otto shook his head. "It was a grenade, Herr Sabat. She didn't look like anything."

I lay back, afraid even to close my eyes.

At this, Father Liu reached over and removed the tray. "I'm sorry we could not get more information," he told me. "It may be that Lady

Pelanot will have learned something from her own people. We will find out when we see her." I did not answer.

He set the tray down and turned back to me. "We have already trespassed on the Enclave's hospitality more than is expedient. You will need to go now with Andrew Wolfbane and Stephen Bloodbear.

I will come to you tomorrow."

"And I," Otto said.

Suddenly I remembered the circumstances of my wounding. How I had left the group in anger. I had violated my own principles by giving way to my emotions, tangled as they had been and scarcely understood by myself, let alone by anyone else.

"You will be welcome," I said now. "And—and I meant it when I said that Lady Pelanot could use the third set of papers.'"

His gaze did not leave my face and I felt a sudden need to reassure him, if I could, that the words of Quele could not harm me. So long as I lived safely within the citadel of my soul, I wanted to tell him, I would be a free man. But under his quiet scrutiny, the words would not come.

"Help me up," I said instead and he did so.

The trip to the club was not easy. A great weakness came over me in the aircar and Bloodbear had to give me a stimulant before we went in. Fortunately, we met no one, having put ourselves on hover at the upper entrance. My prints opened the door.

There was a package waiting outside my apartment and by its size and shape, I knew at once what it would be. Still, Wolfbane insisted on scanning it before it was opened. Afterwards, I had them hang Susanna's picture where I could see it from the bed.

"Check the screen," I told Wolfbane and he found two recorded messages. One was from Susanna and I decided to call her back that evening. The other was from a fellow club member named bor Kladden. He was a retired professor who had beaten me in a few chess games. He, too, had better wait.

I ate a lot and slept some more while Wolfbane and Bloodbear prowled the apartment. Bor Kladden came in the afternoon and I told Heth Andrew to let him in. "This is a friend," I added.

"How close a friend?"

"Close enough to know I don't make my living teaching philosophy. He's seen me laid up before."

Arnese bor Kladden had taught Classics at Continental University for seventy years and now, after five years' retirement, he was only beginning to look his hundred plus. His mind was as sharp as ever. He took Wolfbane's presence in stride and nodded to Bloodbear who had been sitting by the window and rose immediately as the old man came in.

"It's good to see well-mannered youngsters," bor Kladden said to Bloodbear. "But then, Lost Rythans are known for courtesy."

Bloodbear regarded him with new interest and at this, bor Kladden chuckled.

"I've taught every race in the colonies," he said. "And some are less forgettable than others."

"Professor bor Kladden is finishing my own education," I said from the bed, pleased that he had asked them no questions.

His reticence did not quite extend to me. "Speed heal?" He inquired, taking in the empty tray beside my bed.

I nodded. "And how are things with you, Arnese?"

"I complain, of course. But not to you."

"Sorry I can't manage a chess game," I told him. "It would take our minds off our problems. And I'm afraid I'll be going offworld in a couple of days, too."

My visitor pulled up a chair. "Well now," he said, when he had settled himself, "I rather thought you might. You don't stay home too long at a time."

I shrugged. "That's how it is. Find a place you like and then you can't afford to enjoy it."

"You like Bloomhadn?"

I said I did. "Weather and all," I added, knowing that Bloomhadn's lack of weather control was an ongoing irritant among retirees.

Bor Kladden chuckled again. "You'll be in good company this time, at least," he said lightly. "I won't worry about you."

"Arnese," I told him with some earnestness, "you should never worry about me. You burden yourself unnecessarily."

"Yes, yes. And I know what you will say next. That there is only fate and we must take what comes with equanimity." I grinned at him.

"Because you are a most orthodox Stoic. Though I must say you live up to what you believe, which is more than most do."

My grin faded. "No I don't, Arnese. But I would like to."

"We won't argue," he said with a deprecating gesture. "But back to what I was saying before. You've chosen good company." He nodded to Wolfbane who looked thoughtful as he cleared away the remains of my most recent meal and prepared to give me another shot of speed heal.

"You can trust Lost Rythans," he added.

"Arnese," I said, "you are trying to tell me something, aren't you?"

"Yes, Eduardo. Shall I speak?"

"Should Heth Andrew hear this too?"

"If Heth Andrew is what I think he is, then he certainly should." The old man gave both of us a bright-eyed look.

"To avoid mistake—" I began but Wolfbane forestalled me.

"You have guessed correctly, sir," he said. "I am a Faring Guard. I rely on your discretion and your friendship for Eduardo Sabat to keep you from discussing our affairs outside this room."

Bor Kladden smiled. "You didn't need to tell me that," he said.

"Or to flatter me."

"You cannot be serious now," Wolfbane told him. "Flattery is something we never indulge in. That is proverbial, in fact, for we are said to be the most truthful people in the galaxy." He smiled a little as he said that. He had a good smile.

At this, bor Kladden laughed out loud. "Yes," he agreed. "I suppose that's so. But now," he added a moment later, "to business." He turned to me. 'Someone has been asking for you, Eduardo. While you were gone."

"Someone?"

"A very dark man with a very scarred face. In fact, most of what I could see was synthoflesh."

I looked up. "What did he want?"

Bor Kladden made an abortive reach for a snuff box, an anachronism he had given up on his hundredth birthday and still missed. "He said he was a friend of yours and that it was very important that he talk to you."

"Name?"

Bor Kladden shook his head. "I was not sure what to think of him, Eduardo, and so I said only that I did not know when you would return. That was yesterday afternoon."

I would still have been unconscious at the time or maybe still in surgery. "I don't know anyone like that," I said. "But—"

Arnese and I never alluded to the band on my wrist, though he would certainly have known it for what it was. This was no time for reticence. I held up my arm. "Did he have one of these?" I asked. "I couldn't see. He was wearing a coat both times."

"Both?"

"Last night, they broke into the club. Breached the security codes. I had come to check on you—after that, you know. Just in case."

I didn't like that. "You took a risk, Arnese."

"Fate," he said impudently. 'There were two of them outside your door. I couldn't see very well but I'm sure one was the synthoface. They seemed to be quarrelling."

He reached again for his nonexistent snuff and I wondered why he had given up the habit. Surely not for his own health which was excellent.

"They both turned around when they heard me," he went on. "But I must have looked harmless. 'Looking for Sabat?' I asked them. "'Then you're too late. He's gone offworld. Just called me this evening.'

"It was touch and go for a few seconds while they decided whether I was going to turn in an alarm. But I kept things pretty matter of fact—old busybody and all that—and so they left."

This gave me food for thought, but at first the only thing I could think of was an old man confronting two hoods about to break into my apartment. "Arnese—" I began.

"Thought you should know, Eduardo."

"That isn't much to go on," Wolfbane said. "But if the man was not a slave, there will be a track of some kind. He'll have papers if he's from offworld. Synthoflesh on that scale—possibly rebuilt—" He moved off into the other room and I heard him call up the computer.

I turned to my visitor. "Arnese," I asked in a low voice, "just what is a Faring Guard, anyway?"

Bor Kladden sat back, hands groping slightly on his bony knees. "You didn't know? I had thought perhaps you were working for the Star Brothers."

I sank down onto the bed. Sitting up had not been such a good idea just yet. "I'd better not confirm that guess," I told him.

"Of course, of course. None of my business. But you asked about the Faring Guard."

"They're not connected with the Embassy," I said cautiously.

"Not officially," bor Kladden corrected me. "Lost Rythan intelligence is what they are. And don't make a pun on that—"

I shook my head. "I already know better."

"Good. But they'll never cease to surprise you. Did you know they actually hunt with spears? On Lost Rythar, I mean. You should

ask these fellows about the wolfhunt sometime." I said I would do that.

Bor Kladden glanced at the doorway from which we could hear Wolfbane's low voice and an answering voice from the unit. "I ramble, Eduardo. To the point then. The Faring Guard is often detailed to serve the Star Brothers. Lost Rythar has a standing commitment to aid them in every possible way, officially or unofficially. Whether the Star Brothers ask for help or not, actually."

Another piece fell into place. "But what is the source of this commitment?" I asked.

"The Star Brothers," bor Kladden said, "evangelized the entire colony about a century or more back. At great cost to themselves, I might add. It was no easy job."

"So the Lost Rythans are grateful?"

"Certainly they are. They pretty much owe their civilization to the Star Brothers.

"But the Faring Guard," he resumed, "are more than an arm of the government. They are what you might call a penitential society as well. Most of them are former felons."

I looked up in surprise. "Felons?"

"Quite. Lost Rythans don't go in for prisons, and they can't execute everybody who commits a crime, though their justice is pretty bloody at times. Anyway, the Faring Guard is a way for former criminals to redeem their honor. It also gets them out of the way of blood feuds and things like that."

I let out my breath in a low exclamation. "That's pretty impressive, Arnese," I said.

"An interesting system," he agreed. "And one that wouldn't work for many cultures."

"No," I said, thinking of my own checkered past. "Most criminals don't have any honor to redeem."

Bor Kladden got up to go. "I don't suppose I'll see you before you leave?" he said.

"No. But as you say, I'm in good hands."

"Couldn't be better," he agreed cheerfully. "I'm not a Christian myself but—"

I nodded. "Take care of yourself, Arnese."

"Been doing it for a hundred years."

I watched him go and his back was as straight as that of a much younger man. I heard him say something to Wolfbane and then the door slid shut.

I ate again and fell asleep, looking at Susanna's picture. More than ever now, I could feel the storm gathering below that glorious horizon and I dreamed that all the boats along the shore were being made fast. The innocent sky showed nothing, but the sea moved restlessly against the wooden pilings, and the air smelled like ozone or something even more elemental.

In the evening, I got up and dressed.

"A quiet day," Bloodbear greeted me as I came into the living room. He seemed disappointed.

As Wolfbane looked at me, I found myself wondering what these two had done to earn places in the Faring Guard. Robbed? Killed? Surely they were no worse than I, who envied them the bright simplicity of their moral lives. They inhabited a place from which I was forever barred, a place of great sunlit spaces where right was right and wrong was wrong and guilt was followed by repentance as the day followed night.

"Any luck?" I asked Wolfbane, gesturing toward the screen.

"No," he said. "Or actually too much." He held up a sheaf of printouts. "We still can't know for certain whether your visitor is a citizen here. Nor can we determine his race since synthoskin can be made in any form. I have several hundred possible identities."

"No good then," I said and sat down in front of the terminal. My walk from the other room had tired me out.

"No good," Wolfbane agreed and got up to fetch more speed heal. "Father Liu called," he added. "He has booked our passage for tomorrow morning."

"I'll make it, I think," I said, grimacing as he injected the stuff.

"You had another call," he said and keyed in Susanna's logo.

"I'd like to be alone for this one," I said. He and Bloodbear moved off.

For more than a minute, all I saw was a familiar field of lavender with the name Susanna etched across in elfin script. Below, a more businesslike font poured out credits and times, dimensions and dates and prices for her portraits.

And then another scene, apparently recorded, came on. I saw a darkened room, a shadowy form in the foreground. Her hair was down, half obscuring features made ghastly by the glow of the screen before her. A glass and bottle sat at her elbow.

"Eduardo," she said. "Eduardo, I am afraid!"

And then this too dissolved and I saw the face of a patroller. "Eduardo Sabat?" he inquired crisply. "Contract spouse of Susanna Rill?"

I nodded, not understanding.

"I'm afraid I must tell you that Citizen Rill has been found dead in her studio. You'll need to make a formal identification."

I saw Bloodbear watching me from his place at the window and gestured him over. He asked a few questions and established that there had been a break-in at the studio and that her death was no accident.

"Susanna?" I whispered, belatedly finding my voice.

"You'll need to identify the body," the patroller repeated patiently. I felt someone's arm about my shoulders.

For some reason all I could think of was that I had wanted us to adopt a child and now that would never happen. Not unless, like the ancient philosopher, Epictetus, I took on the responsibility myself—

But I was not so courageous as that old man, crippled from torture, poor and wise and good. "Even wolves do not abandon their young," he said. "And shall man?" He had never had a wife.

After that, the speed heal rose up in me and I fainted.

CHAPTER FOUR

I woke as clear-headed as I had ever been, knowing that the speed heal had finally done its work and that when I got up this time,

I would stay up. I was lying fully dressed upon the bed and there at the foot hung Susanna's painting, happiness distilled and sunshine for my heart.

I rolled over and saw Wolfbane sitting at my bedside reading a book, only this time it was my copy of Epictetus and not the Imitation of Christ.

"Hello, Heth Andrew," I said and he poured me a glass of water. Hadn't we gone through this before, some time in the far-off past? But when Otto Zeller materialized beside him, I was forced to return to the present.

"Herr Sabat, I am sorry," Otto said when he saw that I was awake. He looked absolutely shattered. "If I had had any idea our undertaking might have led to this—"

I cut him off with some measure of brutality. "Otto, you didn't know her. She was perfectly capable of getting herself murdered without anyone's help."

"Herr Sabat!"

I got up, not looking at him. "What time is it?"

"Near midnight," Wolfbane said. "Gaed Stephen told the patrollers you would come in the morning."

"I can't do that, Heth Andrew," I said, turning to him. "Otto covered for me on that island incident, but this is too great a risk. My papers won't hold up."

"But this was your wife," he protested, shocked. "Surely you can risk identifying the body."

"My ex-wife actually," I told him. "And seeing her remains won't bring her back." I don't know why I spoke that way, I who ought to have had the ethical advantage over these two. It was their innate kindness that threatened me—the weakness that was their own strength.

I think Otto might have understood in part how I felt, for when he spoke again, it was in a more businesslike tone. "Not seeing her may bring you even more notice," he pointed out. "Had you thought of that, Herr Sabat?"

I thought of it now. "You told them I was ill?"

"They know you were wounded on the island."

"And tomorrow, we leave Sachsen. I'll be gone before they come looking."

"You'll want to come back," Otto pointed out. "Later. Won't you?"

I ran one hand over my hair, the slave band glinting in the muted light. "Later—maybe." Beyond Otto's sturdy form, I saw Father Liu in the doorway. He looked tired.

"Good evening, Mr. Sabat," he said, coming in. "Or morning as the case may be."

"How long have you and Otto been here?"

"We came about an hour ago." To my relief, he did not offer his own condolences or mention the matter at all.

I turned abruptly to Wolfbane. "Alright, Heth Andrew. Is there a connection or not? If there is, maybe we should leave now." "You have a lot of confidence in my abilities, Eduardo." I waited.

"Alright," he said at last. "I will give you my opinion based on a printout of the police report which I, ah, abstracted from the metropolitan computer network." He glanced sidewise and a little guiltily at Father Liu. I found this amusing.

"Nothing was stolen at the studio, though there were signs of what may have been vandalism. The killer, or killers, overrode security codes for the building but there was no break-in per se." "Like they did here," I said. "Bor Kladden told me."

"We do not know that they were the same people, however, Herr Sabat," Otto pointed out.

Wolfbane nodded agreement. "We do not know that," he affirmed. "There was a vid—in the report, I mean. A general view of the studio as found." He swallowed. "I saw the body of course, and the—the other damage."

"What other damage?" I demanded.

"Vandalism, as I mentioned before. The destruction of a painting or two. One had been slashed several times."

His eyes turned almost against his will toward Susanna's painting. "I saw it, Eduardo. A portrait. Your portrait."

I knew the picture he meant. I had never liked it, but Susanna had always said it was a good likeness. And apparently Wolfbane had recognized it even in damaged condition.

"She might," I suggested after a moment's thought, "have done that herself." I did not look at the others. "Was that all?" Wolfbane nodded.

"The damage was recent? Could they tell?"

"Yes." Wolfbane took up Epictetus, turning the pages restlessly. "It might have been as you said, but I do not think so. The alcohol in her blood was very high, certainly too high for her even to defend herself. Though she did possess a weapon, I gather."

"A laser pistol," I said. "One of her friends got it for her." I remembered a night three years ago when I'd had to take it away from her.

"She must have known someone was outside," Wolfbane said.

"She could have called the patrollers."

"But instead she called me."

Wolfbane was silent. I tried to think of other times in my life when worse things than this had happened. This too must be endured, I kept telling myself. It would pass.

But even as I sought consolation in the wisdom of the Stoics, I wondered that there was not more of a struggle. Was I no longer capable of grief?

"It would be better to see her," Otto said at last, hesitantly. "To say goodbye, Herr Sabat."

Never had the barrier between his world and mine seemed so high as it did then. Despite what he had told me of his youth, he had never really passed beyond the tidy sentiments of his home village. No wonder he had failed as a mercenary.

"I'll think about it, Otto," I said, aware of Father Liu still standing in the doorway, watching me. "She'll—they'll cremate her," I added. "Her sister will see to that. It's in her will."

"This is a terrible place," Otto said earnestly. "Bloomhadn."

I ignored him and turned to Wolfbane. "So we'll assume the possibility of a link," I said, trying not to think of someone—Susanna or the murderer?—slashing my portrait in a fit of madness and rage. "What else was in the report? How did she die?"

"She was strangled, Eduardo. But she would have been nearly unconscious by the time they actually got in. Her blood alcohol was that high."

I gazed at her painting and the sun was in my eyes, dazzling after the storm. "There must have been traces. Did he wear gloves?"

"It was done with a wire," Wolfbane said, replacing my book. "Of course the patrollers scooped the area and did a scan of all residue."

"And?"

"So many people had been in and out—it was her studio after all. She met the public there, didn't she?" "What was the verdict?" I asked.

This time he fiddled with an empty speed heal vial. "They're checking everyone of course. Most of what they found matches someone or other, friends and customers."

"But not all?"

"No, Eduardo. But—" I thought the vial would snap in his fingers. "Did you visit her recently?" he asked.

I saw at once what he was getting at. As a corporate slave, my DNA would be unregistered beyond the superficial records I had inserted to back up my forged papers. The sort of search the patrollers were doing would have turned up nothing at all. But I had not been to the studio—not in a year or more. I told Wolfbane that.

"Then there is your answer, Eduardo," he said and this time the vial broke, cutting his thumb. "The most recent sample couldn't be traced."

"So there was more than one slave involved," Father Liu murmured. "And that could mean two at least of your former crew working against us. Or one, now."

"But why would they kill his wife?" Otto asked in perplexity. "There was no reason for such a thing."

"Terrorism? Malice?" Father Liu suggested. "Psychological overkill?"

I brushed past the others and out into the living room. The act was illogical—crazy. It did not fit. And yet, I knew in the deepest part of my soul that it not only fit but that it was inevitable. And a name came to my lips and I would not say it.

Bloodbear looked up from his post by the window. "Someone's out there," he said quietly. "Hovering."

I came to his side at once. He had the window on one-way, turned to infra-red. The flyer made a ghostly image, shining at the edges. I could not see how many people were inside.

"How long has that been there?"

"A minute or two."

"By the window?"

"First they were at the plat door. Then they came along the side."

Wolfbane joined us. His thumb was still bleeding a little and I stared at that red smear against his calloused skin. "I don't like this," he said.

Behind him, Otto glanced quickly around the room. I realized the vid was beeping and hit the sound switch. "Eduardo Sabat—" There was that familiar voice again, husky enough to make my throat ache in sympathy. "You are in danger, Sabat."

"I often am."

"You've got to come out to me now. Hurry!" "Is it coming from the flyer?" Otto breathed. Wolfbane frowned. "He wants us to think so, at least." "Who are you?" I demanded.

"A friend. I can't say more until I know how far I can trust you." "Don't do that," I told him, gesturing the others toward the door. 'I'm hard on friends."

"Sabat—Feullier's been bought out! They're working on the codes! You've got to trust someone!"

I saw the flyer approach the window and ran out the door after Father Liu. Bloodbear wanted to try a shot from the outer platform but Otto shook his head.

"You may have the firepower, Herr Bloodbear," he said, "but we're in the middle of the city. We've had enough publicity already." "Come on," I told them. "Down the shaft and be ready for his friends. How did you come in?"

"Robocab."

I thought for a moment. "Keep going down then. We'll catch the underground from the basement."

We were nearly to the shaft when a hard, white light caught us from the glassite doors on the upper plat. I squinted my eyes against the glare but could make out nothing more than something large outside.

"Run!" Bloodbear shouted from behind, snapping off a shot that tore into the glassite, filling the hallway with an acrid reek.

I felt the wash of a nerve cannon from outside. It was no more than a spasming of muscles at that range, though it pulled sickeningly at my mostly healed wound. Then Wolfbane took my arm and we leaped into the shaft together.

Above us, Bloodbear and Father Liu floated gently in the field, while below, I saw the top of Otto's head. He had a gun in his hand and I saw him tense, ready to go into action the moment we reached the bottom.

But no one met us there. We crossed a tiled foyer, passed a closed cafe where I sometimes ate breakfast, and caught the slidewalk to the station. I do not much like Bloomhadn's underground sections, of which there are tiers upon tiers. Closed in spaces always make me nervous, which is a real defect in a tomb robber. All along the station tunnel, I kept looking back while little things crawled up and down my backbone. Though that particular effect was probably left over from the nerve cannon.

"Here," Otto said suddenly. We got off just in time to catch a module. Luckily there were no other passengers in our compartment and when we alighted somewhere near the harbor, we were on a nearly empty square.

I saw that Otto had not reholstered his weapon which was when I realized that I had left my own stunner behind. I was wearing a grey pullover and the sort of military dungarees I usually favored, with pockets for everything I could possibly need. As luck would have it, all pockets were empty at the moment.

"Now what?" I asked and Wolfbane, who also had a weapon in his hand, gave me a troubled look.

"We might go back to the Embassy Enclave," he said. "Considering the circumstances. But we try to at least keep up appearances—"

"The left hand," Father Liu murmured, smiling faintly, "tries to ignore what the right hand is doing. But," he added, "that isn't always possible."

"We only have to make it until tomorrow," I reminded him. "Just until our shuttle goes up to Sachsen station."

"We could take an earlier one, actually," Father Liu told me.

"Or hole up here," I finished for him. There were places we could go. I had friends at the university—and elsewhere, for that matter. But after what had happened to Susanna, I hesitated to look them up.

Another capsule pulled in and cracked open, disgorging a party of happy spacers with attendant locals. There was much talking and loud laughter, high and jarring in the nearly empty boulevard.

"I think," Wolfbane said quietly, "we should go up now. We can get a robocab nearer the beach."

As Otto agreed, we turned into a street of bars and brothels, still busy at this hour. Though we tried to blend into the crowd, neither Father Liu nor Bloodbear, who was nearly seven feet tall, could have been a normal sight in the neighborhood. Nevertheless, all went well until we reached the park.

"Over here," Wolfbane said and pointed to a hovering row of cabs.

He and Otto mounted at once. Father Liu had just reached for the bar to pull himself up when a group of ragged urchins ran in among us, shouting and jerking about in ghastly imitation of play. Bloodbear and I were separated. I saw him stumble backwards as two skinny girls ran up against him shrieking with laughter as they wrestled a toy skimmer between them.

It must have been near dawn by now and the children were extremely high on loop. I got out of the way of a running boy and stepped off the walk onto the turf. Behind me, a magnolia tree laden with flowers loomed wetly beneath the glowing sky.

A hand fell on my shoulder and I spun about.

"Eduardo Sabat, I arrest you for the murder of Susanna Rill."

I gaped at the patroller's uncertain outline, the distant streetlight glinting on his helmet and the gun in his hand. I had never been arrested on Sachsen before and for a moment my mind went blank.

Someone else took my other arm and began hustling me backward beneath the trees.

"Bloodbear!" I shouted. He and Father Liu turned in my direction. The Lost Rythan raised an uncertain weapon but there were children in his way and I don't think he could see me very well anyway. Then, brushing them aside, he waded forward as Father Liu snatched a little boy out of his path.

One of my captors raised a gun and fired just as another boy ran in front of Bloodbear. I saw the child spin about, throwing up his hands as he fell.

But I had seen something else as well. There was a slave band on the wrist that held the gun!

What I did next was pure reflex. Indeed, I would like to blame it entirely on my conditioning. Twisting away from my other captor, I drove one fist into the killer's face and snatched up his gun as it fell.

And then I shot him, pouring the force of a beam directly into the band until I saw him began to convulse. He died too quickly, I remember thinking as I held down the stud. I was very cool about it and I did not stop until he gave one final spasm, vomiting forth his life's blood.

Slowly I became aware of Bloodbear beside me and of Father Liu. The man in the helmet had run away into the park as Otto and Wolfbane came panting up. The children had long since disappeared— all except one.

Shoving Bloodbear aside, I ran out into the street and knelt beside that one small body.

"It is too late," Otto said. "Again and again it is too late, Herr Sabat."

I did not answer him. Instead I looked up into Bloodbear's haggard face and saw that he was looking at me. "You killed that man," he said.

"And I would do it again," I snarled. "They used these kids! Can't you see they set them up?"

"I saw that."

"They killed a child!" I was still shaking with the horror of it.

"But the band," Bloodbear said. "To shoot into the band! Surely you knew what would happen!"

I looked down at my hands. "Maybe," I said with somewhat less intensity, "I would not do it that way again."

"Come and see if you can identify this man," Wolfbane called softly. "And then we must get away from this place." I got up and came over to him.

He flashed a light on the dead man's face, though I could see him well enough by now in the early morning light. After a moment, I nodded. "Boris," I said. "I never knew him by any other name."

"Two down, then," Otto murmured, looking away. Boris had died hard, no mistaking that, his lips bitten through, his eyes bulging so that one had nearly come out of the socket.

I grew sick at what I had done. I wanted to tell them all, especially Otto, about my conditioning. That I was forced to react with violence whenever a child was threatened or hurt.

But such explanation would change nothing. This death was my doing—one more strand of my fate. And though I would pass away and this that I had done would pass away, yet if all things were made again, as very likely they would be and had always been, it would happen just as it had this time. Nothing I could say or do would change that; to believe otherwise would violate my own creed as a Stoic.

"We had better go," Wolfbane said softly.

"It is hard to leave that child." Otto turned to me. "But we have done it before, Herr Sabat. Abandoned the dead in this verdammte city!"

I did not answer him.

We set one of the robocabs for the shuttleport. When I had settled myself and put away the gun I had taken from Boris, I turned to Wolfbane.

"They could not have known which capsule we would take," I said. "They could not have known where we would be."

"That is so, Eduardo. I have been thinking of that."

"They knew about Susanna's murder."

"But they would if—" Wolfbane was watching me.

I waited for him to go on. I wanted someone else to say the next part.

"Well, Eduardo? Did you think this Boris was the murderer?" His clear eyes met mine and at last I understood him. Like Bloodbear, he had been deeply shocked at my brutality. He wanted to, if not exonerate me, at least to readmit me to his own bright moral world—a world in which there were reasons for things.

For a moment, I thought I was going to burst out laughing. I wondered what Wolfbane had done to earn his place in the Faring Guard. I was willing to bet that if he had killed someone, it would have been a clean kill, the blow struck at the height of long-repented passion. And then I didn't want to laugh anymore. I wanted to tell him the truth and I tried to do so.

"Boris," I said carefully, "was no leader. If he killed her, it was because someone else told him to."

"Do you think he did kill her?"

"I have no way of knowing that, Heth Andrew," I said. "I wasn't thinking about that at all."

"So how could they have found us so quickly?" Otto asked suddenly. Father Liu, who was busy putting something on his hand where one of the children had bitten him, looked up.

"What was that man talking about on your vid? Right before we left the apartment. Something about a buyout—"

I closed my eyes but there was nothing behind the lids except Boris' dead face. I opened them again quickly. "He wanted me to come out to him."

"But at the end," Father Liu persisted, "what was it he said?"

I hesitated. The Star Brothers—or rather Hithia—had hired me to do a job. A well-paid job, it was true, but still I did not owe them my life story. There'd been enough of that thrown about already.

"I'd rather not say," I told him.

Otto gave me a very serious look. "I hope you will reconsider, Herr Sabat. If Father Liu thinks it is important, then you had better tell him."

"It's not connected with our mission. Besides," I added, glancing at the priest in irritation, "the Star Brothers must have enough to do without keeping tabs on every citizen."

Father Liu did not take offense. "But you are not a citizen, Mr. Sabat," he said calmly. "And I was not prying into your personal affairs." He finished with his hand and put away the kit. 'There was reference to codes and a corporate buyout. Now it strikes me that the only codes that would concern you are those of your own wristband."

I sat forward, surprised at the violence of my reaction. "What are you getting at?" My voice came out as hoarse as that of the man in the flyer.

The priest faced me with that same calm he had managed earlier. "I'm not quite sure," he admitted. "Andrew Wolfbane would know better than I, but I was wondering if, without breaking the inner codes, someone might find a way to trace your whereabouts."

My hands clenched on the edge of the seat and I fell silent, aghast at the possibilities this opened up.

Wolfbane hesitated. Then, "What do you think, Gaed Stephen?" he asked, turning to Bloodbear.

Bloodbear frowned, his own grey eyes raised for a moment to my face. Still frowning, he folded his arms and stuck his long legs out before him, standard seats not being designed to accommodate Lost Rythans. "That is possible, Heth Andrew," he said slowly. "It would be a step toward the inner codes, of course."

"A step?" I felt the sweat trickling down my face and could not even bring myself to wipe it off.

"A very small step."

"But I do not understand," Otto said. "Does this mean that these men are acting as slaves? That they have already been brought under control of this new corporation?"

"Most certainly not," Bloodbear said. "If they are working for anyone, they are doing so voluntarily. There are master codes, you see, which would have been modified at the time of purchase. If these had been activated—" He glanced at me and shook his head.

A lot of things occurred to me in that moment, things about as ugly and hopeless as any I had ever encountered. And then, once more, I closed the gates of my inner citadel. I would never be a slave again, I told myself. When life became intolerable, I would leave it— that was the last defense and somehow, when the last moment came, I would.

I felt Father Liu watching me almost as though he read my mind, and I looked back at him with the pitiful defiance of one who defended without hope the gates of a fortress about to crumble around him. I licked my lips, wondering why I was not angry at him. "This complicates things," I said aloud and my voice came out as steady as I had meant it to.

"Not too much, Mr. Sabat," he replied. "We still need you. And later we will help you if we can." He did not elaborate but something in his face gave me sudden hope. Star Brothers, I suspected, did not make idle promises—or threats, for that matter.

"Well," Otto said, "we shall be safe enough in the shuttle. And on the starship, well no one can molest us on a starship." "And maybe on Ponia," Wolfbane added.

"But now I could wish," Father Liu murmured, "that Lady Pelanot were not coming. If only she would reconsider."

"I could come in her place," Bloodbear offered eagerly, reverting once more to the simple warrior that lay not so very far beneath his education and his training in Lost Rythar's secret service. I remembered the way he and Wolfbane had listened to Lady Pelanot's story about the assassin.

But, "I was not quite thinking of you," Father Liu admitted with a self-deprecating smile. "Ah well—at least we are forewarned about future danger."

I forced myself to relax further. "There can't be more than two slaves left alive," I said, trying not to think of Maureen Kavanaugh. "And I find it hard to believe Lady Pelanot's enemies have recruited the entire crew—"

"Why not?" The Star Brother asked me. "They have all worked together before."

"Since our freedom, you mean?"

He nodded. "Weren't you aware of that?"

"No, Father Liu, I wasn't. I have had no real contact with any of them since—since Feullier."

He watched me in his oblique way. "Then you did not know that the others had gone into business for themselves, just as you did. Up until now they have not had your level of success."

"You seem to know a lot."

"I know that there are personal reasons why you and Miss Kavanaugh have never tried to look each other up."

I turned away. "You said you were not going to pry."

"Your wife was murdered, Mr. Sabat. Now I must ask you whether you hold Miss Kavanaugh responsible."

"Responsible?" I stared at him and then had to bite off words he probably wouldn't approve. "I haven't held Maureen responsible for anything in seven or eight years. She is insane."

"True," he agreed, leaving me in doubt as to just how much he really did know. "But somehow she has held the loyalty of your former crew—all save yours, that is. And if someone has hired her to stop you from rescuing Hermradon Pelanot, then this might be a tactic to discourage you."

"Coincidence. Anyway, we are the only people who can get into Godcountry. Of course she would be hired."

"Coincidence? Yes, certainly that is possible." He looked troubled. "But it adds another factor, doesn't it?"

We got out at the shuttle port just as the suns were rising above the sea. Everywhere in Bloomhadn, the night people would be closing up shop and the busy workers of the day would be leaving their beds, unaware of the pounding life that swept around them while they slept.

Otto got us onto the first shuttle into orbit and we ate breakfast at the station, surrounded by moving images of the morning we had left behind. A newscaster told us it would be a sunny day in Bloomhadn, the first in weeks.

CHAPTER FIVE

Waking up on a starship is never easy, but since only the mad can traverse the main channels of the net in anything resembling consciousness, cold sleep is necessary. Or so most believe—though obviously Hermradon had made his own adaptations. But on the whole, starpilots are not sane.

So I came half awake, went through an hour or so of weird dreams, and drank the stuff they give out to make us feel human again. Most of my nightmares were about Godcountry. Naturally.

Father Liu had rented a suite down on Quele's moon and it was there we gathered for the last time. I thought that Lost Rythans seemed to tolerate cold sleep better than most but maybe it was just their zeal for their duties that made them ignore discomfort. Wolfbane was almost quivering with eagerness to be gone and Bloodbear showed a corresponding unrest because he was not to accompany us. I, who hated Quele about as much as a man can hate an entire planet, had no patience with his fidgeting. I dialed myself some coffee and went to sit with Father Liu.

"Is Lady Pelanot meeting us here?" I asked him.

He nodded. "In about an hour I will say Mass here in the suite. It may be the last opportunity for Otto and Andrew Wolfbane before your return."

"You have a talent for understatement," I observed sourly.

"I wonder," he said, "if you know Quele as well as you think you do, Mr. Sabat."

"I know you'd die a very messy death if you were caught down there in a Star Brother's habit," I told him. "They wouldn't even ask you to bow to the gods before they tore you to pieces."

He sat back and looked at me. "Ah yes, you are an expert on Godcountry—and no doubt you know your way around the capital. But, Mr. Sabat, have you considered how you are to get from one to the other?"

Otto was taking care of that part, but I did not say so. I was sure he already knew and that this was just the indirect way he had of coming to a point. So I made a noncommittal noise and waited.

I was rewarded after a few seconds by a rather weary smile. "Think, Mr. Sabat," he said. "You are going down with certain immunities, or at least most of you are—"

We both looked at my wristband and his smile became rueful.

"But," he resumed, "you may be certain those immunities won't hold outside the city. Someone is going to have to transport you and hide you—"

"When I was here before," I said, with a grim smile of my own, "Feullier had a deal going with a local gang. Hijackers and robbers who preyed on the pilgrims, I mean."

Father Liu winced. "Otto has contacts too, of course. We got them for him, and if they are caught, they'll be treated a lot worse than robbers."

I gazed at him darkly. "Tomb robbers," I said, "are buried alive."

"Worse," he repeated. "I should know."

I paused, cup half raised, until I remembered to set it down. "Are you trying to tell me there are already Star Brothers on Quele? Christians?"

"There are Star Brothers everywhere."

"But how do they manage? How do they survive?"

"They don't always survive, Mr. Sabat. We are known for our high mortality rate as well as for our tenacity. So you see you needn't tell me what would happen if I were caught saying Mass down there because it has happened to others. Some of them were my friends."

I digested this slowly. "So we'll be dealing with your own contacts in the city and—"

"And in the villages. All the way to Godcountry."

"Do they know why we're coming?"

"They know you are on a mission for us and that if you succeed, the Faith will be planted openly on a world they will never see."

Before either of us could say more, the door chimed and Wolfbane let in Lady Pelanot. She was no longer wearing a veil and I was startled at the delicacy, the classic beauty of her face. Her race was strange to me, her complexion pale with only a hint of gold—but there was more than a suggestion of that wildness I had seen in the men. She seemed to me in that moment as unpredictable as a tiger. She was also, as I had guessed before, about a decade older than I.

Her small mouth twisted with distaste when she saw me, quickly cancelling the effects of any beauty she might have had in my eyes. As usual, I was tempted to start a quarrel if I could, for I wanted to see the blood rush into her white cheeks, to see her dark eyes snapping as they had done the first time we met. But then I decided it was too much effort. I drank my coffee instead.

Father Liu received her with his usual politeness and Otto too came over and greeted her. "You have prepared yourself well, Lady Pelanot," he said, observing her dark dress and eminently sensible shoes. "You will make a creditable secretary."

"I hope," the priest added, "that you can pass all detection devices?"

"I should," she answered, glancing at Wolfbane. "The Lost Rythan embassy was so good as to send up this outfit before I left Sachsen station."

"Then you'll get through," Bloodbear told her. "And we owe the ambassador a beer."

"Gallons of it," Wolfbane agreed. "But we won't risk paying him."

Father Liu nodded emphatic agreement. "Certainly not. And now, would anyone like to go to confession?"

Otto excused himself and accompanied the priest into the other room. This gave me a feeling as though we were going into battle, and it was true that we might die down there. I had been in Godcountry before, of course, many times. But then I had been a slave with nothing to lose. For the first time, I began to realize that this was different.

And then I thought of Tokot and how someone was working on the master codes. The irony of my present situation brought a grim smile to my lips. I saw Wolfbane watching me soberly.

"Are you ready for Quele, Heth Andrew?" I asked, but then, remembering what Father Liu had told me about the native Christians risking their necks for Hithia, I was sorry I had spoken so glibly.

"I will go to confession, Eduardo, and I will hear Mass. Then I will be ready."

"You have a very simple faith, Heth Andrew."

"Real things are always simple," he said and I was silenced. He had echoed one of my own beliefs and I wondered suddenly if this simplicity wasn't one of the reasons Otto and I hit it off so well.

It was not, I decided, that I denied the complexities around me any more than Otto did. But I knew that everything could be brought down to size if you thought about it enough. Even now with Susanna dead and her murderer yet to be identified, my inner citadel remained in order and life made sense.

"I will pray for you, Eduardo," Wolfbane said abruptly. Then Otto came back and he left me.

***

The guildhall in Quele City was a square stone block set at angles to the quaint wood and brick buildings that lined the streets. It looked like a fortress—or a prison. When our flyer came down on the roof, I think we all had that feeling. It took a few moments before any of us were ready to go in.

Otto, in his new role of Trademaster First-class, led the way, his square face hard and stern. Behind him, Wolfbane paced like a great, shaggy beast, barely held in check by Otto's authority. He looked down his nose at the Quele official who had escorted us and, I was sure he made the man more than a little nervous.

Pelanot and I came last, though she made it very plain we were not paired off. I was beginning to find her brittle hauteur amusing since it came not from my moral but from my social inferiority. She seemed, for such a clever woman, to have very little discernment in the less tangible sphere—which was not a hopeful sign for poor Father Liu who intended to make a Christian of her.

I had taken the oath. When we came through customs, each of us was asked to affirm the supremacy of Quele's gods. This was an act of more political than religious significance to the Quele, who believed that all foreigners were damned anyway. But nevertheless the whole business was repellent enough to Otto and company.

My companions had each refused in turn, of course, offering their guild papers as tokens of immunity. I saw Wolfbane's hands twitch at his sides while this was done and his agonized gaze fairly scorched me as his eyes met mine.

"And your slave?" the Quele—this Quele—had asked, not quite gloating, but obviously enjoying the discomfiture of the aliens.

Wordlessly, I walked over to the niche where a representative group of Quele's pantheon awaited the submission of visitors. I knelt and repeated the formula in Quele, not bothering to read the phonetic printout on the wall. I had done this too many times before.

But this time was different after all. The words left a bad taste in my mouth and that taste was uncomfortably like shame, for I was no longer a slave and I knew it. I might say to myself that words meant nothing, that I had not truly sold myself to the Quele, that my inner fortress was unbreached. But I did not quite believe myself.

At the guildhall, our escort made sure we had reserved rooms and an office before he departed. That departure was none too soon, I think. Wolfbane's smoldering gaze followed him until he was out of sight.

"Well," Otto said, when the Quele had left us alone in our office suite, "let us get down to business as quickly as we can. We do not know when the, ah, other party will turn up. They may be here on Quele already."

"They have all the same problems we have," I pointed out. "And they can't have arrived any earlier."

"That is true," he said. 'But still, there are things to be done. Herr Sabat, you and I must go out into the city and see about one or two matters. My assistant,"—here he indicated Wolfbane—"will set up shop. Who knows but we may sell a bit of agricultural equipment."

"Delivery could be a problem," I said.

"Not at all, Herr Sabat. I am a bona-fide representative of Agro-Sachsen. Andrew Wolfbane and I will be happy to do business with anyone who drops in."

I gave up. Otto was way out of my league when it came to things like this and I knew it.

We took a robocab from the roof, me in my role as interpreter and Otto playing tourist, though as I well knew, there was little to see in Quele City. The entire colony was no more than a variegated blotch on one wilderness continent of a planet too poor to attract immigrants. Only the desperate came here and the Quele quickly absorbed them, or if they were hopeless, chewed them up and spit them back out.

We hovered above the guildhall for a moment. To our left lay the high temple where a line of drab natives could usually be seen filing in at one end while another more irregular line emerged from the other. Quele's gods were fond of burnt offerings and two trails of greasy smoke rose from the temple chimneys day and night. I had forgotten the smell, but now it all came back to me. I felt about Quele City as Otto felt about Bloomhadn, only worse.

"Where to?" I asked Otto.

"High Tree Market. Do you know it?"

I nodded. "It's on the other side of the city. A huge square." I punched in the destination and we set off. Block after block of wood, brick and stone passed beneath us, the buildings mostly flat roofed and no more than a couple stories high.

"There," I said presently, pointing to an oblong of green, "is the park. They have public executions." Otto did not say anything.

"And over here is the Colony Prison." I indicated a gargoyle infested roofline. "Ecclesiastical court across the way—right next to the university."

"These people are literate?" Otto asked sourly. "I would think they used the building to wall up criminals."

I chuckled. "Sorry," I told him. "Just having fun. I haven't been here in a while."

At length we came down at a cab stand, sliding in below the hovering empties, and got out at the edge of the square. Quele tend to be short, stocky types with uniformly brown hair and light-colored eyes. Otto might pass for a native, but neither I nor Wolfbane would stand a chance. I pushed up my sleeve to show the slave band and followed Otto around the square.

We made our way through a crowd of bulky women with fat cheeks and slight moustaches. There were children as well who stared at us as though we were strange animals—and men who apparently regarded all strangers with deep animosity.

"We're looking for the butcher shops," Otto whispered and I nodded.

"You'll smell them when we get close," I said and soon, rounding a corner, my prediction came true with a vengeance.

"Now a fellow called Tapman Troy," Otto told me, unperturbed. "He has a big place. My friends," he added, glancing at me, "have arranged to have us take samples of the meat for Agro-Sachsen's research department."

Suddenly I was glad I hadn't eaten much breakfast.

We found the place at last, but Troy was not there. After an uncomfortable few minutes, a powerful looking brute consented to guide us around—but only after perusing our papers with an intensity that led even me to wonder about the literacy of the Quele. After some time, Otto was finally allowed to produce his sample kit and get started.

"Tell him we had a long walk to get here," Otto said to me as he worked beneath the gimlet eyes of our guide. We had all three moved off into the back part of the building by this time and no one else was around.

I looked at Otto as though he had lost his mind, but did as he said.

Immediately our guide relaxed. "And how do you like the weather?" he enquired with ludicrous and unexpected politeness.

I translated for Otto.

"Much too warm," the latter replied. When I had passed that on, the Quele straightened himself. "You are both most welcome here," he said. I translated while holding fast the swinging carcass of something large and smelly. I waited to see what would happen next.

Calmly Otto scraped off a small sliver of meat and put it into a tube. "Ask him what arrangements have been made," he told me.

"You shall leave the city tonight," the Quele said. "We'll come for you, but don't be surprised at the manner of our coming. We can be pretty creative at times." He grinned suddenly, looking like a different man entirely—not even a Quele.

We followed him down a row of hanging meat and started in among some smaller carcasses that looked to my eye rather like short, fat dwarves. "We'll be waiting," I told him when I had passed this on to Otto.

"You will know us by this." He showed me a knotted leather thong around one brawny wrist. "It is a rosary, the only kind we have on Quele."

Once more I translated for Otto and he paused in his work. "Things will be better for them one day," he said.

"I must get back up front," the Quele said abruptly, reverting to his first role. We heard him bellowing at some unfortunate underling and turned to our own task. Otto was pretty thorough and kept us both at it until midday.

Back at the guildhall, Otto all business and me thinking of lunch despite my nasty morning, troubles awaited us. Klavia Pelanot met us at the office door, her cheeks red enough now, her eyes snapping with fury.

"Your Lost Rythan," she fairly hissed in her rage, "has gotten himself arrested."

Otto came quickly into the room and shut the door. "What was he doing? Proselytizing?" he asked in consternation.

"I doubt it. The charge was manslaughter. Even a Lost Rythan would be more subtle than that!"

"But what happened?"

"He killed someone in a brawl."

"Not a Hithian by any chance?" I asked her. "Did you enquire?"

"Of course I did," she snapped, "and it was a Hithian. It seems our enemies are one step ahead of us again."

"What have you done so far?" I asked her.

"Tried to talk to the authorities. It is slow going with the language barrier, not to mention, this damned translating unit which keeps on making puns—"

"Homophones," Otto said. "But did you find out anything?"

"Nothing. They won't talk to me until I get clearance from the foreign office."

Otto ran one hand through his hair. "I must say, I did not anticipate anything like this so soon," he told me. "How did it happen, Lady Pelanot?"

"Someone came in with a message from you—"

"I sent no message."

"We were suspicious, but Wolfbane went out anyway and you know the rest." She glared at Otto. "He was a Faring Guard, after all, wasn't he? Even I know what that means."

"He was a trained professional."

"And a criminal," she said. "What was he in for, anyway?"

Otto was plainly shocked. "Lady Pelanot! No one asks such a question."

She snorted. "If the Star Brothers hadn't recommended you so highly, I'd begin to wonder what sort of menagerie you—"

To his credit, Otto kept his temper. He turned to me. "You know more about Quele than I do, Herr Sabat. What is your recommendation?"

I thought hard. "He'll be in civil custody," I said at last. "And they will have given him counsel. Quele deal fairly by their lights." "But he was probably set up," Otto pointed out.

"He was probably ambushed on the roof. But you can't get away with the sorts of things here that you can in Bloomhadn."

I felt their eyes on me. "I'd better go in person," I added. "I know more about the workings of Quele justice than you do."

"I'll just bet you do," Pelanot sneered and I turned on her.

"I do," I agreed. "And that applies to other colonies as well. Your nephew broke the law when he entered the tendrils of the net and I am going to break more laws to rescue him. That is why you hired me."

She started to speak and I moved a step toward her. "And if you give Otto any more trouble," I told her, "I'll break the law that says a slave can't throw the autarch's sister out the nearest window."

If I thought that would frighten her, I was wrong. She pulled a glassite blade and faced me. "That might not be so easy, Sabat," she said, but at least her sneer was gone.

I relaxed slightly, a little ashamed of my outburst. "I'll keep that in mind," I told her and turned to go. "You will not wait for me beyond this evening. If I'm not back you'll know the mission is aborted." "I think you will be back, Herr Sabat," Otto said.

Blessing his innocence, I set off on foot and caught a public transport two blocks away. If anyone was tracing my whereabouts, my only hope was to keep moving and not to be caught alone. I got off at the Hall of Justice and told them Agro-Sachsen had sent me.

It took a while but finally I got in to see an undersecretary. This meant once more offering homage to the gods, but not until I bribed someone could I even get the name of Wolfbane's lawyer, Hegor Horton.

"But it's no use," the Quele secretary told me. "Your master will not bow to the gods. How can he be tried if he has no legal rights?"

"He is not a citizen, sir," I pointed out. "That must be his excuse."

"Nor," the Quele said sharply, "are you." I turned away, knowing full well that Wolfbane's immunity would not cover this.

The legal office was in the same building—as probably Wolfbane was himself—and I found Hegor Horton eating lunch at his desk.

"The probe," he told me when I had identified myself. "No trial is possible if he will not cooperate. We would have to assume bad faith."

He referred to the mind probe which was something not even Net Central used openly. But then this was Quele.

Horton picked up another sandwich. "They'll determine his complicity of course and punish him accordingly. We're not," he added, as though reading my mind, "savages. If the probe does not show any capital offense, he will be deported as soon as our justice is satisfied."

"What if he is innocent, sir?"

"No one who refuses to honor the gods is innocent," Horton said dryly.

I turned to go. I had a card on Otto's expense account and the time had come to make use of it. Certainly I had not exaggerated when I said I knew Quele's justice system and, consequently, I also knew exactly when to step outside the law.

"One moment, slave," Horton said, gesturing me back into his office. "You will tell Mr. Wolfbane's partner these things, of course. Everything I've said will be confirmed officially within a few days.

But," he added, "there is something more he should know." I waited, keeping my face as blank as possible.

"Your master has been more than uncooperative. In fact, his behavior has been remarkably offensive. You had better tell his partner that if his attitude does not change, Mr. Wolfbane may pass out of this jurisdiction entirely."

I did not pretend to misunderstand; indeed, I understood a lot more than Horton probably did. "You warned him?" I asked through suddenly dry lips. "You told him what could happen?"

"I did."

I gave Horton my best bow. "Thank-you, sir," I said and meant it.

But now I knew I really had to act fast. Heth Andrew Wolfbane just might have the guts to deliberately commit Quele's most heinous crime—if he understood the courts, that is. If he were accused of blasphemy, he would avoid the probe and all danger of betraying the rest of us, because the other court did not use it. The small matter of an automatic death penalty would hardly deter a Lost Rythan in pursuit of what he considered his duty. My only hope was to extricate him from the civil authorities before it was too late.

I nearly ran to the shaft, careless in my hurry, though the half-healed wound still pulled somewhere deep in my chest. I was three floors down before I realized what I had seen on my way out of the office—a dark man, his face smooth with synthoflesh, staring around a corner at something I could not see.

I moved over into the upstream, remembering belatedly that I was unarmed. But when I emerged, the stranger was gone. After a short search, I gave up.

Back on the street, I took another public car and studied my fellow passengers with the care the situation warranted. No Hithians, no dark men—no foreigners at all. But still, I knew I would have to keep moving.

I got off at a station near the market square Otto and I had visited earlier. Naturally I knew better than to turn this problem over to Otto's contacts. I didn't think they would or could do the things that would be needed to free Wolfbane.

Instead, I was going to call on someone else—someone I hadn't seen in over six years and who might no longer be where I could find him. Someone who might, in short, already have kept a long-delayed appointment with the gallows in the park.

But I was in luck. Descending a flight of narrow stone steps beside a second-hand store, I met a doorman who knew me.

"Long time, Sabat," he said. Grotan was a Quele, scarred with more than one public flogging, not to mention a brand on his left cheek.

I greeted him and asked how he'd been.

"Not too bad. I hear Feullier's gone."

"That's right, Grotan. Nothing left but a crater." He did not move away from the door.

"I'm in business for myself now," I told him. "I can pay for what I need."

Grotan's eyes narrowed thoughtfully. His next brush with the law would probably kill him and he was taking no chances. "You want to see Yordan," he stated.

"That about sums it up," I told him. "You may tell him I have a job for him."

Again I was in luck, because Grotan was as afraid of his boss as he was of the law and he also remembered the generous fee scale Feullier had employed.

We passed through one of Quele's very few dens of vice, a speakeasy where the big thrills were gambling and watching the dancing girls who came in two nights a week. It was pretty heady stuff for Quele City.

I entered a well-remembered sitting room at the back where Grotan left me at a nod from the man who sat peacefully smoking a pipe as he watched the news on the wall.

"Eduardo Sabat!" Yordan said, almost rising. "How are you?"

He hadn't changed much, I decided, as I looked into his genial grandfatherly face. Maybe he had less hair these days and his Quellian spectacles were thicker. But otherwise he was the same. I knew I mustn't let down my guard for one second.

"Have you eaten?" Yordan asked and I said I had not.

He ordered a meal and then sat back, smoking, while I ate. "So you're your own man now?"

I nodded with my mouth full.

"Still in archaeology?"

"Usually."

"But not this time?"

I hesitated, wondering how much I dared tell him. If the Hithians came here, he'd sell me out at a moment's notice—perhaps he already had. But I had no choice about revealing at least a part of my business, if I intended to do any business at all.

"Special job," I said tentatively. "It won't affect things here in Quele City, at least."

"I am glad of that, Eduardo. Very glad. And I am happy to see you doing so well. You always had a professional attitude and I thought it was a shame you had so little opportunity with Feullier."

I hid a smile at this and told him what I needed done. "It will be well worth your while," I added. "I'm on a planetary expense account."

He pursed his lips. "A Lost Rythan? A renegade, I take it."

I did not answer that. "I need him for the moment," I said. 'We're in business together."

"But why doesn't he just give evidence and try to get off?"

"They're like that," I said shortly. "But still I need him."

Yordan's eyes narrowed behind their thick lenses. "There is only one reason he would keep silent," he said after a moment's thought. "He is not a renegade after all, is he? You are working for the Star Brothers."

"You don't expect an answer to that," I observed, after which I named a price for Wolfbane's release.

Yordan puffed on his pipe while I waited. "Star Brothers," he repeated, wondering. "You're a Christian?" I shook my head in irritation.

"But this is very dangerous," he said then. "I've heard they have a finger in every pot!" He seemed to think of the Star Brothers as some sort of giant cartel, an interstellar mob of the first order. I did not try to disabuse him of the notion, for he had lived on Quele all his life and was steeped in the local propaganda. Anyway, his respect—his almost awe at the very idea—could only help me in the long run.

"Well now," he said at last. "Considering the danger, this will have to be a very expensive operation."

I finished off a sandwich and washed it down with the native equivalent of wine. He wanted to haggle and so we haggled. It didn't take long to come to an agreement, considering how much money was at my command. "But," I told Yordan, "there isn't much time. A few hours at most and he'll be where you can't get him."

"Dead? Or—Oh, I see." Yordan raised one eyebrow and looked at me. "A real hothead, then. I've heard Lost Rythans aren't too bright."

"They have that reputation."

"And where will you be?"

I named a working-class pub I had once frequented. "I'll check in," I told him, "every hour or so."

While Yordan's men did their work—of which I did not want to know the details—I planned to lead the scarred man all over the city and hope his tracing of my band wasn't continuous. But when I reached the door, I found I was already too late.

"Someone's out there," Grotan said, halting me with one hand on the latch.

"Someone?"

"Two men. Foreigners."

I paused, deciding. "I'm not up for company right now," I said at last.

For a fee, he led me through another door into a semi underground garment factory where dull-eyed women gazed incuriously at us as we passed. There was a cab stand on the corner where I emerged, but before I went out, I turned to Grotan once more. "What did they look like?" I asked him.

"One had a jacket with a hood—I couldn't see his face, but he was not very tall. And the other was foreign—dark hair and earrings." This last came out with evident disgust. Quele's men didn't go in for jewelry.

Grotan had described a Hithian, though I didn't tell him. As for the other, who could say? My fleeting glimpses of the dark man had not given me any particular impression of his size. I thanked the Quele and took off.

The rests of the day was exhausting. I travelled nearly every mode Quele City could supply, making random patterns which included the bar where I dutifully checked in every hour. I also took time to withdraw a considerable sum from Otto's account and to purchase a small handgun, the best Quele's scanty underground had to offer. Finally, on my fourth stop at the bar, I spotted someone I recognized drinking in a booth. He was alone.

Warily, I approached, seated myself and waited.

"Outside—in a cab."

"I'll have to see for myself," I told him and went out.

But when I viewed Wolfbane's long form draped over the seat, I turned on my companion. "I'm not paying for a corpse," I said, backing away.

"Take it easy, Sabat." Grotan came sauntering over from another cab. "He's on sus—check if you want." He handed me a scanner and I did so.

"Why put him under like this?" I demanded when I had reassured myself that Heth Andrew was alive.

"He came out through the morgue," Grotan explained. "And," he added, shoving aside Wolfbane's clothing to show me a mass of lacerations and bruises, "you might want to leave him alone for a while. He won't like it, waking up like this."

I gave a bleak nod. "He really must have made them mad," I said. "He was on his way to the gods' court lockup," Grotan said. "Just like you thought. Blasphemy. He spit on the gods."

"Good for him," I almost said, but not even Grotan would have liked that. "Thanks," I told him instead. "Tell your boss I'm grateful." I reached in my belt for the scrip.

At that moment, a flyer swooped in and Grotan was neatly decapitated in a line of laser fire. His partner and I blinked at one another as another craft passed over our heads before both disappeared behind a line of warehouses.

"Here," I said, tossing him the scrip. "Get out while you can."

He turned to run, then came back—for he was, after all, a Quele—and handed me a vial. "To bring him to," he explained breathlessly and sprinted away.

I darted into the cab, injected Wolfbane and set the controls for the guildhall just as one of the flyers came streaking back. I leaped to the ground and fired into the approaching bubble, seeing it shatter. Then it was gone and so was my cab with Wolfbane still unconscious inside it.

And then the other flyer came in, circling—and I prepared myself to die.

CHAPTER SIX

I raised the gun, a pitiful thing that only shot bullets, and aimed with both hands together, knowing I did not stand a chance.

I was right. A stunner beam caught me before the flyer came in range of my weapon and I stumbled to the ground, the gun falling from suddenly useless hands. The flyer set down beside me and the dark man got out.

"I wouldn't have to do this, Sabat," his familiar rasp came to me, "if you were a more trusting sort."

"Just who the hell are you?" I managed to get out.

"No time. The cops are on the way." Despite my struggles, which were not very coordinated, he wrestled me into the flyer and took off in a flattened arc that moved us out of the district and in over a zone of apartment buildings. He set us to circle slowly above tidy streets and little shops. Below, a few smaller craft drifted sedately from balcony to balcony.

"They're tracking you, Sabat," the dark man said. "And until we take out their equipment, you haven't a chance."

"Who?" I demanded, levering myself up on one arm only to collapse again as my strength gave way.

"Maureen Kavanaugh has been hired by the Hithian royal family to keep you from rescuing the autarch's son."

I peered up into that scarred face. "I don't know you," I said slowly, "but I think I should. Let me see your arms."

He held them out and his wrists were bare and completely unmarked though, since both were covered in synthoflesh, I couldn't be sure. "You knew me," he said, "as a free contractor. I spoke up for you and Kavanaugh when you got in trouble with the company. But it didn't do any good."

"Amid Steed," I said. "But he's in prison." "I was."

'But—" This time I made it halfway up before I fell back. The stun beam was wearing off. "What happened to you?"

"Flyer crash. They pried me out of the wreckage and the Autonomy of Central Africa was good enough to put me back together again. Then they sentenced me to rehab for a while and gave me a free education at the University of Asia when I was paroled."

"The University of Asia," I repeated. "Isn't that where…?"

"Yes, Sabat. Hermradon and I studied together, or rather I studied under him. Then he went home to start up a project on Hithia and asked me to join him as soon as I graduated."

I finally dragged myself into a sitting position and leaned sideways against the back of the seat. "You work for Hermradon, then?"

"I will. You might say he has my loyalty in advance."

"And you said Maureen had been hired by the royal family? That's doesn't quite fit, you know."

Steed—if it was Steed—leaned back, watching my reaction as he spoke. "I was led to believe," he said slowly, "that the family was somewhat divided. And Hermradon said to trust no one."

"He should know." Then I shook my head. "Steed, I don't dare to believe you. I can't—" I watched his rigid features; only his eyes seemed alive. "You say you crashed somewhere on earth? But what were you doing there, anyway?"

"Fighting a war. I was on the wrong side."

It was on the tip of my tongue to tell him that in my opinion most wars did not have right and wrong sides and further that such a distinction would have had no meaning for a hired soldier. But instead, I merely repeated what he had said. "You were," I mused aloud, "on the wrong side?"

"The bad guys. And I found out when the bio stuff started. That's why I was hired, apparently. They had something that had been smuggled out of Godcountry and then they souped it up. And I—all of us who had been there—was immune because we'd had it already back on Quele."

"Before the bad guys got hold of it, you mean?" I asked. Godcountry was a treasure house of biological oddities and now that I knew also about the net tendrils, it was plain why. Stuff must have been leaking into the wilderness from dozens of worlds for uncounted years.

"So," I said, wincing as my muscles began to twitch. "So you balked at the dirty part."

"Actually, I sabotaged their project," he said. "And then I escaped in a flyer before—as I thought, anyway—anyone knew what I had done."

"But they did know," I said. "Or figured it out. And they shot you down."

"Pretty much. But luckily I crashed on the other side of the border."

"Ah."

He turned away, staring out over the city. "Sabat, they were grateful. I can't tell you how grateful they were. They did the best they could for me. Besides, it made good propaganda for their side."

"Soldier of fortune has change of heart," I murmured.

"Shut up, Sabat."

"Sorry."

"There's nothing more I can do to persuade you we're on the same side now. If you like, I'll drop you off. Obviously we can't stay here without the others turning up."

I stared out the front of the craft and grunted. "Too late," I said and pointed to a dark silhouette skimming above the rooflines.

Steed leaped to the controls and we cut away, the other flyer now in open pursuit. As they gained on us, I could see that I'd messed up their windscreen with my earlier shot, but the two people inside looked pretty healthy.

"Hang on," Steed told me and I did the best I could with still clumsy hands. We went lower, slanting down a canyon of office buildings, down and down until we passed out of the city and into a ravine. There was a river at the bottom.

"We're gaining on them," I said.

"I'm going to try something," Steed told me. "I don't think they can track your band through too much stone and earth. I'm going to follow this river and swing around. There!" He indicated a dark ridge on the horizon.

We kept barely above the water and, as the river looped about, we began to lose sight of the other flyer on the bends. Suddenly Steed brought us up and out, racing around a great mass of broken cliffs where we hovered, wondering if Kavanaugh would keep going.

"Got to risk a run back to the city," Steed said. "Can you use your hands now?"

I flexed my fingers and sat up straight. "I think so."

"Heat gun behind you," he told me and brought us all the way around to cut cross country and back into the Quele City. Meanwhile, I found the weapon but didn't need it. There was no sign of the other flyer.

We flew straight to the guildhall, Steed pausing us to hover above the roof. "Well, Sabat? Am I one of your team?"

I cradled the gun, chewing my underlip. The sun was going down and in the reddish light, I saw that even Steed's eyes were bio constructs. They gave back the light in an unsettling way. "It's not up to me," I said at last. "Otto will have to decide." He still waited.

"Alright. I think you're really Steed."

"What made you decide that?"

I gave him a wry smile. "The way you told me to shut up back there. You did that before. When I was still a slave."

Steed's face did not—could not change, but I heard him chuckle. "So I did. A couple times."

I replaced the weapon since it was too big to carry openly into the guildhall, and then thought to look for the robocab I had sent off with Wolfbane inside. There was, not surprisingly, no sign of it.

"Come on," I said and led him warily down into the building. "We probably don't have much time."

Most of the offices were closed and though a few people still milled about on our floor, the lights had already been dimmed. It was one of the many thrifty habits of the Quele and extended also to such things as a lack of adequate streetlights outside.

No one looked twice at us as we came in. But I did not know how Otto would feel about me bringing in a stranger. Or Lady Pelanot, for that matter, but this was a minor worry.

As usual, my less important cares were forestalled by bigger ones. We had barely reached the suite when the doors burst open and Otto and Pelanot came out with a rather dazed-looking Wolfbane limping behind them. Behind him, two civil police emerged with very businesslike stunners directed at his broad back.

"Uh, oh," I said, but it was too late to retreat. One of the cops jerked his chin in our direction and motioned for us to join the others.

"There was not," Steed murmured to me, "a police flyer on the roof."

"No talking," one of the pair said as a tradesman and a messenger got quickly out of our way.

I gave the speaker a closer scrutiny and saw a bit of knotted leather dangling below one sleeve. "It's okay," I breathed, belatedly recognizing the multi-talented butcher.

Steed shrugged and fell in beside me. Otto didn't even turn, though Lady Pelanot gave us a sharp glance. At that moment, Wolfbane stumbled and swayed slightly, necessitating some action on my part. With a glance at our "captors" as though seeking permission, I moved forward to take one arm while Steed took the other. Between us, we hustled the Lost Rythan into the shaft.

Conveniently, an unmarked hovercraft met us on the roof and we all piled aboard, our pretense of lawmen and felons forgotten. As we took off across the darkening city, I found myself wedged into the angle of a seat with most of Wolfbane lying on top of me. Lady Pelanot crouched on the floor at my feet, clutching a brace bar. She glared up at me.

"You can, of course, account for your actions?" she inquired icily.

"Nice to see you again," I told her and tried to locate Otto in the melee.

There were three Quele aboard, our friend from the butcher shop and two buddies of equally hearty dimensions. One of them was piloting and one was giving Wolfbane something to drink from a flask while the butcher himself sat with Otto. Steed, who had taken the rest of the floor, was watching everyone. I noticed that Otto was armed.

Gingerly, I crawled out from under Wolfbane who groaned and sat up, knocking me over on top of Lady Pelanot. She was even less pleased at this intimacy than she had been on first catching sight of me, and my elbow in her left eye did not help.

Otto looked up as I squeezed down beside Steed. "Ah, Herr Sabat. I knew you would not fail us."

"Thanks, Otto," I said sincerely. "I needed that."

"And your friend here—?"

"Amid Steed. He used to be a free contractor."

"Ah."

I turned to Steed. "You were on Sachsen," I said. "You called me."

"I tried to meet with you," he answered. "But she—Kavanaugh got there first."

I tried to see him in the dimness, recreating his old face in memory. "Maureen," I said, hearing the sound of my own voice as though someone else were speaking. "Maureen was at the studio." Steed did not respond.

"When my wife was killed," I elaborated. "She was there." Amid looked at me. "I didn't even know you had a wife, Sabat. What are you talking about?"

"Maureen must have killed her—or watched as someone else killed her. You didn't even know?"

"No," he said slowly. "I did not know. I was concentrating on you. Not Maureen Kavanaugh."

"There was no reason for it," I told him. 'We didn't even live together. It was crazy."

I realized I was trembling and closed my eyes. But instead of Maureen, I kept seeing the dead face of Boris with one eye hanging out and blood all over his chin. Maybe I was crazy too, I thought. Somehow, Steed must have guessed what I was thinking.

"I don't know what they did to you both that time," he ventured with what may have passed for gentleness, "when they punished you. But you know she was never the same after that, Sabat."

I shook my head. "Sorry, Steed. I don't want to talk about it anymore. I can't."

But then, I did after all, because Steed had been one of the masters and he knew me and he had seen me when I had no dignity of my own, no claim to humanity even—and now it didn't matter. He was okay.

I swallowed and began again. "She broke is all. Most people would." But then I had to stop once more. Maureen had broken not so much from physical pain as from the other things the slave band could do, like mess with our perceptions and make us believe things that weren't real. Things like being buried alive, for instance, in my own case. I don't know just what Maureen's own personal hell had been but obviously it was something worse than mine.

Otto, who had been listening in silence, made his slow way into the conversation. "This Kavanaugh," he said, "she is mad then? A psychopath?"

Steed shrugged. "I think so."

"And she's been hired to sabotage our efforts?"

"Yes," Steed affirmed. "Along with her crew. There were two besides her."

"Then she's the only one left," I murmured. "The others are accounted for."

Lady Pelanot was studying Steed and now she spoke up. "Is there any particular reason we should trust you?" she asked.

He started, seeming to notice for the first time that she was a Hithian. I thought I saw a change come over his face, but could not be sure. Certainly his uniformly rasping voice betrayed nothing as he told her he worked for Hermradon.

"But I could," he added, "ask you the same thing, ma'am."

Lady Pelanot's own face might have been synthoskin for all she showed. She turned to me instead of answering Steed. "You have not told us yet what you spent the money on, Sabat. The withdrawal you made this afternoon."

I gave her a thin smile. "Wolfbane," I said. "Sent to you with my best compliments."

"Herr Wolfbane," Otto explained to me, "remembers nothing after he apparently succumbed to mistreatment by his jailors. He

woke up in a flyer on the guildhall roof."

I glanced over at the Lost Rythan. "Alright now, Heth Andrew?" I asked. "You were slipped one of the sus drugs—that's why you don't remember anything."

"Ah. And that accounts for the headache too," he said. "But how did you manage this, Eduardo? They were going to try me for sacrilege and though I did resist to the best of my ability, I was extremely well guarded at all times."

I shrugged. "Oh, I've got contacts here," I said. "But Hithia paid the bill." Then I grew more serious. "What you tried to do was a very fine thing, Heth Andrew. I'm glad it wasn't necessary."

Wolfbane gave me a slow smile and his eyes lit up. "It was a great satisfaction, Eduardo, to smash the idols. And since I could see no alternative, I indulged my feelings with great energy." His smile turned into a very fierce grin. "I know it is said," he added, "that Lost Rythans are not averse to martyrdom, but in my case, I am grateful to have this honor deferred. After all, it is better to make martyrs of our enemies."

"And did you do that?" I asked, unable to keep from grinning myself.

"I don't think so. We must pay for our pleasures, as you well know, Eduardo, and those Quele are pretty rough. But I did break the captain's collar bone."

His cheerful, bloodthirsty enthusiasm put heart into me. Even Lady Pelanot gave him a grudging look of approval, though she probably hadn't much understanding of his motives. Neither did I quite, having never been exposed before to the sort of religious free-for-all that existed between Christians and Quele.

Otto did not smile. "And so this was done to avoid the probe," he said slowly. "I see. But how did you manage to free him, Herr Sabat?"

"I can't give details," I said. "But the authorities now believe he is dead. In fact my friends retrieved him from the morgue."

The butcher, who had been unable to understand our conversation, now turned to me for an explanation. I told him as much of our affairs as I thought wise. "Where are we going now?" I asked then.

"Factory roof. They'll let you in and send you on in a truck full of shoes. All the way to Spire, on the edge of Godcountry."

"I've been to Spire," I told him, relieved we were not going to travel with a load of his own smelly wares. I did not then know how bad new leather could smell.

We were approaching our drop off. Already the sky showed a few stars. Quele City's dim or nonexistent streetlights left this part of the city pretty dark—stygian, actually, I decided as we flew above the nearly deserted canyon of a street. I peered down into that vast crack where anything might lurk and wondered anew that Otto could not love bright, boisterous Bloomhadn. I wished with all my heart that we were back on Sachsen and not, now that we had finally come to it, on our way to Godcountry. But then, I set those thoughts aside. The thing was to survive and get the job done.

Our lights were cut as soon as we landed and we scrambled out onto the roof in nearly total darkness, glad, for my part, at least, that there was a high parapet. I felt someone beside me and Wolfbane's hand fell on my shoulder as he steadied himself. "Eduardo?" he said softly.

"Right here, Heth Andrew."

"Thank you, Eduardo, for what you did."

"Maybe," I told him, "you will have a chance to reciprocate."

Then the roof door opened and we were ushered inside. By the light of a pressure lantern, I took in what must have been a family group. Two half-grown children offered us food but when I tried to talk to them, they shied away. I was, after all, an alien.

To my relief, Wolfbane's injuries proved superficial, though the Quele had used something on his back and shoulders that left a lot of bruises. Our host shook his head over these as he spread on some pungent salve. Apparently they had seen such injuries before.

Otto, meanwhile, was taken to a storeroom where one of the family pointed out an assortment of gear and weapons from which we could select what we would need. Swallowing the last of some very indifferent ale, I joined him.

"A week or so on foot, Otto," I said. "At least three days in and three days out."

"And the time it takes to find Hermradon."

"That too," I agreed. "But the sacred precincts are not large. We'll hide in the old city—it's already been looted and they don't guard it very closely anymore." I did not add that there wasn't much need to guard the place on account of its well-deserved reputation for being haunted. No sense borrowing trouble.

Otto had more on the ball than I gave him credit for. "You make things sound very straightforward, Herr Sabat," he said mildly. "But we both know they are not."

I picked up a rifle, regretting the heat gun left behind in Steed's flyer. "We will both earn our fees, Otto," I agreed.

He gave me a shrewd look. "Lady Pelanot had much to say about your extravagance this afternoon. She thought you might have run out on us."

"I should have thrown her out the window, after all. But of course this isn't Bloomhadn."

Otto began filling packs for each of us. "This Steed was a friend of yours—before?" he asked then.

"Sort of. There was a barrier, of course. Slave and free. Can't get around that one very well." I helped him divide up a box of ration bars. "But he was always pretty decent." I gave Otto the outlines of Steed's story.

"So he was not originally a black man?"

I shook my head, amused. As a villager, Otto was very conscious of things like that. "The Central Africans rebuilt him in their own image," I said. "Probably there wasn't much left to go on."

Otto nodded thoughtfully. "And you think he's telling the truth?"

"Pretty much. But I'll keep an eye on him."

"You don't trust many people."

I weighed a bush knife in one hand and thought about that.

"No," I said. "I tend to measure other men by myself."

"We are always surprising ourselves, Herr Sabat."

I transferred the knife to my other hand. "Well at least I trust Heth Andrew Wolfbane," I said defensively.

Otto chuckled at this. "Lost Rythans are unique," he told me. "More's the pity."

We left the city in the back of a cargo floater—and it was bad for me. They had made a little cave for us among crates of shoes. And when we and our equipment had been stowed away, the entrance was filled with more crates.

The smell was appalling, but mostly I suffered from my old fear of closed in spaces. This last was so bad that sweat stood out on my forehead and my hands were slick with it. I felt as though I were suffocating.

As we began to move, I heard the others shifting in their places.

Someone fiddled with a bit of pack harness, and there came the clank of a water bottle being stowed. I heard the familiar sound of Otto taking out his rosary beads. But all these things seemed far away.

No one must know that I was afraid. My fear was, after all, irrational. This hot, stifling darkness, the wise old man would have said, is but the raw material on which our moral powers may act—

Suddenly a hand clutched my arm, digging into the flesh in panic. I thought it was Lady Pelanot. She was as claustrophobic as I! Silently I laid my other hand atop hers but she drew away quickly. I heard a sharp intake of breath and then nothing more for the rest of the ride.

When the truck stopped with a jolt, a general stir told me we were all making sure we had weapons to hand. I drew out a native pistol the butcher's friends had given me to replace the one I had lost when Steed stunned me and waited while the boxes were drawn away.

The brisk, piney air was like cold ambrosia after the stench of leather in the truck. "Sabat?" our driver called softly, knowing I spoke Quele. "Sabat?"

I crawled out onto the predawn highway, mist curling around my ankles as I stretched the kinks from my muscles. "What's up?" I asked. "This isn't the village."

The Quele—I think his name was Torman—led me around to the front of the floater and pointed. We were on a stretch of unpaved road, the truck floating about half a meter above the graded surface. Ahead, I made out a sort of road sign with a rounded top.

I peered at the top, trying to read a message there. And then I saw that it was no sign at all. A pole had been roughly driven into the ground—topped by a human head.

CHAPTER SEVEN

Behind me, Otto paused, one hand on my shoulder as he tried to make out what Torman and I were staring at.

"Sabat?" Steed called softly from the truck. "What's up?"

I told him. Godcountry had its own police. The holy rangers, we called them, and they sometimes went in for this sort of thing.

"But we are not in Godcountry, Herr Sabat," Otto protested.

"They patrol the surrounding villages." My shoulder blades drew together of their own accord as though expecting a bullet, but nothing happened. "Otto," I said then, "this is serious, you know. Heads—I mean they don't do this to ordinary criminals. Not even tomb robbers."

Otto moved away from the truck. "That couldn't be the prince, could it? But no," he answered himself. "That is no Hithian."

"Not Hermradon," I agreed, squinting my eyes. "It's an old man."

Abruptly one of the Quele doused the lights, leaving us in inky darkness. "We must go back," Torman said quickly. "We cannot approach the village now." I retailed this to Otto.

"But has this anything to do with us?" he asked as the others emerged from the truck. "What do you think, Herr Sabat?"

"Who knows?" Steed answered for me. "Maybe this guy was just some—some—"

"Nonbeliever?" I suggested and heard Otto draw in his breath.

"Lieber Gott! What if he is a Star Brother!"

I asked Torman about this. One of the crates had spilled and he was throwing boxes back into the truck, dropping shoes in the road.

He shook his head, not pausing in his task. "He is a Quele. We were going to his shop."

I picked up an armful of boxes and, elbowing him aside, stowed them gently into the back. "Then you must return to the city, of course," I said. "And the sooner we part company, the safer you will be."

My eyes had grown used to the starlight and I saw him pause, his arms full of shoes. "You are not to blame for this," he said haltingly. "At least I do not see how you could be. We live in constant danger and this was not entirely unexpected. Only we did not think it would come so soon."

"I see," I said. "And just what," I asked, lowering my voice, "are we likely to find when we get to Spire?"

He shook his head, a gesture barely visible. Neither did he lift his eyes.

I translated our conversation for Otto who turned to him at once. "Tell him, Herr Sabat, that we are sorry. It is likely he has lost other friends this night."

"Maybe," I agreed. "Do you think there was a massacre?"

"You know the Quele better than I do."

I did indeed know the Quele. "Well, Otto," I replied. "There it is."

"We brought cloaks for you," Torman told me, emerging from the front of the truck. "Pilgrims' clothing. Your faces will be masked, but whether the tall one can pass for one of us, I do not know." "No way," I said with a glance at Heth Andrew.

"Then you can't enter Godcountry by the road?"

"No," I said, wishing things could be that easy. "But we'll take the cloaks just in case. And—and thank you. For everything."

The other Quele handed these out from the cab and I told Otto what they were for.

"Hide them beside the road," he said and I did so, covering them with a mat of needles at the base of a twin-topped fir tall enough, I hoped, to be a landmark if I had to come back. I had just finished when I heard the hum of an approaching flyer.

"Everyone into the woods," I shouted as Torman slammed the truck doors and leaped for the cab.

"May God protect you!" he called and with a rush of displaced air, the floater spun about, blowing the dust of the roadway into a whirling cloud. Then it was gone and we were alone.

I crouched where I was, hidden by the darkness under the trees. I heard crashing in the brush beside me and up on the edge of the road I made out the dim profile of someone watching the sky.

"That you, Steed?" I called softly.

"Right."

"See anything?"

"I don't," he said, a weapon appearing suddenly in his hand,

"think it's the rangers."

"How can you tell?"

"The same way I found you, Sabat. I'm picking up on a slave band."

With an oath, I sprang up beside him, drawing my own gun. I did not know what I could do at this range, but forgetting my philosophy, I dreamed only of revenge.

The thing skimmed downward, dimming the stars—and I fired. Susanna's death was in that shot and all the pain of our shattered marriage and hopeless love, but another sort of love intervened. I could not kill Maureen in cold blood and I knew it.

I missed.

Steed had no such compunction and I saw the flyer buck once and right itself as someone leaned out a half-opened hatch and fired on us. Steed fell at once and did not rise as the bright arc of a heat beam played over him. Behind me, Otto and Wolfbane ran up, firing as the flyer turned back. This time I steeled myself and did not miss.

Flames erupted from one side of craft as it slewed sidewise, tilting toward the trees. I did not think I had done that, but who could say. I took aim again and the world fell apart.

For a long time I did not know if there had been a crash or if Kavanaugh had thrown a grenade. In fact, I did not know anything at all.

When next things righted themselves, I was standing in some very cold water. A lot of sand had found its way into my hair and clothing. My hands and knees were scraped raw and something sharp had left a long gouge on one cheek. I had no idea how I had gotten where I was.

Slop, slop. Something was lurching its way upstream. After a moment, I realized it was me. How long had I been walking, or rather stumbling about? And where was everyone else?

I dared not risk calling aloud, so I paused once more to take stock. Water—a current. Obviously I was in a creek and, knowing that we were within a kilometer of Spire, I could at least guess which one.

Above me, the sky was a dim, star hazed streak, fringed with trees. The banks overhung the water and, reaching out one hand, I felt rock. Good. That meant no one could take me from the air.

I considered the direction I had been going, turned about, and began to feel my way back upstream. It wasn't long until I stumbled over a body. Trembling with a mixture of exhaustion and dread, I knelt to reach out an exploratory hand.

Whoever it was was still breathing and, after a moment, I decided it was Otto. With an effort that left me dizzy, I hauled him up onto the narrow shingle and rolled him over. I was rewarded with a stream of muttered north country German and a fist that nearly connected with my eye.

"Take it easy, Otto," I said, reaching out a restraining hand. "It's me, Sabat."

He tried to sit up, failed, and sprawled back onto the sand.

"What—is happened?"

"I'm not sure." Quickly I felt him over. "What hurts, Otto?"

"My head. I must have hit it when I fell—Pass auf!" he yelped suddenly as my probing fingers found charred cloth along one leg. A burn, I thought, and a pretty bad one.

He wriggled away from my touch but then, bracing himself, he let me check things out. "Does it bleed much?" he asked.

"I can't see," I told him, slipping a pressure bandage from my belt and shoving it home. "This should hold things for a while."

He didn't answer but only gripped my wrist. "Listen," he breathed.

The sound of the flyer was very faint, muted by the trees and the overhang. It seemed to be moving away and—was it my imagination or was there an irregularity in that sound? Certainly something was wrong with the engine.

"So they didn't crash," I muttered, wondering if I was glad or sorry. There was no doubt Maureen was doing her best to kill us all.

"Do you think they know where we are?" Otto asked.

I thought this over. "Probably not. We're under a bank and whatever they're using to track me doesn't seem to work through dirt and rock."

"But they are trying to find you in particular?"

I nodded, realized he couldn't see me and told him that was the case. "They must have hit us with something pretty powerful back there, whatever it was," I added.

"Herr Sabat—where are the others?"

I swallowed, remembering. Steed was probably dead and it was my fault. I told Otto this. "I missed the first shot, Otto. There was no reason for that."

"Was there not?"

I shrugged. "You saw what I did to Boris. You know what I can do."

"But that—is it not part of your conditioning to react so whenever a child is hurt?"

"What do you know about my conditioning?" I whispered angrily.

There was a long silence before he spoke again. "I will not lie to you, Herr Sabat. I know what I have seen and I also know what the Star Brothers know." He moved slightly, groaning as his leg dragged over the sand. "It may be that we are alone, Herr Sabat. It may be that we have only a short while to live."

"I'm sorry, Otto," I said. "But you've got to understand that you can't just—just dig into these things that way."

"I hope I do understand. But I know also that a man can only live alone within himself so long before he goes mad."

I was grateful he could not see my face at that moment. "That is exactly where we are meant to live, Otto," I said softly. "Inside ourselves."

But Otto did not answer and when I bent down to check on him, I saw that he had passed out.

I sat back on my heels, listening for the flyer. Instead I heard the faint slopping sound of someone else wading the brook. Somehow I had kept the Quele pistol and now I pulled it out and waited.

The splashes came nearer and then ceased. "I know you are there," a cool voice said and I recognized Klavia Pelanot.

"And you've got me covered," I finished for her, so relieved I almost forgot I didn't like her.

She came up onto the sandy shelf beside me. "Who is that with you?"

"Otto Zeller."

"And that other man? Your criminal friend?"

"I don't know."

A shadow loomed against the sky and a moment later, Heth Andrew joined us. "We've been looking for you, Eduardo," he said.

"You were caught in the blast—"

"So she did throw a grenade?"

"Apparently."

"What's wrong with Zeller?" Pelanot asked, flicking a torch over his face.

"I don't know. Concussion probably. And he's been shot in the leg."

"We've got to get him moving if we can," she said. "Before they come back—or they put the law on us."

"I know," I told her, unsnapping another compartment in my first aid kit. "I'll put a stim disc on him—I've used them before. They're not good but we don't have a choice."

I found Otto's carotid artery and pressed the flat wafer home, activating it with a practiced twist.

"How long will that last?" Heth Andrew asked, balancing himself half out of the water.

"Not long. Maybe until we can find better cover and give him speed heal."

"So what next?" Pelanot persisted. "We can't go to this village, obviously. Had we not better go around it and directly into the preserve?"

"Maybe," I said slowly as Otto began to come around. "But not if we can help it."

"This other party," Heth Andrew spoke up, "surely they cannot take the flyer in?"

"No," I told him, helping Otto to sit up. "Take it easy," I said. "I know it's rough to come to on stim. Give it a chance to take effect."

Otto grunted and looked up at Heth Andrew's shadow. "All here?"

"All but Steed."

"Ah. And now?"

And now it was my turn to lead us, I realized. Otto had done his part and earned his fee. I drew in a deep breath. No one was going to like my next suggestion.

"I think I know where we are," I began. "This is a branch of Hollow Creek and there will be a bridge further on where the road crosses near the village."

"Then we won't want to go there," Pelanot said.

I caught myself toying with the wristband and snatched my hand away. 'We want to go where Maureen—where Miss Kavanaugh does not expect us to go. And where she could not strike if she did." I wished I could see the other's faces as I spoke, but at least mine was invisible to them. There were things I did not want anyone to know just yet about getting into Godcountry.

The problem was that no matter where we entered, my passage into Godcountry was going to be a hard one because the entire perimeter was guarded by a sensor field. I had brought a resonator to get us across undetected, but the resonator did things to the slave band that I tried to forget each time until I had to use the thing again. It was one of the reasons I no longer worked on Quele.

But of course I didn't tell them any of this. It could wait. "I think," I said instead, "that they do not know where we are. They

flew over a while ago and just kept going."

"But if there's been any disturbance in Spire," Heth Andrew pointed out, "fighting, I mean, then strangers will not be very welcome."

"I doubt they've been fighting," I said. "Only killing. And anyway, we won't be strangers. I'll go back for those costumes and we'll become pilgrims."

"You can't pass off a Lost Rythan as a native," Pelanot snapped. "Especially one as uncooperative as Wolfbane."

"I wasn't going to," I told her. "Heth Andrew will have to meet us on the other side of the village."

"So why go in at all?"

I held onto my patience with both hands, biting off the things I was most tempted to say. This was no time for another quarrel and besides, there was no window handy to throw her out.

"Otto needs speed heal, for one thing," I explained. "And I can't give it to him unless he takes in a lot of calories. All we have are protein bars because we were to pick up the rest of our supplies in Spire."

She started to say something but I cut her off.

"And then there's this," I added, shoving the slave band in her face. "Wherever I go, Maureen Kavanaugh will eventually follow. Would you rather meet her in the village or out in the woods?"

"If I had known they were going to hire a slave—"

This I let pass.

"Herr Sabat is right," Otto said. "And you have agreed to follow orders, Lady Pelanot. Now you will do so."

When Otto spoke like that, which he seldom did, the entire atmosphere seemed to change. He was no Lost Rythan—he was much too cool-headed for that—but whatever he had learned in the hills, absorbed as it were through generations of upland village life, had made something of him that both chilled and calmed those under his command. And Lady Pelanot was calmed, though not entirely silenced.

"But," she still protested, though more quietly, "would it not be safer to cut straight to the border from here? Then we wouldn't have to break up the party."

"You don't," I said with less heat than I would have believed possible a few moments before, "just march into the preserve. Not from anywhere."

"This road," Heth Andrew said slowly, "it goes on through the village?"

"And into Godcountry," I agreed. "But we'll never be able to pass that way even in disguise. Not all the way across the border." I did not add that Otto's scruples were a major impediment at this point. After all, I was beginning to wonder if I should not have more scruples of my own. Anyway, there was still the problem of a Lost Rythan nearly two meters tall and not at all likely to bow to any of Quele's gods.

"The perimeter, I take it, is guarded?" Heth Andrew said.

I told him about the field. "It would alert the rangers and—other things." I told him also that I had a resonator.

"Most impressive, Herr Sabat," Otto said and even Heth Andrew made an appreciative noise. Things like that were highly illegal and not very easy to obtain. They were also expensive. But this one had once belonged to Feullier.

"Otto," I added, before they could ask any more questions, "is equipped to deal with android guards." Otto and I had worked together on other worlds and I knew that his implants were not strictly legal either. Though he usually kept his activities within the law, I might add. At least the moral law.

"Does Kavanaugh have a resonator too?" Pelanot asked.

"Of course she does. We were seldom able to come in as pilgrims in the old days. It was too risky."

"So she'll follow on foot?"

"She won't be in any shape to make trouble right away," I said. "And I'm going to need help getting through myself when the time comes."

I turned to Wolfbane. "Otto will need all his concentration, Heth Andrew, so it will be up to you."

"You will be incapacitated, Eduardo?"

"Somewhat."

"How long?" Pelanot demanded. "And in what way?"

"Hours," I told her shortly, remembering her own fear when we had been shut up in the truck. How could I really make them see that the band worked on my own inner weakness—that I carried my personal doom wired into my flesh? How Maureen would cope, I couldn't imagine.

"Now," I went on quickly in order to avoid more questions, "Heth Andrew will need to leave the creek before the bridge—"

I gave him coordinates and directed him to meet us north of the village, among the orchards. "It isn't harvest time and you should be safe enough if you're careful."

When he had gone, I told the others I would go up for the cloaks. "It's nearly dawn," I added, "and I don't think the other party will dare show themselves on the road unless they have disguises of their own."

I could see a little by now though the sun had not risen, and I made the ascent from the creek very quickly. But when I emerged from the last thicket, neither the signpost nor the double topped tree were anywhere in sight.

I dared not risk standing up on the highway, so I stayed in the ditch, moving uphill and to the left because I thought we had been on an ascent when we stopped the night before. To my relief my efforts were rewarded at last by the sight of that grim trophy, backed by the first magenta promise of the dawn.

Turning, I soon oriented myself and realized I was standing almost directly opposite the tree where I had hidden our disguises. Quickly I retrieved everything and began casting about for Steed's body. There was no sign of it, though I did find a heat gun lying in the grass.

I was just moving back into the woods with my burden when I heard the approaching hum of a floater—perhaps such another as we had ridden in last night. There was barely time to conceal myself before a great, open sled crested the hill and drew even with the signpost.

It was a pilgrim party. Twenty or so costumed figures sat on the bed of the floater while one of the perfect ones, swathed in white, harangued them. Though I could hear little of his discourse, its subject was plain enough.

In the broadening light, a faint nimbus feathered about the head on the post—longish hair gone whiter even than the robes of the perfect one.

The face was fine-cut for a Quele, the teeth showing as rigor mortis set in. I might have played chess with such a man back at the Crescent Club in Bloomhadn. Or I might have listened to him speak of things I had never known before—might have listened spellbound as I sometimes did to my old friend from the university.

But this was not Bloomhadn. Here the head of an old man might be hacked from its body and thrust upon a pole, wisdom poured out like blood upon the ground. And then I remembered the dead boy in the alley and shrugged. If there was a lesson here, I was too tired to learn it.

The perfect one spoke for a long time. When the floater finally moved off, the first sun of Quele was a deep crimson smear, pulsing on the horizon.

I hurried back to the others, pausing only to search once more for any sign of Steed. There was none. Surely Maureen had not landed, and if the rangers had been here, they would have hunted the rest of us out of our hiding places. I added one more worry to my list and then let it go. The matter was out of my hands.

I called to Otto and Lady Pelanot as I slid back down the bank, dragging the cloaks in a bundle behind me. "Don't let them fall in the water," I hissed as I scrambled to my feet in a shower of sand. 'How is Otto?"

"I'm alright, Herr Sabat."

"What took you so long?" Pelanot demanded angrily, her arms full of cloaks. "It's almost daylight!"

I told her about the pilgrims. "And now," I added, "we'd better get going before that stim wears off. The bridge isn't too far and then we'll take the road."

"But can we do this?" Otto asked. "We know so little, Lady Pelanot and I. We do not even speak the language."

"Pilgrims don't say much," I told him. "The perfect ones do all the talking."

"No sign of Kavanaugh out there?" Lady Pelanot asked and I shook my head. I was helping Otto along while she carried everything, and our footing beneath the overhang was none too certain.

"They'll have to ditch the flyer," I added. "And even if they're in the village by now, Maureen won't dare try anything." I gave a mirthless smile. "She knows as well as I do what happens to anyone who defiles the holy places."

"I think I can get along now, Herr Sabat," Otto said, letting go of my arm. "There is the bridge ahead." He was limping badly but that would be alright. A lot of the pilgrims had things wrong with them.

"Time to get dressed, then."

There were masks built into our cowl-like head coverings and everything was voluminous enough to conceal even the heat gun. I did not intend to give it up unless I had to. We stepped out onto the bridge.

"Spire," I said, indicating a sprawl of plastiblock and wood, surrounded by cleared fields. Beyond lay a long belt of trees and the low hills of Godcountry. There was a fairy tale quality to this, our first glimpse of the forbidden land. But I, at least, had seen it before and was not in a fairy tale mood.

"Come on," I said and led the others across the bridge and into the village. We turned off the main road almost at once and onto a street of workshops and storage sheds. No one seemed to be at work yet and we passed quickly by small knots of villagers who fell silent when they saw our pilgrims' attire. A stench of burning hung over the place and there were far too many flies.

"So," Otto muttered in my ear when he had passed. "How do you read this?"

"A lot of new martyrs for your church, Otto. That's probably what you smell."

"For God's sake, Herr Sabat! Can't you show some respect?"

"Sorry. But what did you expect after seeing that guy on the pole? These people are complete barbarians."

Klavia Pelanot had gone ahead of us and I saw her waiting at the next corner, peering down another street. "Is that the square?" she asked when we came up with her. She pointed in the direction of a milling crowd of villagers which also included some rangers and a few pilgrims.

"Yes that's the square. But we're going the other way." I steered her up a narrow lane, past a garden and onto a parallel road.

"Where?" she asked, shrugging off my grip. "Where are we going?"

"Graveyard. Pilgrims often go to places like that. A lot of them come here to die, you know."

"But I thought they were buried out in Godcountry," Otto protested.

"Only the rich. That's why the looting is so good."

After this, Otto fell silent and concentrated on staying on his feet while Lady Pelanot made a point of not walking beside me. We passed through a smaller square where nervous peasants hurried by, not looking at us or at each other. A sled piled with feed sacks was parked on one side and some children were playing there. Or rather, they were quarrelling. Everyone wanted to be the rangers, apparently, and no one would be the blasphemer. I didn't blame them.

At last, I found the turning and we joined a group of pilgrims passing along a wide, tree-shaded lane. Ahead loomed a very solemn looking gate.

"This is it," I said unnecessarily. "We need a place to rest and some food. We'll find it all here."

Inside, the tombs of the poor made a small city. It was, I knew, a city of identical windowless houses where the dead were shelved neatly one atop another, but from the outside, it didn't look so bad. A wire fence surrounded the necropolis and on the far side an orchard of low trees stretched halfway to the main forest wall.

The others stared at that, but my own attention was caught by one of the perfect ones headed in our direction.

"Bow," I hissed.

For a moment, I feared they would not comply, Otto because he couldn't and Lady Pelanot for obvious reasons. But we must have satisfied him because he moved on after a brief acknowledgment.

"Those trees there are the border, aren't they?" Lady Pelanot whispered when he had gone.

"Not quite," I told her. "It's a little further in but not much."

"Such a short distance to cross—and nothing to be seen."

"You'll see plenty," I promised her. "And as for distance, it's further than it looks." I turned away to study the enclosure itself.

Nothing could have contrasted more with the blooming countryside than this bare place of unrelieved grey. A few people were in sight, dun-colored forms, moving slowly as though they had used up the last of their strength in getting here.

"We'll keep out of sight as much as we can," I murmured. "They close the gate at night and we'll go over the fence when everyone's gone. Heth Andrew should be out there somewhere," I added, pointing to a distant orchard.

By now Otto was swaying where he stood and I took his arm. "We've got to get under cover. You need rest and I need to look at that leg of yours in better light."

Glancing around, I tried the door of the nearest tomb.

"What are you doing?" Lady Pelanot hissed, her voice gone shrill with horror and disgust. Apparently I had touched a cultural nerve.

"They don't have hotels here," I said shortly.

"You can't take us into a tomb!"

Otto was leaning heavily on me by now and it looked like I would have to risk more stim if I wanted him to keep going. He'd done very well so far, mainly because he was Otto, I suppose, but now he was plainly at the end of his strength.

"It's not," I said with some effort at patience, "as though they leave the bodies scattered around. They're all bundled up in shrouds and the bottom shelf is always left empty."

She made a sound of disgust. "I'm sure you would know," she said.

"Herr Sabat," Otto said quietly, "let us seek elsewhere for shelter. There must be other buildings. Storage sheds, perhaps."

With a little grimace, I turned away, pausing to let a small party of pilgrims pass by in the narrow street. There was that quality in Otto, an unpretentious decency that sometimes shamed but never offended me and that made me yield to him at once.

"Would a new tomb be alright?" I asked them. "An empty one? There should be some at the other end."

"That will be fine, Herr Sabat." Only it came out all blurred when he said it and I barely caught him as he staggered against me. A couple of pilgrims paused and offered to help but I shook my head.

Between us, Lady Pelanot and I got him down another street and into a section of half-finished tomb houses. To my relief, no workmen were about. The first door I tried opened easily, but even at this, Klavia Pelanot hesitated.

"You don't have to stay," I told her through gritted teeth. "But if Otto doesn't make it, the mission's off."

Without a word, she helped me get him inside and onto the bottom shelf.

"Shut the door," I ordered, hunting about for a little torch I had stowed in my pocket. Of course I had lost it.

Otto had one. Pelanot would not close the door until I turned it on. I could not see her face, of course, though I threw off my own mask and Otto's, leaving her to the dubious privacy of her own. I knew by her posture that she was afraid.

With seeming casualness I flicked the light upward to show her how high the roof was and then turned my attention to Otto. His leg was pretty bad by now and the first thing I did was give him an antibiotic. "You need speed heal," I said as I applied burn spray. 'Now."

He nodded, his features drawn taut in the uncertain light. I thought his cheeks were flushed and when I felt his forehead it was hot. I shot him up, hoping I would be able to procure the calories he was going to need during the next few hours.

"I'll have to leave you alone with him," I told Lady Pelanot as I examined Otto's scalp. As I expected, there was quite a knot behind one ear and some blood had got matted in his hair.

She nodded.

"Don't give him ration tabs, even if he asks for them. He's got to have real food."

Again she nodded.

I glanced down at Otto one last time and saw that his eyes were closed. It seemed like a good idea to bundle the hood of his robe beneath his head, but maybe I was just stalling because I didn't know whether to trust him to Pelanot's care or not. I gestured her outside.

In the sunlight, she straightened, drew in a breath and turned to me expectantly. I thought I saw anger—and impatience—in the movement, but maybe I was wrong. Anyway all I could think of in that moment was that we were nothing but tools to her, that our lives had no value except as we were useful in finding her nephew.

"Lady Pelanot, I—"

That was no good. I could not tell this woman I shared her claustrophobia—that I understood this much, at least, though I had no qualms about the company of the dead. She would despise my sympathy.

I began again. "Otto is a friend of mine," I said this time. "And besides he has a family. Children and a wife."

Still she said nothing. I remembered belatedly what she had told us earlier of her own children.

"Just stay with him," I muttered gruffly, turning away. "You know what happens if he dies—and if it is your fault, I swear you will die too."

Mask in place and the heat gun slung over my back beneath the robe, I paused to take my direction.. The necropolis was fairly large and there were many signs of construction in progress as I made my way back to the main concourse. A lot more people were about by now—villagers, workmen and pilgrims. I smelled the smell of fresh bread and hastened my steps.

Soon I came into a small square of shops where villagers offered maps, food and trinkets for sale. A few rangers stood about, reminding me that all was not well back in town. Also there were quite a few of the perfect ones circulating among the crowd, likely for the same reason.

Coming abreast of a small bakery, I pointed to what I wanted, pretending I had made a vow of silence. This earned me a sort of deference I did not deserve and could not mock, much as I despised the Quele in general.

Further on, I bought a map, just in case anything new had happened while I was gone. Still, it was not likely a map would tell me anything I didn't already know about Godcountry itself, I thought grimly. Stowing the thing with the bread, I headed back toward the construction area, walking briskly, already planning our next move. I should have known things were not going to be that easy—

Ahead of me, a chain crossed the road into the unfinished section—a chain that had not been there before. Beside it, two rangers eyed the crowd with an air of bored brutality, enervated by the night's atrocities, but as ever, ready to commit more. Construction workers scrambled out behind them and I wondered how long it would be before Otto and Lady Pelanot were discovered.

I was just taking all this in when fate decided to test my mettle by adding a further complication. One of the perfect ones had detached himself from the crowd and was headed unmistakably in my direction. I could not pretend to misunderstand his gesture as he signaled me peremptorily to wait. So, wondering how quickly I could untangle the heat gun from my robe and how long I would last when I did, I waited, rangers at my back, for whatever was to come.

CHAPTER EIGHT

The perfect one planted himself about six feet away, eyeing me silently through the holes in his mask. Behind us, the guards had ceased to fidget and come to attention.

I bowed slightly, easing the straps of the gun off one shoulder, withdrawing my hand into one hanging sleeve. Whatever else happened, I was resolved that this particular perfect one would go to his reward.

He gestured toward the chain and, after a moment, one of the rangers unhooked it, waiting expectantly for further orders.

None came. Before I could wriggle free my weapon, my arm was taken in a grip much stronger than I had expected and I was steered, still in complete silence, back up the unfinished road. Another nod secured the chain behind us, but this time one of the rangers dared speak.

"Do you require assistance, sir?" His answer was a curt refusal.

It was not uncommon here for the perfect ones to single out a pilgrim whose demeanor did not suit them. And though I had done my best to comport myself as a bona-fide member of this company, the truth was that I was not even a Quele.

Apparently the rangers were also wondering what I had done wrong. The perfect one had a nerve whip belted around his waist and had already taken it in hand. The idea that I would resist did not occur to anyone except me.

I paced beside my captor, relieved that the rangers were not to accompany us. I prepared myself to act as soon as we had passed out of sight of the guards.

We turned into a lane of half-finished tombs and the Quele tightened his grip. I winced but did not struggle—there were still too many workers about. Also, I had not expected the man to be so strong.

He seemed intent on privacy and this also suited me. We turned several times before he halted in a small square formed of stone blocks and sacks of mortar.

I did not wait for the next development. With a lunge that nearly dislocated my shoulder, I rolled free, tripped over the robe and righted myself, shoving frantically at the heavy cloth to bring up my weapon. In another few seconds, I'd have put the biggest hole I could right through that white robe.

"You always were hasty, Sabat."

I stared into the triangular muzzle of a stunner and slowly relaxed. "Do you realize," I got out, breathing heavily, "that I nearly killed you?"

Steed chuckled. "If you could only see your face!"

I realized that my mask was indeed askew, revealing to all the world—if the world had been watching—that I was manifestly a foreigner. I sat down. A few hours ago I had been searching for Steed's dead body. Never again, I promised myself, would I jump to conclusions on such a colossal scale. Never again—until next time. Life was like that. My small store of wisdom was augmented slowly if at all.

"You can, I hope," I panted with what dignity I could manage, "account for your survival? I saw them shoot you down."

The stunner disappeared. "You saw right, Sabat. But you forgot that I had been re-engineered."

I stared at his cloaked form. "You mean you're a cyborg?"

"Not entirely." Was it my imagination or did he sound really angry this time? I decided not to pursue this line of enquiry. Instead, I asked him how he'd found me and whether or not the former owner of his costume was still alive.

"You know how I found you, Sabat. The same way I did before. And as to your second question, no."

Suddenly I was very glad we were both on the same side.

Before we could get any more chummy, however, our reunion was interrupted by the advent of another perfect one who stood stock still in astonishment at the tableau before him.

I had just presence of mind enough to conceal the heat gun—

but there was no time to cover my face. Steed drew his whip and stood over me as the Quele approached.

"What have you found, brother?" this one cried in the cant of the perfect. His voice was that of an old man.

I spoke up quickly, lest Steed's deplorable accent betray him. "Please sir," I whined, letting him see the slave bracelet, "I've done no harm and only seek asylum."

"Asylum?" The perfect one's voice sounded as though he thought I was mad. But then he recollected himself. "A tomb robber!" he cried. "Ah, brother, you have caught one of the defilers of the dead!"

He didn't have time to finish his congratulations. Steed's whip caught him in a sidewise rictus and I hit him over the head with the heat gun.

For a moment of two, we stood over the body and stared at one another. Then, "Did you kill him, Sabat?"

"I don't think so."

"Let's get him under cover." He picked up the Quele and looked around.

"Here," I said, pointing to another row of tombs. These had no doors as yet, nor were they roofed, but we could stash the perfect one on an upper shelf for the time being.

"He might wake up," Steed said as I helped him hoist his burden inside.

"I thought of that."

"We'll need the rest of the day and part of the night, Sabat."

"Stun him."

Steed said no more and neither did I. I don't know what he was thinking, but I was remembering Kiel, the guy they buried alive. I climbed back down and the smell of a stunner came and went before Steed joined me. Maybe we had both had enough killing for a while.

Quickly I told him what we had done so far. "Otto," I added, "needs food." I realized then that I had dropped the buns back near the entrance to our road.

"I'll go back for more," Steed offered but I vetoed that.

"You've got too much of an accent," I told him as I put my costume right.

"Sabat, there's something you need to know before you go out there."

I paused, looking at him through the eyeholes of my mask.

"You're not the only offworlder passing for a Quele."

"You know?"

"Yes. I don't know if they've located you yet and it may be that their equipment is still in the flyer. Out there somewhere, I mean. In the orchards." He gestured vaguely in that direction.

"So Maureen knows or guesses I'm in Spire but can't narrow it down?"

He nodded.

"But could you locate her?"

"It's built in, sort of. Yes, I could do that if you wanted me to."

I thought of Otto and Lady Pelanot out in the empty part of the necropolis, maybe at the mercy right now of Maureen and her Hithian assassins.

"But of course you couldn't do anything without betraying yourself," Steed pointed out.

I came to a decision. "We'll go together," I told him. "For bread, I mean. And if she's out there, I'll want to know. But we've both got to cross the border, Steed. She and I will be on even terms then."

"Yes. But first you've got to get to the border, don't forget."

"Tonight, when everyone is gone."

"We won't have the advantage when she reconnects with her team and equipment."

I shrugged. "We can only do so much, Steed. First, Otto."

We went out together after food, making sure the lane was empty and, choosing a different route, re-entered the diminutive market square.

I bought more bread and some fruit while Steed circulated among the crowd. But when he rejoined me, he only shook his head. If Maureen had come into the necropolis, she was gone now.

The road we took this time was not blocked off—apparently the guards had been securing the area for a funeral procession. From our present vantage, we could just see the tail end of the mourners leaving the necropolis to pass onto the main road to Godcountry.

I led Steed past a crew of workers hauling stone and headed back to the corner of our own little street. Here I paused, peering around a facade to make sure all was well.

The tomb where I had left Otto and Lady Pelanot looked no different from the outside. Either she was in there or else had run away entirely.

I smiled to myself at this. To choose between her own sturdy courage and mine, I knew who I'd back. It was only her temper I mistrusted.

"Come on," I whispered, hurrying down the street and onto the little porch. I saw that the door was open a crack and, remembering my own reaction to meeting Steed, quickly pulled off my own mask.

The door was flung wide at once and she stood before me, unmasked now and as pale as any corpse. But though her eyes were large and dark, they regarded me steadily enough from their skull-like shadows.

"How is Otto?" I demanded as Steed came up behind me, still covered up in his costume.

She stared at him, reaching for a weapon. Impatiently, I told her who he was.

"Now tell me about Otto," I said.

"He—he's alright. But did you bring food?"

I shoved a loaf of bread into her hands and followed her inside. Otto was where I'd left him. His fever was gone and he eyed the food like one of the jackals I had once seen on earth, fighting over a dead donkey.

"That's alright, then," I said as Lady Pelanot produced a dagger and cut him a slice. I wondered briefly if this was the assassin's knife she had kept all those years but maybe I, in my turn, was growing a bit light-headed. Certainly it had been a hard day.

While Otto fed, I sat back and let Steed tell his story which turned out to be a strange one. He had, as I had truly witnessed, been cut down. There were burns on his skin and clothing to attest to this.

"Only it is not really my skin," he told us, his dark face immobile as ever. "I was injured of course, but not in the same way I would have been before."

I winced, looking at those burns. Likely he'd known his share of physical suffering after the flyer crash back on Earth.

"I stayed where I was," he went on. "Nothing so innocent as a fresh corpse and anyway I couldn't get up just then. A little while later, something exploded."

That was where my own memory stopped—until I woke up in the creek. I waited curiously to have the gaps filled in.

"The flyer was already gone," Steed went on. "I think it was a delayed thing."

"So they never landed?"

"Not then and not there. You hurt their machine, Sabat. You hurt it good."

"But not enough to crash it."

Steed shrugged. "So after that, I tried to get up again and couldn't."

"Where was I?"

"Down the hill, I guess. I think you hit a tree. Everyone was gone as far as I could see and I was all alone."

"What did you do?"

Steed threw off his robes and took a seat at Otto's feet. "I went to sleep," he said.

I stared at him. "You mean you passed out?"

"In a way, but it was deliberate. I made some connections and then I checked out while my body repaired itself." Again that unmoved face, but I thought I heard something in his voice that had not been there before. Perhaps Steed wasn't as blasé about these things as he pretended.

"So then," he finished, "I woke up a couple hours later and there was some guy standing over me with a nerve whip. I took it away from him—and a cloak and a skimmer—and then I went on into the village."

"You just took it?"

·"Well he used it when I woke up, but it didn't do much. He thought I was a tomb robber."

"You were," I said. "Remember?"

"Right. So anyway, here I am."

I thought this over. "Steed, I didn't see any body. Of the Quele, I mean."

"Oh that. You would have if you'd looked up. I put him in a tree."

By this time, Otto had finished the bread and I risked another shot of speed heal. As I expected, it put him out.

"You'd better get some rest too, Sabat," Steed said. "We've got a long wait and you don't look so good yourself."

"What about you?"

"I don't normally sleep. That other thing—that was total suspension of everything. Temporary annihilation. Not regular sleep."

I grunted. "Well I may not be able to sleep either." But he was right about me. I hadn't slept in a while and things were beginning to look surreal. I climbed to the shelf above Otto's and stretched out.

Below, I heard Lady Pelanot asking Steed something and the rumble of his replies, but the words were too low to hear. I shifted on the stone, bunching my Quele cloak beneath me, trying to get comfortable.

It was no use. My body thrummed with tension, not just because I was going into Godcountry but because Maureen would be there too.

I imagined her somewhere in the village or beyond, out among the orchards maybe. She wouldn't dare cross by day and of course she couldn't bring the flyer through the field at any time. But would she be able to haul in what she used to track me? I was afraid she could.

And meanwhile, might she narrow down my location and return to the necropolis? But that was pure paranoia. Maureen wasn't stupid. She'd want to get out of this alive if she could—wouldn't she? But I had no real answer to that one.

And now, I started to worry about Wolfbane. Would he be where I'd told him to be? Or would he, after the way of his people, find or be found by some new trouble?

And so it went. Trying to rest was torture until at last I stopped worrying about externals and forced myself to enter into the place of truth. And the truth was that I was afraid.

Why had I taken this job? Why had I returned to this place of all places, the one I hated most?

Was it for the money? To please Otto? Why hadn't I just refused him the moment he mentioned Quele?

I closed my eyes and there was the Sacred Compound as I had last seen it from the hillside above, dark smoke rising in a column from the temple square where they were branding Kiel preparatory to consigning him to the underworld. Maureen was beside me, fighting the grip of the contractors and the other slaves until one of them finally knocked her out.

Could that have been when she finally snapped? Was it possible that what they did to us later did no more than set the seal on the collapse of her tottering sanity? For we had been forced to remain long after Kiel would have choked out his life in the pits beneath the tombs, struggling against the weight of the soil, blinded by the eternal dark, gasping at the last filthy dregs of the air.

Sweating, I sat up. I'd almost drifted off, smelled the smoke, heard the roar of the crowd, joined myself with Kiel as he was dragged to the hole—

It was better to stay awake, I decided, than to dream, and I almost swung one leg over the edge to get up.

But I couldn't do that. I had not slept in a day and a half and tonight I would take this party through the sensor field. If I could, that is.

Still, I could not rest. I kept thinking of Kiel and how it was to be a slave, always at the mercy of them, the faceless corporation. Two slaves had disobeyed an order and tried to break into the temple lock-up. Two slaves had tried to rescue another slave and failed. The whole team had had to leave the area ahead of schedule because of what those two had done. The company was not pleased.

But it was a real individual person who keyed in the discipline orders. A real person made the decision and a real person carried it out. Someone closed the door on that bare, little room where I was and someone else punched in a code. Human fingers touched those keys. Only the monsters who came later were innocent, for they had their origin in my own brain.

I felt the stone beneath my hands as I rolled over onto my back. The resonator had always done funny things to the slave band, but after that time, it was worse. Each time I used the thing, there came an echo of that crawling horror, as though a bone had been broken and healed but could never be as strong again as it had been.

I heard a movement below and a moment later, Steed's face appeared over the edge. "Still awake, Sabat?"

"Yeah."

"I let Lady Pelanot keep watch out on the porch."

"Good idea. And Otto?"

"Still asleep."

I made room for him to come up and seat himself beside me. "Never thought we'd work together again, you and me."

"Same here. And as usual, we find ourselves sitting in a tomb."

"Just like old times."

I did not answer at once, the fingers of my left hand finding the familiar ridges of the band. Then, "I never said thank-you, Steed. For that time. You tried."

"Things were never the same after that, were they?"

I shook my head. We could barely see each other in the dim light from below. I tried to remember what Steed had looked like before his accident. He had been a skinny guy with dark hair, I recalled, always kept short. He walked like he had once been a soldier. "Things," I said, "are still not the same."

"Sabat, you're in charge of this operation. Don't think I've forgotten that."

I forced myself to quit fondling the band. "I'm glad you're here, Steed," I told him. "You've been over there before. The others—" I shrugged.

"Okay. So let's plan accordingly," he suggested. "What do you want us to do when we get through?"

"There will be the robot patrollers inside. Probably not too many rangers." I was thinking aloud. "Otto handles mechanical stuff, robots and all."

"Ah."

"He's a pro, Steed. He's got implants and things." I looked up. "What about you?"

"I've got some. But if his are special, they'll be better than mine. My friends had hoped, when they fixed me up, that I'd go straight."

I chuckled. "Okay. So Otto's got to be functional."

"He seems to be doing alright."

I hoped Steed was right. "But it'll be hard on him, just the hike and all, I mean. We had better lay up for a while once we're in."

"Fine with me."

"As for myself," I went on, still thinking out loud, "I should be able to take over sometime tomorrow—if the crossing isn't too bad, that is."

"And then?"

I considered. "It has been a while, Steed. You know Godcountry. Anything at all could have happened."

"So we check things out first."

"We do that. And later, we make camp up in the hills above the compound. And then I go in—alone."

"As a pilgrim?"

"Right. No one else speaks the language but you. And your accent is a lot worse than mine."

"You always did have a gift for languages," Steed agreed. "Okay, then, so far. You spy things out first."

"He should be in the temple lock-up," I went on steadily. "Like Kiel."

Steed did not answer. He only cocked his head to one side.

"I've learned a few tricks since then," I added. "But I work alone."

We sat in silence for a while and then Steed got down. I tried once more to rest and this time my weariness overcame me. The result was a light, dream-riddled sleep where the butter yellow suns of Sachsen receded into space and the golden sun of earth poured down in its place, illuminating the columns and facades of cities that were no more. I tried to find my father, but he had gone away.

"But surely," I cried, "he left some message for me?"

The sky seemed to laugh and the ever-present sea tossed itself playfully onto the sand. "You are the message," it said.

Angrily, I plunged myself into that other sea, the sea of stars, and swam away from that place, vowing I would never look back. Before I had a chance to break that resolve, Steed woke me. Relieved, I got up at once.

"Dark outside," he said. "The others are still asleep." "Uh," I grunted, wishing for a drink of water.

"Kavanaugh passed by earlier."

I came awake so suddenly that I nearly fell off the ledge. "Here?"

"Outside the fence. In the orchards."

"You think she knows where we are?"

"If she does, she never came to check. She's gone now."

"Gone?"

"Up the hill, Sabat. Out of my range."

I bit back a curse. "Why didn't you wake me?" I demanded.

"What difference would it make?" he countered. "If she went over the border at sunset, then she took an extra risk. And anyway, she won't be in any shape to bother us for a while."

"The Hithians will."

Steed shrugged. "Shall I wake everyone?"

I slid off the ledge and stood looking down at Otto. Lady Pelanot was a huddled form on the floor, as near the door as she could manage. The night air blew in upon her face, smelling of dampness and ripening fruit.

I jerked my head in her direction, signaling that Steed should wake her while I turned my attention to Otto. He woke as easily as he always did, his eyes clear.

"Ah, Herr Sabat. Is it time, then?"

"Yes, Otto."

"Shall we need our disguises?"

"Only mine. I'll pack it up and carry it." I was painfully aware that we had not dared pick up the remainder of our supplies and that things were going to be hard out there. All we had were our weapons and some emergency stuff got at the capital. Oh well, I decided, if it came down to sleeping on the ground and knocking over a rabbit or two, we would manage.

On this optimistic note, I opened the door and saw at once that Quele itself had a surprise for us. Beyond the porch, it was pouring rain—and the darkness outside was total. I crouched in the doorway for a moment listening to the wind and wondering what to do next.

Belatedly I remembered that I was in charge of this particular job and no one was going to tell me what to do. I closed my eyes and tried to remember just how far it was to the fence. Then I set off, the others trailing behind. We were soaked within minutes and as I felt my way along the lanes of half-finished tombs, I tried not to think about what would happen if I got lost. Or what Lady Pelanot would say, which was even worse.

We crossed two side streets, but still no fence. By now, we could see a little in the reflection from the clouds, but as I said before, Quele are thrifty and the streetlights of Spire must have been very few and far between.

And then I saw a light that should not have been there.

"Inside," Steed hissed, pulling us into a tomb. He left the door cracked open as we all crowded behind him.

"It's moving," he said. "Must be the rangers."

"Maybe they found that guy." Quickly I told Otto about the perfect one we had stunned.

The light paused on the corner of our lane and I heard two people arguing in Quele. It was too far to hear them very well but I did catch a word or two. "Manch" for instance, which meant, roughly, "jackal".

I wondered if this were a new name for us tomb robbers. We had been called a lot of things in the past. The real manch, I remembered, was nothing but a wild dog, hardly worth a midnight search. All they ever did was eat garbage and howl.

But there was that word again and a couple more times in plural. And I noticed that the group was staying together. The whole thing puzzled me.

Finally they moved off.

Steed eased our door shut and flicked on a light. The tomb we were in was both painted and frescoed. A multitude of gods glowered from the walls and, on the lower bench, a long bundle lay wrapped in bright cotton. Oops, I thought. And I'd told Lady Pelanot the Quele never did that.

With a shriek, she flung herself on the door which, to our combined dismay, had latched and would not open.

"It's alright," Steed said. "There's a catch up here."

Belatedly, I remembered we had run into this sort of thing before, out in Godcountry. After all, why should the thing be locked from the inside?

As Steed worked the mechanism, I dared one covert glance at Lady Pelanot. Her eyes were dilated, her face ghastly. I had a feeling that amounted to an intuition that she was not going to forgive us for seeing her fear so plainly. And somehow I knew that I was the one she would blame the most.

Steed killed the light and swung open the door. Even I was glad to get out—doubly so because I could no longer see Lady Pelanot's face.

"We went too far west," I said. "I know where we are now— we've left the construction area. If we catch the lane at the corner, we'll come to the fence."

Watching carefully for any more signs of the rangers, I led the group what I hoped was due north until we passed a final pair of maintenance buildings and, groping before me, felt the thick wire of the fence.

"We'll climb," I said quickly. By now I was shivering a little, for the wind had turned chilly and I was soaking wet. From somewhere within the necropolis, I heard the howl of a manch and it was answered from somewhere else, whether inside or out, I could not tell. I set one foot into the wire.

As we climbed higher—for the fence was a tall one out of respect for the dead—I could see more and more of the necropolis behind us. Several streets away, the rangers were still searching for, I hoped, something other than us.

Beyond our little neighborhood, the shops were closed, lit only by a set of frugal glow poles at the four corners of the square. Spire itself was no more than a pearly glow beyond a screen of trees.

I swung one leg over the topmost bar and turned to help Lady Pelanot who was nearly beside me. But she seemed not at all hampered by the dress the Lost Rythans had given her and drew away from my hand as though I were a particularly disgusting animal. I concentrated on the climb down.

At the bottom, we all squelched through sodden grass. The rain poured, the tall weeds slapped and tangled about our legs, and a multitude of ripening burrs attached themselves to our clothing. Jackals howled, a lion—pretty far off—gave a coughing roar, and the wind made a periodic gust that drowned everything else out. It was not a very good beginning for our trek into Godcountry.

Indeed, I thought sourly, things were bearing less and less resemblance to my carefully laid plans. Morale was low and probably still plummeting, my nose was beginning to drip, and aside from the advent of a rabid jackal, the only other development I could reasonably expect would be Maureen and her Hithians, firing heat guns as they came.

At which point, these final touches were added to the night's adventures—or so it seemed to me at the time. Something raced past—several somethings—low and on four legs. The beam of a laser arced out, cutting one of them down. I saw the dark form leap high and fall back, thrashing. It looked like a mighty big specimen.

"Hit the ground," Otto hissed and we all hunkered down in the wet, burr-infested grass as a troop of hunters loped past.

"What the—?" Steed rolled over and sat up.

"Only a Quele would go hunting in the rain," I muttered, pulling a few burrs out of my hair.

"We're not," Steed observed, "where we should be, are we Sabat?"

"I've noticed that."

We were in fact, west of the orchards, having come out onto an unplanted strip of common. I believe it would have been used for grazing sheep, a fact which probably accounted for the jackal hunters.

I sat up and gave Steed the coordinates I had given Heth Andrew and he set them in his direction finder while Otto looked on. I had yet to hear one complaint from good old Otto, though Lady Pelanot's silence was more eloquent. Her ill will radiated in waves I could almost feel.

Finally we set off, the sounds of the hunt fading away as we slogged back toward the orchards. Water ran down the back of my neck, soaking nicely into the top of a turtleneck where it joined several gallons that were already there.

Of course the orchards were fenced, though happily the thrifty Quele used nothing worse than barbed wire to keep the sheep out. They saved the fancy high tech stuff for Godcountry itself.

So we ran into the wire, or rather Lady Pelanot did and had to be untangled. She spurned my assistance again but permitted Steed to cut away a swatch of her skirt. Meanwhile, venting my own feelings, I stamped down the barrier and walked across, tripping over a dead jackal as I emerged beneath the overloaded boughs of a variform apple tree. The others followed more carefully.

At least we had found a little shelter from the rain—just enough to make the sudden drips and spatters more startling. The season was advancing, I gathered, judging by the rotten fruit beneath the trees. I wondered how Heth Andrew was making out.

"Not far now," Steed said in answer to my wonders. "If he's there, that is."

We advanced, tree by sopping tree, until things opened out into a sort of clearing where trailers full of empty crates waited patiently for the harvest. Of the Lost Rythan, there was no sign.

"Okay," I said. "We wait. After all, the hunters might have passed this way. Heth Andrew could be hiding."

"I hear something," Lady Pelanot whispered. "Listen!" I listened to the wind.

"Do you think it's wolves?" Otto asked but Steed laid one hand on his arm.

"Wait!" By this I knew he was using his enhanced audio.

"They're everywhere," he breathed at last. "This is something new, Sabat. I hardly remember these things before."

"There were never this many manch," I agreed. 'But we're armed."

"I don't," Otto put in with some hesitation, "think we should remain here. Did you give Herr Wolfbane co-ordinates for this exact place?"

I glanced in Steed's direction.

"Not quite," he said. "We'll check."

We went back under the trees and the wind got louder, only it wasn't the wind at all. And we found Heth Andrew in trouble. So were we.

He hailed us from the upper branches of a tree and I marveled that, large as he was, he had not broken it down. The ground beneath was littered with apples and dead jackals, while a laser pistol lay where he had apparently dropped it. I did not stop to pick it up. Instead, I grabbed Lady Pelanot and thrust her at the nearest tree.

"Climb!" I hissed and tried to find Otto.

I was almost too late on that one and had to shoot two jackals before I could boost him up another tree and follow, with the manch nipping at my legs. Steed, meanwhile, had his own troubles, but I could do nothing to help him. He made it at last onto a safe perch of his own.

"They chew you up?" I called.

"Some."

"How many, do you think?"

"Out here? Who knows. Godcountry must have really spilled over this time."

I did not answer. I was wet and cold and acutely aware that the hunters were still out there somewhere. We had enough noise going in our bit of the orchard to bring every ranger outside of Spire— unless of course, they were otherwise occupied. We seemed to be having a jackal convention.

The rain finally slacked off and a chilly wind began to blow. Manch howled and cold water dripped down on me from the leaves above. There was too much noise to talk to Heth Andrew, though of course I had a few questions to ask him. Mostly, though, I thought about Godcountry and how it was less than two kilometers away and as unreachable as the stars without the net.

"What do you think about shooting as many as we can?" Otto shouted to me at last.

I thought this over. Would we even have enough charge to spare? And how much attention would we attract if we did? The matter required careful consideration, I told myself, but before I could come to a decision, we were rescued.

The advent of a troop of hunters did not exactly raise my spirits at the moment. For a few seconds, I even considered shooting them, but fortunately, second thoughts intervened.

The Quele made short work of our attackers, killing many and driving the rest further into the orchard. At last, they turned their attention to the trees.

A light played over me but I kept my face averted, praying they would not discover Wolfbane and Lady Pelanot, neither of whom could pass for a Quele shepherd by any stretch of bad light or stupidity.

To forestall explanations, I wriggled about as though to climb down, calling out thanks in my best imitation of the local dialect. I did not even try to account for my presence, only hoping I would not be taken for an apple thief.

"Are you injured?" one of the rangers asked without much interest. Plainly he was much more intent on following the rest of the pack.

I told him I was fine and then he saw Otto, clinging to a branch above me.

"Not alone, then?"

"My brother," I said quickly, still averting my face. A good look at Otto's features might best allay any suspicions, I thought.

I waited, hoping no more questions would follow. I saw that the other hunters were slicing ears from the dead dogs and guessed there was a bounty on the things. Good. Our presence in the apple orchard at midnight was not going to look so strange after all.

Due to some miracle, no one found Heth Andrew's pistol— or Heth Andrew himself, either. With a final wave, the last of our rescuers departed and I slid down, clinging to my tree trunk with trembling hands.

"Let's get out of here," I said and we did so.

We heard many jackals in the distance as we passed northward through the orchards of Spire. As we emerged at last onto the wasteland that became Godcountry's border, they seemed a bit louder.

"Maybe," Steed muttered, "they ate Kavanaugh."

Heth Andrew had apparently seen nothing of the other party and did not know whether they had gone through or not. "But I saw dead dogs this morning," he added. "Burned, not shot. And no one had cut off their ears."

We climbed a small ridge and entered a belt of trees. Steed, who had made the crossing before, paused at once. I motioned the others to halt.

"This is it," I said. "The sensor field begins just above." "You said you could neutralize it," Lady Pelanot stated.

"Not quite that," I told her. "The resonator actually neutralizes us—the impression our presence would make on the field. And to do this," I added, "we must stay together. Its range isn't very great."

"No scouting ahead," Steed added. "If one of us gets separated, the alarms will go off."

While he was talking, I sat down and unclipped the thing from my belt, weighing it in my hands as I spoke. "While we cross and immediately afterward—say a few hours—you will follow Amid Steed's orders."

I turned to him. "Find a sheltered place like we were talking about before. Defensible and all that. We all need a rest."

"Herr Sabat," Otto said quietly, "you have not told us very much about the side effects of this device."

"No," I said, "I haven't." And before he could ask further, I closed the switch.

CHAPTER NINE

The world seemed to recede from me then. Knowing that this was probably my imagination did not help. It never did.

"Alright so far?" Steed asked and I nodded tightly.

"Let's go, then."

We went on up the hill where trees cut off the sky, eating up the clouds as well as the glow of a newly risen moon. I knew those trees for the trees of Godcountry. They were like no others I had ever seen, for the winds of chaos blew and sighed among their branches.

Wolfbane stalked slightly ahead of us. Had he been an animal, his hackles would be rising about now. So would Lady Pelanot's. Her slim ramrod back was just visible somewhere to the side of Wolfbane. As for Otto, he stayed with me.

"Your—leg?" I asked him, shaping my words slowly as we neared the treeless crest. I was like a man intoxicated and I knew I must be careful or things would fall apart. Maybe they would anyway.

"I am alright, Herr Sabat."

Behind us, Steed hovered like a guardian spirit. I felt his alien gaze on my back and it was almost like old times.

The forest fell away abruptly into a low tangle of something like gorse—only Steed and I knew that it was not—and the unfettered wind sang in our ears. Below lay a dark, barren valley, almost a gorge, bounded by more hills. I knew those hills were there, even though they were invisible in the darkness, just as I had known we would come out of the trees and into the wind.

"We're still inside the field," Steed said to Otto. "But be ready for android patrols when we climb again. Just in case." Actually the patrols would be further up if things had not changed in the years since I was last here. But of course if Kavanaugh and her party had stirred them up when they came through, that would be another matter.

Otto peered ahead, curiously, I thought, though he seemed more weary than anything else. Or maybe it was only the wind that made him falter.

I turned about for another glimpse of the forest we had left behind. I could not see the lights of Spire anymore, but I knew that at any moment, the rustling wind might strip those trees, tearing away all cover—even the very flesh from our bones.

I heard Steed say something more to Otto, but the wind blew away his words. Suddenly his face was beside mine. "Sabat? Can you hear me?"

I gaped at him and raised one hand. Already the wind had blown away the flesh. I stared, fascinated at the naked bones.

"Sabat, it's the resonator. Remember?" He loomed closer, dark upon dark. "The resonator, Sabat. Whatever you see isn't real. Keep that in mind."

His words unraveled past me, catching on the naked branches of the trees until they shredded away and were lost.

"You're going to be okay, Sabat. Soon it will be over."

I nodded, trying to remember. I had pushed the switch and now we were in the pangs of this strange birth—going into— Godcountry.

At that name, the wind stood still, its power held in place, towers and pinnacles of force poised above us. I let Otto take my arm as we began the descent. But even as I placed one booted foot before another, the wind returned, screaming over the shattered hills, tearing away my breath and my mind.

Why had I done this thing? I wanted to cry out. By all the hypothetical gods, why had I come back to Quele? Or was it—and this thought filled me with a dreary horror—was it that I had never left?

All my life as a free man—and it was not a long one, comprising no more than a few years subtime—passed before my memory and was gone. Susanna and the club, chess games with Arnese bor

Kladden, quiet talk and wine drunk in the purlieus of Bloomhadn Park, the sunlight that always made my city new. I groped for these precious things in the wind and the dark, but they were gone.

And still we moved onward, descending. Wolfbane's tigerish presence drifted in and out of my perception. Lady Pelanot seemed more than ever like a demon, but Otto still remained to me as he always was, calm and sturdy at my side.

Sometimes the others paused and spoke but I could no longer hear what anyone said. A pain had come upon me, so gradually that I was still not sure it was entirely physical. My head ached and my arms and legs began to cramp so that I staggered as I walked.

"Not much further—"

I thought it was Steed who had spoken but it was not. A shadow walked beside me—and in all that barren place, there was no one else!

"Where," I got out through chattering teeth, "are we going?"

"Back, Eduardo. Back to Godcountry."

In a moment of clarity, I turned on the thing. "I chose," I told it. "I pressed that switch and I knew the resonator would mess with the slave band. It's a—a bad trip is all."

My answer was silence, so I stopped and forced my companion to stop likewise. In the sourceless light of that place, I saw that he wore pilgrims' dress, the face covered by a mask and hood.

"Show yourself," I commanded.

"Do you really wish me to?"

The voice I heard was Maureen's and, groping for a weapon with one hand, I seized upon the cloth with the other and tugged it away.

No eyes looked into mine, for there were none in that ruin of bone and hair. It was the head I had seen beside the roadway, only much weathered now and stripped of the quiet pathos it had worn when I first saw it.

"Welcome home," it said. "Welcome to Godcountry, Eduardo Sabat."

I struggled in a grip gone bone hard, my head thrown back with the rictus of my limbs.

"Sabat!"

The words were distant, icy cold and far away.

"It's the re—eeeeeeesonnnnn—" The sound stretched and broke, but I grew still in the grip of that which held me.

"Yes," I said, remembering. I had a job to do: I must walk.

Obediently, I did so.

But the shadow would not leave me alone.

"You return," it said, "to the holy places."

"I spit on the holy places."

"You do not dare. You are no Lost Rythan; you are a slave." I shook my head doggedly. "That's over," I said.

On my other side, I heard a laugh, but I did not turn. I knew very well Susanna walked there and I would rather have passed through the temple fire than meet her now. It was too late for us.

She had other ideas, apparently. "You have always been a slave," she taunted, and there was that in her voice that challenged me, that even attempted in a ghastly way, to allure me.

"Go away. Your time has passed."

"Always a slave! Always always always—"

But I would not look. Anyway, everything was changing again and somehow I was back at Feullier, in the holding cell with the quiet words of the discipline officer still echoing in my ears.

"Disobeyed a direct order—caused an expedition to abort—" I stared at the slave band on my wrist.

"Disobeyed—caused loss to—the company."

The walls drew inward and darkness, like a solid thing began to gather in the corners of my cell. I felt gritty stone beneath my hands and knew it for the stone of Quele. My worst fears had come to pass and I was buried alive!

I sucked in a lungful of precious air, trying not to think about the brick and stone that pressed above me. Eyes bulging with terror, I stifled a scream. Screams, after all, used up oxygen. But I knew I could not bear this!

And then without warning, I passed into a still deeper place, that inner citadel where the sun shone upon eternity and I was free. "Whenever a tyrant threatens death or exile," the wise old man had asked, "does he threaten you then? Or is it only your body?"

I could barely feel my body. I seemed to be all brain and straining senses—but I tried dutifully to persuade myself that these things were nothing to me, death and pain and terror. But how could I believe? The room was shrinking—eternity itself was shrinking until even the sun went out.

"But I've been here before," I faltered. "I remember it. It will pass away. It is only an effect of the resonator on the slave band." I crouched behind my words, raising my blinded eyes to that which I could not see—the starry night on the edge of Godcountry.

"Fool," the shadow mocked. "You were always here and there is no other place for you. This is your inner citadel and it does not pass."

The words seemed to suck the last of the air from my tomb. But, gasping, I let anger overpower me, as I had done before.

"So be it!" I cried. "But still this place is mine!"

In answer, the walls moved again—I heard them grinding inward. Stifling, I placed one hand against the stone. "Not this—not this!" I wanted to whisper, but I did not. I clenched my teeth together instead.

I knew even as I had known before, that this was not real. But my knowledge was worthless! The wise old man was wrong! To know a thing does not free us from our fear of it—it only gives us more to fear. I was suffocating and I would soon be crushed and, real or not, those things towered above my intellect, cutting off all semblance of reason, all hope of light.

"Tomb robber! How many times have you violated the peace of the dead?" a voice said in Quele.

I tried to turn, but there was no longer space enough. If I panicked now, I would surely die, throwing myself against the stone until I had battered away my miserable life. But what other hope was there?

"If suffering be beyond endurance—"

It was the true voice of Epictetus this time; he had not abandoned me, then, after all. "If suffering be beyond endurance," I quoted through swollen lips, "the door is open. It is fit that the final door should be open—thus we escape all trouble—"

But even this dread hope did not allay my present fear. I twisted in the dark and felt at last the stone against my back and sides.

"You could die. You could have died before."

"It was not—so bad that time."

"Liar!" I no longer knew who spoke to me, but in that place where madness lapped against my frailty, no company could be unwelcome except my own.

I answered the charge, speaking quickly to put off that moment when I would cease to be a man at all and flit forever wailing among the ruins of the citadel that had once been mine. "How," I whispered, "am I a liar?"

"It was not in you to take your life, Eduardo. It is not now."

"But that is the right of all! The foundation of my freedom!"

"If death is the foundation of your freedom, you are too great a fool to live!"

If death—

Suddenly I saw myself as I really was and that seeing was the most dreadful thing I had ever known.

For my citadel did shatter and the pride that had sustained it—I groveled in the dark, blind and crushed beneath the ruins.

No, I could not die. Death was no escape, no dissolution of a material soul as I had tried to believe. There was only the long curse of immortality—and memory.

Memory! I writhed with it. The life I had tried to live with Susanna, whom I had never loved and could not love, rose up to accuse me. Oh, she had known well enough, I saw now, poor woman.

And the murder of Boris! He had been nothing to me. It was the slave band I had wanted to destroy! Was there no end to the way I used and cast aside the lives of others?

I knew where my strength had come from, that first time in the cell at Feullier. How dared I pity Maureen her madness, when it was for her sake I had come out of that dark place believing I was whole. Believing a lie when the truth was that I, too, had been broken! No wonder our love turned to hate! I had thrust my lie upon her and later I had abandoned her because she would not believe me!

But this was too much for me—a man can only bear so much truth. Writhing, I felt the stone come away like bits of cheese beneath my scrabbling fingers. I opened my eyes and rain fell in my face like tears.

"He's coming around."

Above me, the sky was a net of stars. The water was tears—or maybe sweat. My fingers hurt and, levering myself up, I saw that they were bleeding.

Someone held an arm about my shoulders and forced a canteen to my lips. Whatever was in it—and I thought it was schnapps, which I detest—brought me quickly to my senses.

"We're—through?"

"Through the field," Steed's voice affirmed, though I could not see him. 'But not out of the border zone."

"Ah."

"Can you get up?"

I tried to rise, and fell into a convulsion. Someone had to shove a rag in my mouth to keep me from biting my tongue. I gathered this had happened once already, judging by the efficiency with which they handled me.

When I had myself once more under control, I was flat on the ground. "How did I get this far?" I asked Otto.

"Herr Wolfbane carried you. Don't you remember anything?"

I shook my head. "Where is he now?"

"Down the hill with Lady Pelanot. He heard something and went to investigate."

"The other party, do you think?" I was trying my best to focus on things outside myself, but it was all too easy to slip back into the resonator-induced state of unreality. Memory—

When I closed my eyes I saw her on the beach beside me. We made one shadow on the sand. The sea, Homer's own wine dark sea, washed gently against the North African shore, tossing bits of foam against our legs.

First we had been friends and then we were lovers. Still later, we were both. I do not think she loved our studies particularly, for the voices of the ancients did not sound in her ears as they did in mine. But for my sake, she stood there on the shore and listened to the surf while the hot yellow sunlight poured down on us like the blessings of the gods.

Her hand was tanned on the back and freckled. Mine was dark, the fingers long and as yet unscarred. The slave band gave back the sunlight in a crazy pattern that kept changing when I moved.

"We must move on, Eduardo," Steed said and the sun sparkles became starlight once more. "There is still the robot patrol."

"Is Otto ready?" I asked. "Has he activated his sensors?"

"Right. Now, up you come." Steed reached down and hauled me into a sitting position. When the stars stopped spinning, I put his hands aside and climbed to my feet. I turned to Otto and saw that he was not in much better shape than I. Worse, perhaps, since I was at least unwounded.

He had the sensor built into his brain, along with a few other things. He would track the robot assigned to this area, halt it and reprogram it. If his strength did not run out, that is. If he could not do it, we would have to wait until it found us and, likely by that time, we would have enough on our hands already.

As I stood, getting my bearings, a form materialized in the gloom and I recognized Lady Pelanot. She glanced in my direction, but did not address me. "The Lost Rythan will be along," she said to Otto. "He is cleaning a goat."

For a moment, I was afraid I might be slipping into another dream, until Steed spoke up.

"What did you say?"

"Goat," she snapped. "Or the local equivalent, anyway. Breakfast."

At this point, Heth Andrew appeared, a gory bundle slung over one shoulder. After all I had been through, the sight of him nearly brought tears to my eyes.

"Eduardo," he cried heartily, reaching one hand to steady me. "You are back among us!"

"That," I told him, "is a mixed blessing." My joints felt as though I had been on the rack, and something was very wrong with my sense of balance. But these things were nothing compared to the terrible truths I had looked upon and must now live with.

Quickly I set all that aside. Later, I told myself. And if I got killed on this expedition, then never. "Thank you," I told Heth Andrew, "for helping me through the field."

"You did not tell us, Eduardo, that the resonator would be so hard on you."

I shrugged. "What good would it have done to tell you?"

Steed spoke up at this and his voice was serious. "It was never this bad before, Sabat, was it? Or I would have said something to the others."

I clenched my teeth. "It's been a while," I told him. "That probably accounts for it."

"You were out of your head."

I closed my eyes, forcing calmness. Though all my philosophy lay in ruins, the habits by which I had lived were too strong not to sustain me in this crisis. I answered him with a calmness born not of knowledge but of will.

"I am not," I said, "out of my head now, Steed."

He shrugged. I knew very well what he was thinking—that there would be a return trip. If something really had gone wrong between the band and the resonator, I might not survive.

To say that this did not frighten me would be stretching the truth, but I didn't let it show. In one way, I was like a man mortally wounded, yet in another, I seemed to be drawing for the first time in my life on the true and naked core of my own personality. Paradoxically, having lost my false sense of inner freedom, I was truly free in a way I had never known before. Possibly I was insane as well, but that no longer mattered. And that knowledge was more of a relief than I could ever have believed.

So we set off, a pair of rising moons giving us enough double-shadowed illumination to avoid stumbling as we climbed the first of a series of low hills.

Otto paused from time to time, listening for the sentry. But he was also weakening. I considered giving him more stim but that isn't such a good thing, especially with speed heal, and so I did not do it.

We were crossing a dark stream bed when Otto fell suddenly to his knees. I rushed to his side, but he had not collapsed. Something lay there among the stones before him—a broken form, sprawled in the moonlight, one arm severed, the head lying nearby. A great hole was melted in the metalplast torso.

"The sentry?" Steed asked and Otto nodded.

"Heat gun, Herr Steed. Not very subtle."

I did not say anything. It was obvious who had taken out the guard and Otto was right. It was not very subtle. And now the question was—where was she now?

Steed looked up at me. "I don't sense the band, Sabat. She must have gone on. They could be pretty far in by now."

Still I did not speak. Maureen had just endured what I endured or something like it, and yet she or her crew had already destroyed the sentry. But then, she had already made that most painful crossing between sanity and madness and so it might not mean as much to her as it did to me.

"Let's get out of here," I said. We made our way between two bare hills, higher than the others and fringed with great, round-topped trees like tufts of wooly hair. This was a landmark I knew even by moonlight.

Otto's strength gave out before we passed around the flank of the nearest hill and Steed had to pick him up and carry him. Wolfbane offered, of course, but even he was tiring. Besides, he still lugged his kill across one shoulder, slouching like a great, shaggy bear.

At length, I located the entrance to a long valley I knew, and from there a cutting which led into a much wider gap between the hills. We had not gone into this place often, back in the old days, because we usually made camp on the hillside above the temple complex. But there were ruins here that would shelter us. A few degenerates, hardly deserving the name of tribesmen lived in brush shelters on the other hill, shunning the ruins entirely.

I told Lady Pelanot and Heth Andrew about the ruins.

"Are there—tombs?" she asked quickly.

'I don't know. This place was abandoned so long ago, I don't even think they were related to the Quele."

She asked no more, but only trudged on, slightly behind Wolfbane. If I hadn't been so tired, I might have pitied her a little. She was, after all, a primitive herself. And the alien night was full of ghosts. Certainly Wolfbane felt them—and so did I.

We came to the first of the roofless houses as the sky began to lighten with dawn. A chill mist rose about our feet and the turf, or whatever it was, was soaking wet. I chose a house with a clay floor, though even here, the grass had made inroads. I had Steed lay Otto in the driest corner.

"D'you think his wound is infected?" Steed asked as we examined him by the light of Steed's torch.

I shrugged. "I think he's exhausted. We all are."

Wolfbane slung down our breakfast—which was looking less appetizing as the light broadened—and looked around.

I knew at once that the hut was very ugly, though I could not have said why exactly. The walls were of naked brick, the roof nearly gone, with enough poles and tiles remaining to shelter the corners of the main room. There was a dismal regularity about the architecture, a total lack of any sort of aesthetic sense that depressed me. I almost wished we had found a cave instead.

I could see that Lady Pelanot was not pleased either, though how the architecture of a house could so affect anyone was beyond me. It was no uglier than Quele City, this dead village, but its effect on me was a lot worse.

"I will take the first watch," Steed said, rising from Otto's corner. He, at least, seemed not to be affected by our surroundings.

"You must be—" I was about to say tired, but then I remembered that he was no longer quite human. He had told me so himself.

I looked up suddenly into his strangely rigid face where his artificial eyes met mine. Was I seeking some confirmation that he was indeed the same man who had once been my overseer? I could not repress a shiver, but maybe he did not see it. Suddenly I hoped not.

"Okay, Steed," I said. "You take the first watch."

He turned away, moving about the hut as he poked into a couple archways and kicked at a pile of rubble on the floor. "We never really looked into these houses, did we, Sabat?"

"No."

"Probably everything's been looted already."

My head ached. "I'm going to stretch out." I fished a pill from my first aid kit and swallowed it dry. "Wake me if something happens."

I saw Lady Pelanot settle herself gingerly in another angle of the room while Wolfbane busied himself laying out the meat. "I'll build a fire when the sun is higher," he told me. "Too tired to be hungry now anyway."

I watched him for a while, half-asleep. His dim outline seemed like the shape of all men who had ever cleaned goats and laid fires, on all the worlds there had ever been. I closed my eyes.

For once, I did not dream of the wise old man, save only as someone dim and far away. I wanted to call to him. After all, I was his son, wasn't I? But no words would come. Epictetus glanced my way once, his face as immobile as Steed's and I knew by this that he was only a shade, wandering among the quiet halls of Hades, and that he no longer remembered me.

"But it could have been different," I whispered. "You didn't have to settle for this."

I woke sitting with my head on my knees, a pose the dead often assumed in Godcountry. Here on the other side of the border, where the great ones slept, they did not stretch themselves out in their tombs like the poor in the village. They sat among their treasures as though they were living men who had fallen asleep.

But I was not thinking about the dead—at least not the human dead. An unsettling thought had brought me out of sleep—the memory of the damaged robot Otto had found. What if Maureen had left it there for us to find? Had she reprogrammed it or not? Were the rangers hurrying to the scene? Was the guard redoubled about the temple complex? Was she really as mad as I thought?

Then I came fully awake and shook off these useless worries. What would be would be, and we would face it when it came. I concentrated on my own aching body instead. The dead, I thought sourly, were lucky, for they, at least, could stay put.

At last, I staggered to my feet and went over to check on Otto. The sun was well risen now and in its light, I saw that he was still sleeping. He looked terrible.

Then, moving creakily, I tried to locate the others. Wolfbane and Steed were gone, but Lady Pelanot was in her corner, watching me.

Her unveiled face had lost none of its determination.

"Where are Steed and Heth Andrew?" I asked.

"I am not sure."

I tried to rub some of the stiffness out of my arms and shoulders. My hands were still raw from scratching at the ground during the earlier part of the night.

"Do you still trust this Steed?" she asked me abruptly.

"I don't have any reason not to, Lady Pelanot." I eyed her closely. "Do you?"

She shrugged. "He looks like a devil," she said. "But I don't suppose that would matter to one of your sort." I shook my head. "I've never seen a devil." "Tell me about this place," she commanded then.

"I don't know much," I admitted. "It was once a village is all."

"But where did the people go?"

"Who can say? Maybe the crops died and they had to move. Things change very quickly in Godcountry." "It is like no other place in the galaxy?"

I hid my amusement. "I wouldn't say that, Lady Pelanot," I told her seriously. 'The galaxy is a big place."

"But these people. Were they human?"

I thought I began to understand her. She would, of course, be xenophobic to an extreme, and travelling among the stars was no casual event in her life. "Anyone who can build a house must be human," I told her. "And all humans come from the same ancestors. There never was a truly alien race, even though there have been mutations among the different colonies."

She stared into her lap. "So," she said. "All begin as human beings. But when do they stop? When are they not human anymore, Sabat?"

I gave this some thought. Even Heth Andrew must seem like an alien to her, I thought. Of us all, I was the one most likely to fit her racial standards, and I did not come all that close. But probably she was still thinking of Steed.

I chose my words with care. "We all," I said, "have different opinions about that. Otto would say that human stock never ceases to be human."

"And you?"

"My opinions cannot matter to you, Lady Pelanot."

"Answer me." Her dark eyes and the will that lay behind them were so compelling that I obeyed.

"I am not sure," I told her truthfully. "I suppose we cease to be human when we decide to be something else. Something less."

She gave a grim chuckle. "Something less? Why not more?"

"There is no more," I said evenly. "Not for us."

"That," she said contemptuously, "is what I would expect from a slave."

For a moment, I was furious, but my anger evaporated as quickly as it came. "Ask Otto, then," I said. "After all, his faith will soon be yours."

To my surprise, she laughed outright. "I am not talking about faith," she said. 'You have seen evil, Sabat. And can you believe there is nothing better than humanity?"

I turned away. "Not here at any rate," I said lightly.

Again she chuckled. "Well struck, slave. And I suppose you would have looted this place if there had been anything to loot?"

"Probably."

"How does it feel to rob the dead?"

"They don't mind."

She stared at me. "I was—asking," she said. "Mr. Sabat."

Her use of that "mister" did not escape, though it amused me. "In that case, you deserve an answer," I told her. I thought for a moment. "At first it felt shameful, I think. In fact, it still does a little. But you could hardly expect me to have lived by my feelings, could you?"

"Why not?"

"Because that would be a luxury," I started to say. Then, "No, you really want to know, don't you?" I told her about how I had been originally being trained as a tutor—a classical scholar. "But Feullier," I added, "was not interested in scholarship."

"And so they broke you."

"Why do you say that?" I asked, my voice suddenly brittle.

She did not answer at once and when she did, the distance had come back between us. "I did not hire a scholar," she said. "Only a tomb robber. So that's alright."

"I think I'd better look for the others," I told her abruptly. "And we need water." Quickly I strode away.

I found Steed standing by the village well, one hand on the broken coping. He was so still that I had a strange feeling watching him. I had said that being human meant you could build houses, but it meant something more. Termites built houses. Bees and beavers built houses. Being human meant that you could decide not to build anything, even if you died of exposure.

It meant also that you could laugh, as Steed still did, and that you could cry. I wondered what sort of tears his eyes would produce. And I looked at the edge of him, there against the sky.

"Ah, Sabat," he said when he saw me. "I was just coming back to wake you."

I grunted.

He dipped one hand into a cracked stone basin. "I think the other party may have camped further up the valley," he said. "Or at least someone did. There was smoke for a while."

I stared at the stone and tried to picture women coming to fill identical stone jars—or were they men?—identical people, anyway, who lived in identical huts. People who had forgotten, perhaps that they were human. Or people who had never known in the first place.

"She got here first," I said.

"Presumably."

Suddenly Steed turned back, staring down at the quiet village. Our hut was hidden by a rise, but I thought I heard something. A cry?

Turning almost together, we sprinted down the hill and into the ruins—too late.

CHAPTER TEN

I could hear the silence in the ruined hut as I drew up panting behind Steed. My breath was overloud in my ears but I heard no other sound. I was afraid of what I would see when I looked in through the ruined door—but there was nothing at all.

Nothing, that is, except our few belongings, the brushwood laid to cook out breakfast, and the dressed meat that was to provide it. Otto and Lady Pelanot had vanished.

Steed glanced at me, his eyes catching the light momentarily before he turned away. I began casting about at once for a trail, leaving him to use whatever enhanced senses had been given him. But neither of us turned up a thing.

Quele's morning advanced around us, the suns nearly as bright as the Sachsen cluster, the shadows far more distinct than they were on Otto's more humid world. I stood with my back to the light and studied the ruins.

Bits of wall, fallen roofs, regular, though broken doorframes. Here and there I made out part of a stone fence. Everywhere the strange vegetation had moved in, greening the streets, grasping the stone and rotted wood with reaching tendrils, weighting them down with the woody burden of centuries' growth. I still couldn't figure out why the place was so repellent.

Even now, when the original dwellers had been gone so long, no animals denned here. The regularity of the architecture could still be seen—an almost hivelike pattern—but nowhere could I make out so much as a game trail. Only the birds twittered unmusically overhead. I turned to Steed.

He seemed as mystified as I, though I'm still not sure he felt what I did as we stood in the ruined village. "Godcountry," he muttered, though, and it sounded like a curse.

I shook off my fancies. "Where is Wolfbane?" I said. "Do you know?"

"Scouting."

I ran one hand through my hair, swearing inwardly. "Do you think they got him, too?" I asked. "Whoever—"

"Whoever?"

We both glanced around once more. We were not dealing with ghosts, I reminded myself. My friend and my employer had been carried off by flesh and blood and whoever did it might be still around.

I tried to look at the village through different eyes, hoping to see beyond my own hatred of Godcountry and its dread wonders. The village, aside from being an ugly place, was manifestly indefensible. Even when it was first built, it could never have been meant as a fortress. Either there were no rival tribes or else whoever had lived here depended on some other sort of defense. We had no other defense.

"Come on, Steed," I said. "We're sitting ducks here in the ruins."

"Who do you think it was, Sabat?"

"Maureen," I snapped. "Who else?"

He paused, his eyes unfocused while he accessed one of the implants in his head. I waited, holding my impatience in check as well as I could.

"Nothing," he said at last. "Not a thing, Sabat. I can't pick up her wristband at all." He turned his impassive gaze on my face.

"You can't pick up Maureen's band?"

He shook his head. "Either she's out of range or something is between us. Something solid." I looked away.

"It isn't just the band," he said. "I can't hear anything but a few birds. It's so quiet out there!"

I went back into the hut. Otto had been asleep, I remembered, when I left. His sleeping bag was still warm, as though he had just left it. I looked in Lady Pelanot's corner and found nothing except her pack.

Not quite. I spotted an object there on the broken clay floor and bent to retrieve it. It was the Hithian dagger—not the glassite thing she had pulled on me back in Quele City, but another one. The one she had kept, maybe, all those years.

I saw that the blade was smeared—and the handle. A few drops of blood had fallen on the pack but any that went on the floor would have soaked in by now the way the surface was crumbling away. Somehow, as I held the weapon in my hand, I did not believe the blood was her own.

"Rangers?" Steed hazarded. "After what Kavanaugh's outfit did to that robot, it might only be a matter of time until they came."

"Maybe. We still don't know if she reprogrammed the thing before she tore it apart."

Steed waited. By this I knew it was still my show. I was responsible for the success of our mission and I was responsible for the lives of my companions. I had come a long way since my last visit to Godcountry.

I cleaned Lady Pelanot's knife and put it carefully into one of my pockets. Our next step seemed plain to me, especially since we had been unable to locate so much as a trail to follow. It was time to visit the primitives over on the hill. Specifically, a man named Casarot. He had once been a friend of mine.

Casarot was chief of a tribe of degenerates who eked out a precarious existence outside the laws of Quele. I'd guess he was descended from criminals escaped into Godcountry so long ago they had forgotten their origins. His people had retained nothing but a strong dislike for the law and a deep suspicion for anything having to do with the religion of Quele. I told Steed what I was going to do.

He considered. "It's been a while, Sabat. Six years or more. He might be dead, you know."

I shrugged. "Where else is there to start? We can't do our job without Otto—he's the one who gets us offplanet, remember?"

"Right. And then there's Hermradon's aunt."

Much as she had held her own so far, I bitterly regretted her presence in our party. But what was done was done. I led the way down an overgrown boulevard, trying not to look too closely at the rubbled houses. The emptiness of the place unsettled me, as though the original dwellers had had no spirits to leave behind. The village, I fancied, would have been just as empty when they lived here. But that in itself was a sort of haunting—that emptiness where emptiness should not be.

The ruins ended as abruptly as they had begun, another anomaly as far as I was concerned. I breathed a sigh of relief as we left that place and began to climb once more into the hills. The place we sought now lay in another, broader valley where I hoped to find the Spoinye—rejected of the gods—pasturing their goats. It was their usual grazing ground for this time of year.

Steed apparently did not tire, though I did. We paused at midday for a drink and a bar each of trail ration. All around us, the oddly variegated trees and shrubs bloomed or declined grotesquely as only the trees and shrubs of Godcountry can do. It was a place of change, continual and rapid, as one species superseded another in an endless chain of sudden appearances and equally sudden declines.

I tried not to think of Otto and Lady Pelanot in Maureen's hands. After all, I had watched Maureen lose her humanity, year after year until our final release. Never had she been allowed to be a woman—not after Feullier bought our contracts. And now she was a monster.

So I had that on my mind—the sure knowledge that she would kill my companions as soon as they had ceased to be of use to her. But then a further uncertainty crept in. What if she did not have them at all?

The whole setup was wrong somehow, judging by what I had seen of the Hithians so far. For after all, what use would Otto be to them alive? Wouldn't it be more like them to just cut his throat and take Lady Pelanot? And even then—why not kill both of them? If Maureen had murdered Susanna, she would hardly stop at killing any of my friends she could get hold of.

And there I was, back at that vision of Maureen creeping into the studio—or Boris—or both of them. Maureen couldn't know, of course, that Otto was one of my closest friends, but what if she got it into her head that Lady Pelanot and I were lovers? She was just mad enough to think something like that.

"We should try to spot the herdsmen before dark," Steed said, his still face turned toward the hillside above us. Casarot's valley lay on the other side.

I grunted, glad to be drawn back to my more immediate concerns. But I was still sore from the crossing and did not look forward to the steep climb. And then there was yet another problem to consider.

This was, I told myself, Godcountry. We had been mighty lucky so far not to have run into one of the nastier surprises this place could throw at us. I suppose I was waiting for a blow that did not come, but I found myself tensing every moment.

I scrambled to my feet and turned about slowly, studying the clumps of trees, the flowering vines, the turf that was not turf. A bird or two glided above a distant copse, oversized, I would guess, at this distance—the birds, I mean. But there was nothing else to see.

No deer, or what passed for deer, no tracks of wild cows. Nothing. "You feel it, Steed?" I asked him. "The quiet?"

"Yes. But it's been that way here before. A change in fodder takes out the animals. A new disease maybe." "Or a new predator?" I suggested.

"We'd have seen signs of that."

Without answering, I set myself to climb. Steed had been right about Casarot; he might not be around anymore. But we had no other lead unless we dug up the foundations of the village and turned over every single stone in the valley. Still, the quiet got on my nerves.

We had nearly reached the crest of our hill when I spotted something in the brush. The trees had given way to some sort of springy, purple stuff set with thorns that caught on our trousers and boots and cut our hands when we freed ourselves. Lacking Steed's modified epidermis, I donned gloves.

Suddenly there was movement further up the slope. I nodded to Steed, pointing silently.

"Leatherbunnies," he said, drawing a weapon. Godcountry's leatherbunny, a nonclassified hybrid somewhere in that dim zone between reptile and mammal, bore more resemblance to the first part of its name than to the last. We had christened it ourselves because it had ears like a rabbit.

Unlike a rabbit, it was a carnivore and ran in packs. I drew my own pistol and glanced around uneasily. The purple thorns impeded our movements.

Abruptly the thing sprang—clearing the ground in great wallaby-like jumps, ears flapping, claws extended, and some sort of foamy drool flying from its jaws.

Tangled as I was, I fell back, tripped and nearly went down before Steed shot it. The leatherbunny fell at my feet but not before its fangs had actually grazed my hand.

I stared at the foam on my glove as Steed waded up to me. "What the—" I croaked.

"Didn't think they could go mad," he said. "Did it bite you?"

I shook my head. "I don't think so, anyway." I stepped back from the dead animal. It was nearly the size of a small jackal, the hind legs oversized, the front smaller and thinner. You could see it was sick by the way it had slobbered all over its face. The glazing eyes were half covered by white film. It smelled pretty bad too.

"Close call," Steed said. "And a loner—?" We both looked around, but nothing moved in the sea of ragged purple.

"An epidemic?" I hazarded, but I knew that wasn't right. There would have been bodies, wouldn't there?

"Just a fluke. Something new from wherever." Steed reholstered his own weapon.

"Just a minute," I said, yanking the thorns loose from my pants as I stepped backward. "I'm going to disinfect this glove."

Actually, I wanted to throw it away, but that would be foolish. Besides, I might even be immune to leatherbunny germs.

Steed pulled out a spray and let me have it, glove and sleeve. The stuff smelled stronger than whatever was on me, but that wasn't much comfort. I turned away from the corpse, staring along the way it had come. Sure enough, there was a run beneath the vines. I decided to follow it.

The track was floored with naked ground, visible in the places where the purple stuff didn't quite meet above it. It made a little trail, climbing the hill to a place where there were more rocks than thorns.

It ended in a hole.

"Come here, Steed," I called and he did so.

We both watched that hole, but nothing came out except the smell. This time it was a lot worse, not only the smell of disease but death. Plenty of it.

"Well that confirms our guess," Steed said. "Some new germ has come in from the net."

We had both been inoculated with unicine and it was good stuff, covering or at least lessening the effects of most types of virus and a lot of fungus as well. But only a fool took chances. We moved away from the hole.

"I have a feeling about this, Steed," I said. "I'm going up on top—" I mounted the slight rise above the den entrance and walked along the ridge above. I didn't have far to go before I located another entrance.

Here, at least, were bones, but they were not leatherbunnies. They were all scattered about and gnawed where the bunnies had fed, some time back, judging by the way the local beetles had cleaned up the joints. I had no idea what animals had provided this feast, but in Godcountry it could have been anything.

"Look over there," Steed said quietly, pointing.

I toed a rib cage and something rattled and fell out. It was an arrow or dart, broken off. I found the other end nearby.

"Casarot's people?" Steed asked.

"I don't think so," I said slowly. "Look at that fletching. And the design." There were bands of color like none I had seen so far on Quele. I could have sworn that whatever bird supplied those gold and black feathers had not flown anywhere over Godcountry the last time I was here.

"Something new," I said. Gingerly I retrieved the arrow and handed it to him.

He studied it. "Oh boy," he muttered. "Looks like the net is working overtime."

The amber feather gleamed in the sun. A little breeze stirred our hair. Above us, the blue dome of the sky, darker than the sky of Sachsen and of a purer hue, remained empty. Always before when I had come to this place, I had been a member of a crew, a bit of Feullier's machinery intent on my own job and little else. Now the sheer alienness of Quele—of Godcountry itself—really hit me. I felt the skin tighten over my back and resisted an impulse to whirl about and see what was behind us.

"Let's find Casarot," I said. "If he's still here."

We climbed the last ridge to where we could look down into the adjoining valley. Some of the purple stuff was already growing in patches here and on the hillside, but so far it had not cut very far into the grassland below. To my relief, we spotted a few animals grazing in a tight herd some distance away.

"Come on," I told Steed. "But be careful."

"The herd's smaller," he observed. "Or are we too early in the year?"

"We're not early."

There was no way to hide our approach from the herdsmen. But though I had always gotten along with Casarot's people, I did not lose that tight feeling.

When the inevitable happened and we found ourselves confronting two of the shaggy tribesmen, it took a real effort not to reach for a weapon. This was especially true as the pair did not look friendly at all. Both held drawn bows—and you can bet I checked the color of their arrows. But the shafts were unadorned, the feathers solid black, just as I remembered them.

Steed and I held out our hands in the universal greeting of those who walked outside the laws of Quele, but neither tribesman relaxed. "Why you come here?" one of them demanded in the patois of the outcast.

"Casarot," I said. "I need to see him."

To my relief, no one told me he was dead. But the bowstrings remained taut. "You are—?"

"Sabat."

The name registered. "Feullier?"

I shook my head. "Feullier is gone," I told them. "I am free now."

"Sabat," one of them repeated. "You had magic band on one arm—to hurt you if you disobey."

I held up my wrist. "It's still there," I said. "But the magic is gone."

At sight of the slave band, both arrows were lowered a bit, menacing my legs instead of my heart. "You come."

We went—down through the herd and across the ford of a small river. Casarot's sheep were not looking as well as usual, though nothing really throve in Godcountry. My misgivings intensified.

The day was about gone and we were confronted with another of Quele's hellish sunsets by the time we reached Casarot's summer camp among the shattered hills at the end of the valley.

We were left under guard to wait while he was told of our coming which gave me a chance to look things over. Casarot's people looked no better than the stock, and there were not so many of them as there had been before. Especially children, I thought. I counted only about ten or so.

Finally we were relieved of our weapons and taken into Casarot's hut, a half tent of brushwood and hides. For a moment or two, I could see nothing in the gloom. Then I made out the figures of Casarot's two wives, perched stolidly on either side of a pallet.

"Eduardo Sabat," a thin voice whispered and I braced myself to come forward.

"Hello, Casarot," I said.

In six years, the once vigorous leader of the outcasts had been replaced by a shriveled old man. I tried not to let my surprise show, for after all, this was Godcountry. One of the wives, I saw, was new.

Her predecessor must have died.

"I not think—you return—Sabat."

"Nor I."

"You—free now?"

I hunkered down beside him. "I am free of Feullier," I said.

He grinned at this and I saw many more gaps where his teeth had been. "A new thing for you—to be free."

"It isn't all it's cracked up to be."

At this he laughed a little, coughed and reached for my arm. The slave band caught the light of his smoky little lamp in two gleams like the red eyes of some prowling beast—a beast that watched me now and never let me out of its sight. "Free is inside," he said. "You tell me this once."

"Maybe I did."

He nodded slowly. "Freedom like—peeling a bulb," he said. "You pull until nothing left in your hand."

I did not answer him. I had not come here to discuss philosophy with a savage.

"Empty," he repeated. "Clean. Then you see what come into your hand."

I was ashamed. Here was a man whose life had been nothing but suffering with danger upon danger and no escape beyond the stars and no one except himself to fall back on. He was prematurely old and soon he would die without any of the comforts of civilization. The strange animals of Godcountry would feed on his corpse.

And yet he held out to me a hope greater than my own despair, fruit of a life more worthy than mine had ever been. I shook my head. "My hand is empty, Casarot. And maybe—maybe it always was. Maybe that's the best thing."

"There are—terrible things out there—among the stars?"

"Men are terrible enough, Casarot. Surely you have found that already."

"You speak from dark place."

I did not deny it. "But I am here," I said. "And now I ask you to tell me what has happened. The animals, I mean, and those arrows I saw, not like yours."

His face changed at this. "Unmen," he said. "Shael. Born of a mad god and cast out from heaven. They come like sickness."

I nodded. This was pretty much what I had expected. I told him about the leatherbunnies.

"Yes. That is the way of unmen. They bring sick." "On purpose?" I asked incredulously.

"Who can say? They kill many animals. Clear land—spy on the Quele."

"They spy on the temple complex? On the pilgrims?"

He did not answer right away and I saw that he was afraid. Steed and I exchanged glances at this point. "Ask what they look like," Steed suggested.

I tried this tack and managed to extract a little more information. The Shael were primitives, apparently, though more advanced than Casarot's people and of a different race. Obviously they and some small part of their own ecology had been picked up from some as yet uncontacted world by the ubiquitous net tendrils and dumped here. They used crossbows and lived in a very regimented society, kidnapping local people to augment their scanty population.

"You keep an eye on them?" Steed asked Casarot, but got no answer.

"We need your help," I said then. "Someone has taken our friends and we have no way to find them. They left no trail."

There was a long silence after this—so long I was afraid Casarot had dozed off. But finally he seemed to come to a decision.

"They take. It is their way." He glanced at one of his wives, but she looked down. "They take my son."

I stood up, shocked. "Your son?"

"Yes. Take women for wives, maybe. Take others for other things."

I stared at him.

"They dead, Sabat. All dead. I know this, Sabat." He tried to sit up and one of the wives held him. "You go back to stars! Now!" To my utter consternation, he was weeping.

"Casarot!" I knelt back down so that our faces were on a level. "I can't go back. These are my friends—and until I see their dead

bodies, I must do all that I can to save them."

Once more he clutched at me with one skinny hand. "Soon I go to gods," he said. "To hell of outcasts. But this death—it is worse!"

I looked into his eyes as he said this, and I believed him. Whatever it was he feared—and I could not know what it was—I knew that he spoke the truth. I sat back on my heels, thinking.

"You keep an eye on these people," Steed said to Casarot. "You know for certain then that they took Lady Pelanot and Zeller?"

Casarot lay back down, exhausted, but one of the wives spoke up. She was the one who had looked down when Casarot mentioned his son and I remembered now the infant she had had at her breast when last I saw her.

"We know," she said. "They take other camp too."

It was as though an electric charge had gone through me. "What did you say?" I almost shouted. "Do you mean Maureen Kavanaugh?"

She did not start. "Star people," she said. "Like you."

I grabbed her by the shoulders. "Who saw? Find him for me now!"

Still her calm face did not change. After a moment I let her go.

"Casarot!" I turned to my old friend. "Surely I can just talk to him!"

The old man sighed. "Why for you must die, Sabat? You free now as you say."

"Maybe—Maybe I won't die," I said. "And if I do—isn't that part of being free too, Casarot?"

"I wonder," he said then, "what god will take you at the end, Eduardo Sabat."

I felt as though he had struck me—or taken me up in arms once powerful but now sadly shrunken, and shaken me until my teeth rattled in my head. I could not say a word. How strange that someone like Casarot could, with a word or two, pierce straight to the empty heart of me.

"Who," I said evenly, "saw? Tell me who it is, Casarot. I must know more."

But all the while I watched his face, I was thinking about how there was no god in me after all, as the Stoics had taught. Neither I nor the world was remotely divine and all my pantheism had never been more than a glib theory—something I may have wanted to believe, for whatever reason, but which meant nothing to me now.

"You talk to Jenn," Casarot said at length, never taking his deep-socketed eyes from my face. "Maybe he talk to you, maybe not."

A guard was dispatched, and while we waited, Casarot had our weapons returned to us. Presently a young man came in. I could tell he was one of the wild ones, those of Casarot's people who took an extra step down from the pitiable degeneracy in which they were born.

Jenn watched us furtively out of gold flecked eyes, his tangled hair and thin beard crawling with vermin. He wore the rags of a Quele burial robe, belted with a leather thong in which he had stuck a throwing knife. His feet were bare, calloused, and filthy.

"You show us camp of other star people?" Steed asked and Jenn nodded. I was relieved—both that he would and that Steed had had sense enough not to mention the Shael right off the bat.

Casarot spread his hands. "Good, good," he said. "Jenn sees much, Sabat."

Jenn may have seen much, but he did not, apparently, talk much.

When I turned around, he was gone.

"Come on," Steed called from outside and I followed.

***

Maureen's camp was about where we had expected it to be, further down the valley from the ruins. We reached it sometime in the wee hours, having stopped earlier for a brief rest. Fortunately, our guide knew a shortcut through the hills and we avoided the purple thorns entirely.

I kicked at a mound of still warm ashes, unearthing a few coals. Bedding lay about and here, at least, we saw signs of a struggle. But of the party itself, and their abductors, there was no trace.

We were about to turn away when Jenn raised his head suddenly—and vanished. I was standing right beside him and the speed with which he disappeared seemed almost preternatural—at least until I saw him beckon from behind a tree.

Steed pulled out his gun and I did likewise. Something made a brief shadow in the moonlight.

"Stop or you're dead," I told it in Quele and prepared to fire.

"Eduardo!" A moment later, Wolfbane's burly form was before me. I almost hugged him in my relief.

"Heth Andrew! Where have you been?"

"Out and around. Waiting to see what would come to me."

Steed and I drew him back beneath the trees. "This is Jenn," I said, indicating our guide. "A native of this place."

Wolfbane peered at him for a moment. "Tell me what happened here," he said. "Do you know?" "Did you go back to our own camp?" He nodded.

Quickly I told him about Casarot and what he had said, and about the disappearance of Otto and Lady Pelanot. "But now tell us what you have been doing," I said when I had finished.

"We," he corrected. "I, too, have a companion. The pilot—

Hermradon's pilot, I mean. You remember he had one?" "Where is he?" I demanded, looking around.

"I had to tie him up back there."

I saved my questions, though I had many, and followed the Lost Rythan to a sort of overhang where someone lay, pushed up against the back wall, watching us with eyes that glittered in the light of Steed's torch. The pilot's face was flat, the cheekbones high, and beaded with sweat, his perfectly black hair and thin moustache equally damp.

He looked like a pilot, alright, I thought. They were all of the same genetically altered race. Obviously this one had missed a few doses of the drug most pilots needed to keep themselves even marginally sane. No wonder Wolfbane had had to tie him up.

"Have you questioned him?" I asked.

Heth Andrew nodded. "But he doesn't make a lot of sense, Eduardo. Not even for a pilot."

I looked down at the man again. "What about Hermradon?" I demanded. "Do you know where he is, ah—what's your name, anyway?"

The pilot continued to regard me for a moment, and then, quite suddenly, he chuckled. "The dead," he told me, "are nameless."

"His name is Qitsork," Heth Andrew said. "Father Liu told me."

I turned back to the madman. "So you are dead?" I asked him, seeking some sort of ground on which we could communicate. "How did you die? What about Hermradon? Is he dead too?"

"The dark between the stars came into my head. They let it in and now the hole will not close again."

"Who let it in?"

"The not-men. They took my rockweed and the dark came in."

I froze at the name not-men for it was almost the same term

Casarot had used. "You were with them?" I whispered. "With the Shael? And do they have Hermradon, then?"

He goggled at me for a moment and then his face went blank. "Hermradon is lost. He escaped the binding," he said in a flat voice unlike the one he had been using before. "But only the dead escape— in the end."

"What," I asked then through dry lips, "is the binding?"

His eyes grew wide and his face worked while the lips skinned back from his teeth in a grotesque grin reminiscent of rigor mortis.

"Ask the dead," he muttered and then changed again so that I found myself confronting a lunatic. This time his chuckle became howling laughter. "No good!" he got out. "Everyone knows pilots are mad! No good at all!"

Our guide, Jenn, had begun edging away at the first chuckle, and the racket the pilot was making now nearly sent him into his disappearing act. I tried to catch his eye, though what I could do to reassure him escaped me at the moment.

"Put the pilot out," I told Steed and he did so with the stunner he still carried. In the sudden silence, we all stared at one another, wondering what to do next. Finally, I turned back to Jenn, my own weapon in my hand. "You can talk," I said in Quele. "Even if you don't understand basic, you can talk to me."

He nodded, glancing uneasily at the pilot's still form. "You've seen madmen before, haven't you?" Again that nod.

"And you are not afraid of them, surely?"

"Not mad," he said, sidling away from the pilot's vicinity. "Unalive."

"Him?" I said, jerking my head in the pilot's direction.

A nod. "Touched."

The pilot was that alright, I agreed, but likely Jenn meant something more. "You mean he's been to the Shael, don't you?" I said.

Again a nod.

"Can you take us to them? To their camp or village?"

Jenn swallowed, his lean Adam's apple bobbing in the light of Steed's torch.

I peered into his face. "You can, can't you? You've been spying on their camp!"

At this, he made a sudden leap, disappearing before Steed could get off a single shot with the stunner.

Someone laid a hand on my arm, and I looked around to meet Wolfbane's troubled eyes. "You frightened him, Eduardo. Whatever you said, you frightened him beyond what he could bear."

I put away my own weapon. "A man," I said loudly in Quele, "is loyal to his chief. He does not run away when his people are in danger."

I waited, feeling like a hypocrite. What, after all, did I know of loyalty? I was as much an outcast as Hermradon't pilot. But I was angry and desperate and if Jenn had come into sight, I cannot swear that I would not have sent off a shot of my own.

Steed looked at me questioningly and I nodded. "Casarot must know," he said equally loudly, "that we are starmen. We have guns to kill the Shael. Maybe we can save Casarot's people!"

Wolfbane moved away from us. "Jenn," he called out, "I do not speak your language—"

I translated for him.

"Jenn," he went on, "I, too, am afraid. I who am twice your size! I do not know if we can protect you or ourselves, but we go on because we have a job to do."

We all waited, listening, but there was no sound.

"Jenn," he said again, more softly. "You fear that which you think is worse than death. But I will tell you what is truly worse than to die. To live without honor is worse—to betray those who trusted you."

I translated this too and, a moment later, our guide reappeared as silently as he had gone. I saw Wolfbane's right hand move in the sign Christians made when they invoked their god, but with his left, he wiped sweat from his face. Apparently he had been none too sure he would succeed.

"You will guide us to the Shael?" Steed asked quietly.

Jenn nodded, his unkempt hair falling over his eyes.

"We'll need some rest and—" I indicated the pilot. "What about him?"

Wolfbane bent down and unbound his prisoner. "I think we should leave him for now, Eduardo," he said. "I found him wandering in the woods and he seemed to be doing alright. I think he's been living on his own for a while.'"

"But won't the Shael be looking for him?" I asked.

Wolfbane shook his head. "From things he said, I think they had him once already, but when they saw that whatever they did to the others wouldn't work in his case, they must have let him go. Or at least not pursued him too closely when he escaped."

"Whatever they did," I repeated. "Just what do you think about these people, Heth Andrew?"

"I don't know yet. But I fear some sort of assault on identity—don't you?"

"Brainwashing?"

He frowned. "Something like that."

"Then we're in a hurry," Steed said. "I'll keep watch until dawn and then—"

"No," I told him suddenly. "We'll start now." I was thinking of Maureen. How could I help it? After all that had been done to her already, the thought of this final assault on what remained of her personality made me sick. Maybe she was my enemy, but it came to me now that I was not hers.

Our guide set a grueling pace, the more surprising since he was such a poor specimen. Truly had Wolfbane made his claim that he was twice Jenn's size and he was a lot more healthy besides. Yet we both had trouble keeping up. Only Steed kept on at the same steady pace, never showing the least sign of weariness.

The suns rose in our faces as we crossed a high saddle among the hills. We were far above the valleys now, and in the dawnlight we had a magnificent view of Godcountry.

Far to the south lay Spire, nearly hidden beyond the orchards. Below us, the hills fell away in a greenish haze. I tried to make out the temple square at the end of the pilgrims' road from Spire, but I could not see it.

"Up there," Jenn said at last, pointing to a barren slope. "Valley of unmen on other side." "Will they have sentries?" He laid one hand on his knife.

"They bleed, I take it," Steed said dryly as Jenn led us to a sort of gorge among the jumbled boulders of the hillside.

We walked on scree and gravel that slid away beneath out feet. The rock walls on either side were not high enough to hide us from view and we had to stoop as we went. This was especially hard for Wolfbane because our passage was narrow and crooked as well. Lost Rythans were not made to maneuver in small spaces.

It was midmorning before we reached the top of the hill. The land dropped off before us in a vertical fall, nearly precipitating poor Heth Andrew to a nasty death on the rocks below. He caught himself in time, however, falling backward as he braced his hands on the sides of the gorge. A meter or so below, a narrow ledge crossed the face of the cliff and this, I gathered, was to be our road down.

Jenn made no apology for the near mishap and apparently none was expected. Without comment, the Lost Rythan swung himself over and began the descent.

"Sentries?" Steed asked as we followed.

"Not here," Jenn said tersely. "This way mine."

"So this is your own way in? They've got another road, then?" Jenn nodded.

"Maybe," I suggested from my position behind Wolfbane and Jenn, "we should know if your road has any more surprises?" Jenn grunted interrogatively.

"I mean what else is between us and the Shael," I explained patiently, trying not to look down too often as I inched my way along.

"Trees—dark."

I waited for some addition to this cryptic statement, but there was none. Soon I saw for myself what he had meant, as the ledge widened and we came level with the dark tops of some sort of pines. The foliage was a deep and luminous green—almost jewel-toned where the sun hit it. But below, all was black, bark and needles a dull, wet-looking black. We descended into shadow and abruptly the ledge was gone. We had reached the forest floor.

"They kill trees," Jenn said abruptly. "Make empty ground—put in seeds."

This was a pretty long speech for him and he gave it with some intensity. I translated for Wolfbane.

"How do they kill the trees?" he asked and I passed this on.

"Make sick. All these sick."

I peered at a massive trunk beside me, but could see nothing amiss. Gingerly I put out one hand—something one seldom does in Godcountry—and touched the bark. To my surprise and disgust, it came away in pulpy shreds, showing the decaying cambium beneath. The whole tree was rotten!

Steed shook one of the drooping lower branches and was rewarded by a shower of needles. I gathered the trees were pretty much dead already; they just hadn't turned brown.

"They must be actually trying to remake the ecology," Steed said. "To fit whatever they left behind. But how anyone could even try in a place like Godcountry—"

"My impression," I told him as I wiped my hands on my trousers, "was that they were a bit unusual. You saw Casarot's face when he mentioned them, didn't you?"

A faint noise sent Steed whirling about as he and Wolfbane drew weapons almost simultaneously. I was only seconds behind, but all of us were too late.

Jenn had vanished as usual, and the three of us were left staring into the muzzles of a nerve gun and a laser rifle. Both were held by Quele rangers.

CHAPTER ELEVEN

It didn't seem like a good idea to keep on aiming our own lesser firepower at our would-be captors, but on the other hand, there were three of us—not counting Jenn, who could be anywhere—and only two of them. And one of them was wounded, I saw now.

But still, it was a standoff.

The younger ranger—the unwounded one—seemed as surprised to see us as we were to see him. I expected to hear the familiar cry of "tomb robber" and was not disappointed.

"You will," the young man said, when he had made his point, "drop those weapons and submit yourselves to the justice of Quele."

When it became obvious that none of us had much confidence in Quele's justice, he began to jitter a little with the gun. I was afraid we were going to have a shootout then and there. But something else, and I swear it was not fear of us at least, caused the wounded one to lay one hand on the arm of his companion.

His square face was drawn with more than physical pain and his eyes were absolutely haunted. "Do not fire, Leon," he said hoarsely.

"The others will hear."

I almost glanced in the direction he indicated.

"You've been keeping an eye on them—over there?" I asked the younger ranger and he flushed, a darkening barely visible in the dim light of the forest floor.

"That does not concern you, unbeliever," he said coldly. Then, seeing the slave band on my arm, the look on his face became even uglier. "If your masters seek to league themselves with the cursed ones," he added, "they are greater fools than we thought."

"I have no masters," I told him, the pistol fitting comfortably in my hand, my aim never wavering.

"Why are you here?" the other ranger asked, steadying himself against a tree. The rotting bark crumbled at his touch, powdering away in greasy crumbs, and he sprang away in disgust. But I noticed that he could not repress a groan at the sudden movement.

Steed and I exchanged a glance. "Why are they here?" he asked.

Before I could frame a question, Leon stiffened, his hands twitching on the nerve gun he held. Apparently it had just registered that one of us was a Lost Rythan. Our presumed status as tomb robbers was exchanged for something more sinister.

"So," he said softly, "evil draws evil, I see."

"Don't be an ass," I said sharply, glad Heth Andrew did not understand Quele. "From all I've heard so far about the Shael, you'd be a lot better off in Lost Rythan hands than theirs. And I think you know it."

The older ranger forestalled Leon's reply. "You are right, slave," he said wearily, "and we will not pretend otherwise. The presence of this infidel makes it unlikely that you are out to make any sort of alliance with the cursed-ones."

I kept my eyes on his rifle. So much, then had we gained. But it wasn't a whole lot. After all, adhering to Heth Andrew's religion, or any offworld faith for that matter, was still a crime.

"My name," I told him, wanting to clear this up before we went on, "is not 'slave'. I told you that already."

"Your pardon," the Quele said, a small movement quirking one corner of his lips. "We shall introduce ourselves." He nodded in Leon's direction. "Apprentice Ordon. And I am Sergeant Hekor."

"Sabat," I told him. "And Steed." I pointed. "And Heth Andrew Wolfbane."

"We must move away from here," Hekor said. "It is too near the settlement." He seemed at a loss to continue.

"Truce?" I suggested, one eye on the apprentice.

"There is no provision for making peace with outsiders." Hekor frowned slightly. "I do not see how—"

"You don't have any choice," I pointed out. "If you try to take us, we all fall into the hands of the Shael."

The apprentice gripped his own weapon more tightly. "No, alien. That we do not. Not alive, anyway."

"Ah." I thought for a moment. "Let's have a temporary thing then, a cessation of hostilities. Obviously, you're alone out here and so are we. And whatever we're up against is more than either of us expected."

"It is true," Hekor said slowly, "that I would like to hear your story. For I believe that if you were tomb robbers, you would not have come into this valley. I offer you a temporary truce until we are clear of the area."

Leon didn't look too happy at this. "By what can they swear?" he demanded belligerently.

"By their honor," Hekor told him, his eyes on mine. "For though the gods will surely strike them in the next life, yet they may buy a time of grace in this."

Now I was really glad Heth Andrew did not understand Quele.

"By our honor, then," I said and Steed nodded agreement.

"The Lost Rythan?"

I made an edited translation for Heth Andrew and he gave a shrug. "Let the Quele do likewise then," he said shortly. "They needn't bring in their gods."

So we made peace with our enemies, there in the rotting forest of that nameless valley. Then, because it seemed right to me, I put away my gun and began helping the wounded man along. But as we neared the cliff face, I realized that the cleft by which we had come was completely hidden and that we would have to search for it if we were to use it. I decided not to mention it to the rangers.

"Where to?" I asked the sergeant.

"This way." Leon led us parallel to the stone until we rounded a rubbled point and left the forest behind. Our destination was no more prepossessing than the dreary country we had left, for we found ourselves in a brush-covered wilderness hemmed in on both sides by the lowering hills.

"Our camp is ahead," the apprentice said, gesturing.

By now, both Wolfbane and I were supporting the sergeant. I wanted to ask whether they had applied a pressure bandage, for the Quele was bleeding quite a bit from his side and no longer even tried to speak. What, I wondered, had happened back there? And were we likely to be pursued?

Finally we came upon a small cache of supplies in a sheltered spot against the cliff wall, now no more than a low escarpment at the base of a hill. We laid Hekor down and I had a look at him.

The wound was a deep one, the head of a crossbow bolt still lodged where I did not dare to touch it. He was breathing shallowly and I feared internal bleeding.

Steed and I made him as comfortable as we could while the apprentice looked on, biting his lip and trying to hide his dismay as he saw the extent of the sergeant's injuries.

"Shall I give him something?" I asked. But neither Quele would consent to this.

"Now," Steed said, when we had settled ourselves where we could watch the way we had come, "it is time to talk."

The apprentice looked at him, mouth working as he weighed duty against expediency. If he had not been a Quele, I would have felt sorry for him.

Steed must have had better feelings than I, for he offered to go first. Quickly he recounted recent events, leaving out all mention of Hermradon and our mission, of course.

Leon and the sergeant exchanged meaningful looks when Steed had finished.

"The rest of your party," Hekor whispered. "Prisoners?" Steed and I nodded.

"Ours too. We had come to investigate—" His voice trailed off and the apprentice took up the tale.

"There were rumors," he said, looking as though he didn't like the taste of his words, "among the savages here."

It didn't surprise me to learn that the rangers had some minimal contact with the local tribesmen. I suppose they had to grant some sort of concessions in order to protect the pilgrims.

"We heard those rumors ourselves," I said.

"We went up when a flyover showed cleared land," Leon went on. "Where none had been before, I mean. So we wanted a closer look. We try to monitor any changes in Godcountry."

"And that is why you are here now?"

"We found a sort of village. Risshe, we call them, not Shael as the natives do. Risshe because—" He licked his lips. "We have stories, old legends almost, of these. They came once before, long ago. Like a plague, the soulless ones. The cursed."

"Before?" Steed asked sharply. "Is there any proof of this?"

"They leave behind the pattern of their emptiness. Ruins. You have seen them, I am sure."

"The village!" I exclaimed. "Of course!" I remembered my own loathing for the place and I thought now of what had happened there, beginning to understand.

Leon looked as though he had trapped a confession out of me, which in a way, he had. "Is that why you came?" he asked. "Are you archeologists?"

I shook my head. I had not really told him why we were here, only that our friends had disappeared and we were trying to find them. That, so far as I could judge, was enough.

"You've been watching them, you say," Steed prompted. "And did you see any offworlders among the—the cursed ones?"

I saw the younger man's face harden, his eyes flicking away from Steed's face. I thought he was not going to answer, but whatever fear it was that rode him proved too much for his Quellian reluctance to discuss these things with an outsider. "I saw," he admitted, but still, he would not look at us.

"And what did you see, exactly?" Steed asked him with some gentleness.

But Leon only shook his head. He was, as I had noted already, a lip biter and now he worked away as though he hadn't tasted a good lip in quite a while.

"Well," I said, trying a new tack, "can you at least tell us what happened to you and the sergeant? Obviously you had a run in with these—Risshe."

The apprentice gulped in one shuddering lungful of air. "They spotted us," he said. "Sevor Graton—another apprentice was killed."

I heard something in the Quele's voice I did not quite understand. For some reason, we both glanced at the sergeant but Hekor's eyes were closed and he did not rouse when I checked to see if he was still breathing.

He was, but only barely. Short, quick breaths, almost panting.

"So this Graton was killed. And the sergeant was wounded." I let go of Hekor's arm and sat back on my heels. "But you got away, at least."

"Yes," Leon said. "We got away." He looked at Hekor again.

Wolfbane, too, had been staring at the sergeant's face and now he asked for a translation of what Leon had told us. I gave it.

A dark, brooding look came into the Lost Rythan's eyes as he continued to watch Hekor's dying. "Ask the apprentice," he said quietly, "how his companion died."

I stared at him. "The Risshe killed him."

"Ask him."

I complied but was not prepared for the Quele's reaction to Wolfbane's innocent sounding question. The apprentice turned perfectly white and I thought he was going to attack Heth Andrew. "How dare you!"

I gaped at him, confused. "It's alright, apprentice," I said hastily. "We've kept our truce—remember?"

Leon swallowed. "Your friends," he said flatly, "are no more. Do you understand, alien? You have lost them and you must think of them as dead!"

"So I was told already," I said. "But that doesn't answer Heth Andrew's question."

"You should have listened to whoever told you!"

"Alright, Apprentice, I know the Shael—or the Risshe—have some way to destroy personality. They brainwash their prisoners and if that fails they kill them."

Leon smiled at this, a mirthless grimace that did not sit well on his young face. "You speak as one of the so-called scientists of Earth or Sachsen—or whatever gods-forsaken place spawned you."

"Earth," I said. "Now tell me about the Risshe."

"They are the eaters of souls. The bringers of the living death." "Now," Steed murmured, "we are getting somewhere." I translated for Wolfbane.

"Ask him again, Eduardo," he said quietly, "how his companion died."

I did so.

"Exactly as the Lost Rythan has guessed," the apprentice said, glancing once more at his unconscious superior. "Hekor shot him. None ever fall willingly into the hands of the Risshe. He would have done the same for one of us."

Once more my gaze turned to Hekor's face and it did not surprise me to see that dark hollows had come there beside his nose and beneath his eyes. He was going fast.

"So," Steed muttered. "That bad."

"But his wound," I said. "That was the Risshe?"

The apprentice nodded. "He had to make sure that Graton was dead."

I fell silent, thinking of Otto, of Lady Pelanot. Of Maureen.

"Apprentice," Steed said slowly, "you told us you had been watching the camp for some time. And you saw—foreigners. You must have seen our people brought in."

"I saw aliens among the Risshe."

"Were they—?" I did not know how to ask what I needed to know. Possessed? Unalive? Brainwashed? I looked at the apprentice helplessly.

"They were not restrained in any way," he said. "I saw them walk freely about the camp."

At this I could no longer fight off the fear that crawled in my brain. Had Maureen become a monster twice over? Or Otto? I began to understand the true pathos of certain tales I had heard. How a man might drive a stake through the heart of his beloved, though every blow of the hammer struck likewise into his own. And I resolved that she would end as the Quele had ended if that was what must be. I would see to it, I swore, and other suchlike melodramatic follies—for even then I would not own that it was too late, that Maureen had died through my fault as well as Feullier's and from that death there would be no rising.

Meanwhile Steed translated for Wolfbane. The Lost Rythan used a word in his own language. I do not know what that word meant, but it was as ugly as any I had ever heard on earth. His eyes brooded on the sergeant as he spoke and I, too, glanced at the man who yet clung to life, though the death of his comrade lay on his soul.

"Heth Andrew," I said at last, "do you think we can be sure—that they can be sure that the condition, whatever it is, is irreversible?"

He did not take his eyes off Hekor. "Give these people credit for some intelligence, Eduardo. This is their own world and they say they have dealt with these Risshe before."

Steed alone seemed unaffected by the sense of crawling horror that chilled the rest of us. He turned to the apprentice, his face as usual, impassive. "You say you saw aliens," he said, as though he had been thinking this over. "What exactly did they look like?" Leon shrugged. "A little like him." He pointed to me.

"Hithians, maybe. But no others? No women? Or men who might have passed for your own people?" He shook his head.

"But your legends," Steed pursued. "What exactly do they say?"

The apprentice managed a grim smile at this. "We are not using legends as our guide," he said.

"Ah. Then you have been studying these people for some time?"

"Not at their own base. But we had several tribesmen in our care for a time, and we took a Risshe as well."

"You did?" I exclaimed, turning back to him eagerly. "What do they look like? Where did you get him? Did he talk to you?"

"It—for I will not call the thing human even though it looks like a man—it died. As for the others, they died too, despite all we could do for them."

"No one talked?" Steed asked.

"I didn't say that."

Knowing the rangers, I could guess how the Risshe, at least, had died. But naturally I kept quiet.

Steed took him up. "What did you learn?" he asked.

"From the Risshe, very little. It did not speak Quele, for one thing, but only some dialect of the tribesmen. And for another, it was truly alien—more I mean, than such as you." An expression of distaste crossed his features. "Even if we had spoken the same language, I doubt we could have understood each other."

Once more I did not say anything, but all the while he spoke, I was wondering about this. Was the apprentice only distancing himself from the Risshe or were these really something apart from the human and human-derived races of the settled worlds? No such thing had ever been found, so far as I knew.

"When the thing died," Leon went on, "the tribesmen seemed much affected. They are primitives, of course. But they literally gave up and died too."

Steed considered this. "There was obviously some link between them. But you did question the tribesmen before they died, didn't you? What did they have to say?"

The apprentice shrugged. "That they had been made again. That they were at peace. They said they were the lucky ones and that those who could not achieve this peace were put to death."

Apparently the Quele did not know about the pilot. But then he would hardly count.

"So," Steed said, summing up, "we know they must have Kavanaugh's party. And probably Zeller and Pelanot. But—"

I sat forward eagerly. "But it may not be too late, Steed. And the Quele didn't actually see Maureen!"

"Which could mean she is dead," he pointed out. "And even if she isn't—"

"What?" I demanded.

"I don't have to tell you," Steed said more gently. "She's gone, Sabat. Just like the man said. "You know that already."

But my anger was roused at this. I conceived a sudden and irrational hatred for this man who had once been one of the masters such that I think I could even have killed him at that moment. That's what I mean about not being too stable myself.

Fortunately, Wolfbane laid a hand on my arm and at the sight of him, I was restored. "Alright," I said, shaking myself. "Alright, Heth Andrew."

Steed did not say anything more but I knew well enough what he was thinking. Maureen had killed my wife—either by her own hand or that of Boris. And I had shown no mercy to Boris.

"There is hope, at least, for the others," Steed conceded. "For Zeller and Pelanot. But possibly not much time." He had spoken Quele, and the apprentice had looked up at this, licking his lips.

I turned to him. "Steed has a point," I said. "What are your plans for after our parting?"

"I—" He looked as though he had not thought so far ahead.

"You were going to report in, weren't you? Do you have a com?"

He did not look well. "I did," he admitted. "It got broken when the sergeant fell."

"Were you alone on this? Just you three with no backup?"

"We were more than three. Another was taken, either dead or alive, I don't know." He swallowed. "There are certain formalities, you see. Things that are normally forbidden here in Godcountry. Fliers and such."

I understood. We were in a holy place, defiling it by our very presence. Though I hoped the Quele would not remember that fact just now.

"So, you've got to hike down to the temple complex?"

The Quele bit his lip again. "Obviously I can't leave the sergeant."

"The sergeant," I told him, "is going to leave us if he doesn't stop bleeding."

"I—yes, that is so."

"We can't save him," I said slowly. "But we can save the others. If we act now."

"But there are only four of us," the Quele protested. "What can we do?"

I was thinking the same thing. The enemy had nothing more sophisticated than a crossbow, while we had—I counted four lasers, a stunner, a nerve gun, and my Quellian pistol among us. Too bad there were not enough people to use everything.

I told Wolfbane what was in the offing and he agreed with me. He had moved over to sit by the sergeant, reaching from time to time to check the man's pulse.

"Eduardo," he said after some thought, "ask the apprentice whether these people are camped on the edge of the forest." They were.

At this, Wolfbane nodded to himself. "The trees are dead," he murmured. "Now I wonder how well they might burn."

I wondered too, and decided they would. Well enough to incinerate us all, most likely, but at least the temple guard would have to fly out, ban or no ban, and check. And if the forest fire was big enough, they would have to do something about it.

I put the idea to the Quele, but he did not look too happy.

"It might work," Steed said. "And if the village itself is threatened."

Or even if they think it is, that would make quite a diversion." I agreed. "But we must have a plan," I said.

"The plan should be easy enough," Wolfbane said when I had translated our conversation for him. "One of us must set the fire from the cliff face and the others will station themselves about the Risshe camp."

"And then the one who sets the fire," Steed added, "will circle around to help the rest."

"We need a rendezvous," I told him. "Could we get back here without going through the fire zone?" We put that to the Quele.

"Yes," he said reluctantly. "We were fleeing before, hiding among the trees. But we did not use that route when we normally went to spy on the Risshe. There is a short cut over the hill."

"You'll show us," Steed said. He looked up at the sky, calculating. "It's midafternoon. We'll need to wait for dark, I suppose."

"Just a minute," I said to him in Basic. "We've got to straighten out a few things." I glanced at the Quele before I went on. "First, what about Hermradon? Do the temple guard have him in custody or not?"

Steed shrugged. "The apprentice wouldn't know that, would he? Anyway, didn't the pilot say—?"

"No," I answered, "he didn't, really."

Steed thought about this. "I don't know if we should ask him, Sabat," he said at last.

"It should be alright," Wolfbane argued. "A search party—that's all we really are. An illegal search party, but at least that is something the Quele would understand."

I considered. Wolfbane was probably right. To admit that we were looking for Hermradon would at least absolve us of anything worse. But on the other hand, our lives were already forfeit from the moment we crossed the frontier into Godcountry. The only legal difference might be in how they executed us if we were caught.

I decided to risk it.

The Quele's eyes narrowed at my "confession" and I watched him readjust his ideas about us. But, as I had hoped, his final expression seemed to be relief.

"You have wasted your efforts," he said succinctly. "The Risshe do not have your employer." I waited.

"If you thought to rescue him," the Quele went on, "you should know that he has been a prisoner of the temple for some days past."

I went ahead and told him about meeting the pilot, but he knew nothing of that. "Still, as for this so-called prince, he is lost to you. You would have to take him from the temple guard itself."

I tried to maintain an expressionless face as he spoke, but something must have showed. After all, our original plan had been to do that very thing.

There was an uncomfortable silence, broken by Steed.

"For the information you have given us, you have our thanks," he said. "And for your present help, understood of course that you act out of necessity."

"Basic decency," I added. "Not even criminals should be left in the hands of creatures like these."

The Quele got up. "Our truce still holds," he allowed. "There is no need to say more." He glanced at Wolfbane and me. "Who is to start the fire?" he asked.

"I will," Steed said. "I move the fastest."

"Then I had better show you the way over the hill. We may need your help later."

The two set off, leaving me alone with Wolfbane and the sergeant.

"How is he?" I asked when they had gone.

"Not much longer, Eduardo."

The heat of the day had passed and in the afternoon light, the Quele's face was pinched and bluish, his breathing no longer visible.

"What do you think we should do," I asked Wolfbane, "when we have, ah, finished in the camp?"

"You mean about the apprentice? I've been thinking about that. We can't just stun him and leave him."

I shook my head. "Heth Andrew, we are in a pretty tight spot. If Otto is lost—Remember he is the one who made arrangements to get us back offworld."

"I know those arrangements too, Eduardo. He didn't set this up alone."

I let out a sigh. "I had hoped you would. But I was going to say that, after the mess we left behind in Spire, do you think it would be safe to go back there?"

"We won't be going back to Spire," he said. "There are other villages on the perimeter."

So that was alright. I wouldn't have to look up any more of my old friends at the capital and get them killed.

I leaned against a rock and tried to rest while, across from me, Wolfbane took out a rosary and continued his death watch. A gentle breeze cooled us, bringing a faint effluvium from the rotting trees and a hint of something else. I recognized the spicy scent of the flowers by the river, something I remembered from years before.

With a small rattle, the beads fell into Wolfbane's lap. The sergeant moved slightly, making a strange whistling sound somewhere in his throat, and then it was over. Wolfbane closed the man's eyes with the finality of a task completed and resumed his prayers. Neither of us said anything.

I remember the suns had gone orange and violet as they crowded the hilltop, while the unmusical birds of Godcountry signaled the end of the day.

A few stars were showing when the others returned and, now that there was nothing more to wait for, we prepared ourselves to tackle the Risshe.

CHAPTER TWELVE

I found it very difficult, when we came to it, to leave the sergeant behind. It was not that he wouldn't wait for us, I tried to tell myself. But we all, we humans, seemed to have this feeling that the dead should not lie alone. At least, not at first.

Steed set off the way we had come, back around the escarpment to the forest, but the rest of us took the hill path, climbing awkwardly in the dusk while alien stars began to prick the sky above us. From the river, night singers filled the air with their haunting cry, "Chee-ap! Ho-twit-aaah!"

This too, I remembered from before. God. How it all came back to me now, far more strongly even than it had when we made the crossing! And though I hated this place with all my being, yet I knew I was a part of it and it was a part of me, even as the slave band I wore and might never lay aside.

Steed signaled me when he reached his position, though we had no way to actually speak to one another. The rest of us were still among the rocks, circling wide to come upon the camp from behind.

The Risshe had entrenched themselves in a sort of notch on the far side of the valley, with rock on three sides and the forest on the fourth. No doubt they intended to farm the entire valley floor. Who knows—it might even have been their eventual plan to burn down the trees themselves.

At last we reached our position, a shelf from which we could look down on the brush covered roofs of the settlement. Even here in what was obviously a temporary camp, there was a stark regularity to the placement of these shelters. Also I saw very few campfires.

We were too far away and the light was too poor to see any people, but I could imagine them, moving about down there in the starlight, silent, efficient and ruthless.

"There is a way down," the apprentice said. It was the first time he had spoken since we left our own camp. His voice came out low and hoarse.

I turned to him. "Shall I signal Steed that we are ready?"

He hesitated. "We never came here in the dark before."

I waited for him to say something more but he did not. I wondered if he felt it too—the utter wrongness of what lay below. On my other side, Wolfbane was a dark shadow, his face in profile, limned with starlight. I touched his arm and he did not turn.

"They are vile, Eduardo," he murmured. "We ought to burn them as well."

I started at this barbarity. "We've got to get Otto," I said sharply. "And the others."

"Eduardo," he persisted, turning until I could no longer distinguish his features, "even this Quele knows. Look at him. He is as frightened as that poor native we had for a guide. He knows these are devils."

I forced myself to remember Wolfbane's origins. His was a harsh world, a place where violent death was an everyday occurrence. Bor Klath had mentioned the wolfhunt and I had heard tales of how the Lost Rythans climbed great mountain peaks and even flew about in primitive aircraft, their technology being centuries behind that of Sachsen, and all for the sheer joy of risking their necks. That they were also given to bloodfeuds, despite all the Star Brothers could do, and that some were even killed in duels. And they were superstitious—

So now I wondered if Wolfbane's civilized veneer—for it was no more than that for all his intelligence and education—might have been stripped away entirely. Was he reverting to some primal type that set him on a level with the tribesmen of Godcountry?

"Heth Andrew," I said, choosing my words carefully, "I feel it too that something is very wrong here. I felt it in the ruins. But we cannot let that interfere with what we have come to do."

The Lost Rythan did not move. "I don't know," he said slowly, "whether there is any hope for our companions. But I do know that what has been done here, what these people have chosen for themselves—this cries out to God!"

"Then let God settle it," I told him curtly. "There are only three of us and even if we were an army, we're not going to massacre the Risshe!"

Once more I dared touch his arm. "Heth Andrew, we cannot set things right. We can only try to save our friends."

He shrugged. "Of course, Eduardo. That is our first duty."

I turned to the apprentice. The Quele had not understood our argument but it was plain he would have agreed with Wolfbane. A new hardness had come into his face that went beyond fear. His voice was steady when he spoke.

"The central huts," he said. "Tell the Lost Rythan. It was there we saw the aliens."

I passed this on.

"There is a lower ledge where we watched before. It will be harder to reach in the dark, but our way is very well hidden from those below. But after that part, there will be no cover the rest of the way down."

"It's dark," I told him. "We'll just have to risk it."

Slipping one leg over the edge, the Quele felt about for a foothold. "This isn't far," he said. "Then we climb down a crack in the rock face."

I followed him, relieved when I came into a place where the stars were cut off and our footing was more or less firm. Heth Andrew followed, remarkably agile despite his size. I did not speak to him.

After a longish descent, we emerged onto the lower ledge, much nearer the ground. From here we could hear movement but no voices—not, I think, that we couldn't have, but because no one spoke.

A group of the Risshe, dim forms in the murk, were gathered on the far edge of the village, apparently staring in the direction of the forest. For the first time I smelled smoke.

"Get ready," I told the apprentice, "but don't go yet. We want to give Steed as much time as we can."

More of the Risshe came out and stood, hands at sides, facing the northwest. Their silence began to get on my nerves.

Would they even react as we hoped when they realized that the entire forest was burning? Our plan depended on a certain amount of confusion, but these cold-blooded automata looked as though they didn't know the meaning of the word.

The smoke was rising out beyond the trees and we could hear a dull roaring far off but coming our way. At last the Risshe began to move. First one or two and then a whole troop set off to investigate.

"Heth Andrew," I murmured, "you may get your wish after all. Look how close those trees are to the village. This place is going to be an oven!"

"They'll climb."

I smiled grimly. "So will we." I started down, glancing over my shoulder from time to time. Was the sky beginning to glow behind me, or did I imagine that? Certainly smoke was rasping in my throat, causing my eyes to water so that I had to pause and wipe them.

I slid the last few feet, wincing as I skinned an elbow on the rock. I had landed in a mat of creeping thorns and that was not so pleasant either. As silently as I could, I pulled myself free, trying to spot more of the stuff before I stepped in it.

The light was tricky, though a moon or two had risen. To my left, Wolfbane came on as silently as I, while the smoke-laden breeze stirred his long hair. More than ever, he began to resemble some great, hulking relic from the dawn of time. I tried to remember him quietly reading at my bedside, or pursuing some necessary bit of information via my computer, and found that I no longer could.

Above us, the apprentice took one last survey of the camp before he too slid downward. Just in time, I gestured him away from the thorn patch. We gathered at the base of a rock fall. Directly before us lay the backs of a row of timber-framed huts.

"Let's go," I whispered to Wolfbane.

We left our cover. I ducked around the nearest hut, emerging cautiously to peer out into the street. I saw the apprentice advancing, but Wolfbane had already disappeared into the night.

The Quele gave me an all clear sign, so I came out into the open. No cookfires burned here but somewhere, not so far off, bread was baking. A child cried and was quickly silenced. The sound was an odd one, a sort of high-pitched mewling that made me wonder if there were illness here. Then I set this worry aside and passed into another lane, arrow straight and also empty.

The apprentice pointed. Ahead lay a larger structure, surrounded by a crude veranda where people moved about, tending small fires. It appeared to be a communal kitchen.

Even as I watched, the cooks abandoned their posts one by one, moving toward the forest side of the village. To my surprise, they were all male.

I leaped up onto the veranda and had a look inside, but the place was empty. We went on around the building and into a sort of square made up of neat rows of huts on three sides, the cookhouse on the fourth.

"Is this the center?" I whispered. The apprentice nodded.

But before I could make a move toward any of those dark doorways, a sudden increase in the light showed me that we weren't alone. Three men stood almost directly across the square, apparently guarding one of the houses.

I studied them carefully. This was my first clear view of the Risshe and I tried to make out what it was about them that struck such revulsion into those who came in contact with the group. Apparently the deformity was not a visible one. They seemed to be short, sturdy men in coarse tunics, their shaven heads gleaming in the faint glow of the forest fire, their eyes invisible.

Without a word, the apprentice attacked and I found myself in a fight even before I finished my observations. One of the Risshe went down at once, caught full in the chest by the Quele's nerve gun. I shot another one myself. The third swung some sort of club which I barely avoided before the apprentice disabled him too.

I did not wait for more. Hurdling the body, I shoved against the door of the hut the Risshe had been guarding. I fiddled for a moment with a crude latch and then kicked it open.

All was dark within. "Otto?" I called softly. "Maureen?"

Something rustled. I braced myself just in time as someone ran against me. I was knocked out the door by the impact, stumbled to one knee and raised my gun.

Behind me, the Quele fired first. Afterwards, he flashed a torch and I saw that he'd shot a Hithian. I turned the man over, but he did not open his eyes. I could not tell if the blankness in his face was the effect of the nerve gun or something else.

"Shine that inside," I told the apprentice and he did so. A huddled mound lay against a side wall, a man apparently sleeping or else dead.

I approached warily, gun in hand, and reached over to grasp one shoulder. To my relief, I felt a slight tremor and knew by this that at least I wasn't dealing with a corpse.

With a heave, I rolled him over. The Quele's light showed us a pale face, drawn with weariness. Lank brown hair lay plastered across a broad, high forehead. It was Otto.

I shook him until his eyes came open, but he did not know me. "Otto!" I shouted in his face. "You've got to get up!"

Even inside the hut, I could feel the heat of the approaching forest fire. Sweat pricked and itched beneath my arms as I hauled at Otto's limp form.

"Too late," the apprentice said and I knew he was going to bolt if I didn't do something.

Steeling myself, I drew back and let Otto have a good old-fashioned box on the ear. It was something I had often experienced in my youth at the slave school on Earth.

This time, I thought I saw a glimmer of recognition come into Otto's dull eyes. "Was gibt's?" he mumbled.

"Get up," I said again.

At this, he tried to help himself, but for all his efforts, he could not stay on his feet. He crawled out of the hut and stopped in the doorway, blinking at the light.

"Herr Sabat?" His voice was thick, as though he must shape words with effort.

"Yes, yes," I said quickly. "I'm here, Otto. Now where is Lady Pelanot?"

He shook his head. "Dreaming, Herr Sabat. Lieber Gott! Those dreams—"

"It's over now," I told him.

He looked up at me then and for that one last moment, he was himself. "Go," he told me. "You cannot help us!"

Then his features blurred once more with the effects of whatever the Risshe had done to him. "There is no escape," he murmured, "from those dreams."

A great rage came on me at this as though I were possessed by the god I had once foolishly thought I was. I shoved the Quellian pistol in Otto's face.

"You'll wake up," I said. "Or I drive you into the fire!"

Beyond us, on the forest side of the village, a wall of flames surged and roared, while showers of sparks fell from the glowing sky. Indeed we had miscalculated, for the fire fairly leaped from the last straggling thickets running through the brush right up to the village. A few huts were already burning and things did not look promising for the remainder.

From a side street, three Risshe came running up, swinging some sort of truncheons. The weapons were not very impressive, but the assurance with which they carried them suggested that these were emblems of an authority not hitherto questioned.

One of the three pointed at Otto and gave a sharp command.

With a groan, he rose slowly, first to his knees and then to his feet. I saw that he as going to attack me, a look of anguish on his face quickly replaced with a sort of blankness that was worse.

At this, my rage became a new and icy thing, no longer the hot fury it had been. I reversed the pistol, striking Otto even as he lunged for me with clawed fingers. He collapsed at once.

"You'll pay for that blow!" I shouted at the Risshe. But of course they didn't understand my words, only the look of murder in my face.

The apprentice got off one shot before his gun was struck from his hands. I ran to his aid, taking a glancing blow from one of the truncheons. I dared not fire lest I hit the Quele, but I struck out with my gun again, breaking the nose of one of the Risshe. To my disgust, the man did not even cry out. He only fell back, struggling to retrieve his club while the blood gushed over his face and dripped down his chin.

I kicked the truncheon away, ducked a blow from his companion, and rolled aside as the apprentice made a lunge at his own attacker. I saw him seize the man and batter his head against the doorframe of a burning house.

With the butt of my pistol, I put the other two out of commission and called off the Quele, who still kept smashing the head of his enemy against the wood long after he was dead.

"Help me with Otto," I said. "We've got to get back to the cliff wall!"

Wordlessly the apprentice pointed. I turned and swore. Behind us the square was filling with women and children, driven out of the huts at last, coughing in the smoke as they came on. Even if I could have broken free of my conditioning enough to fire on them, it would have done no good. There were too many, and I could see in their eyes that they were going to kill us.

"Run!" I told the apprentice as, hoisting Otto onto my shoulders, I headed for a break in the houses. To my surprise, I almost made it.

Somebody latched onto my leg and I stumbled, Otto's dead weight sliding to the ground as I turned and cuffed aside one of the children. I felt a wrench even as I did so, at least until I got a closer look. It was female, and for the first time I saw that the women and girls, if they could be called that, were far different from the males, far more alien.

My leg hurt and there was blood on the sharp teeth of the child. It was licking hungrily as it rose from where it had fallen, snuffling through a flat, slit-nostriled nose. Its overlarge eyes gleamed in the firelight, flat and almost faceted.

They surrounded me, those children, hissing and snarling. I could not kill them, even now. I would like to think this was more than my conditioning and that there was a core of pity in me that lay below the hated compulsions of slavery. But probably that would be a lie.

The apprentice, unencumbered by any such prohibition, fired and fired again while I straddled Otto's body, which I had been obliged to ease to the ground. I knew the moment I went down, we'd both be torn to pieces.

A squad of the men came in behind the women, herding them away from the flames. They saw me at once and began to shove their way through the crowd, truncheons ready. If anyone had a bow, I did not see it, but, remembering the sergeant, I felt myself stiffen, fearing I would be skewered any moment.

With a scream, the apprentice broke free of a group of slavering children and lurched to my side. He was bleeding in a dozen places and so was I.

"Look!" he cried.

I turned to where he pointed just in time to see Heth Andrew wade into the Risshe.

The Lost Rythan had lost his gun, or used up the charge, and now he wielded one of the truncheons, laying about him heartily. I could hear heads cracking even above the roar of the fire.

Unfortunately, one of those heads was mine. I did not hear the sound as somebody's stick came down just above my right ear, but after that, things got surreal. Heth Andrew fought and the apprentice fought, and after a while, Steed showed up. It was very hot, I remember, and I shot some of the men.

"Come on Sabat! We're gonna roast!" I felt hands dragging me to my feet. By some miracle, Steed had gotten Otto up and moving, and now he began helping me out of the square. Our attackers were mostly gone or down or else they had other things to worry about. A lot of huts were burning now and I could hardly see for the smoke.

Slowly my head cleared. We were nearing the cliffside and only a few as yet unburned huts lay between us and our way out. But I wasn't looking for a way out. I turned back to the burning village, searching for Maureen. Instead, I saw Lady Pelanot, dagger in hand, backlighted by the fire so that she looked like a she-demon from hell.

Her face was perfectly blank.

"Look out Steed!" I cried, but I was too late.

I saw the blade plunge home as Steed turned, bringing one arm up to strike her down. And then there were only Otto and me and the fire. Otto swayed for a moment, passing one hand over his eyes before he, too, collapsed.

I knelt beside Lady Pelanot. No wonder the Quele preferred death to falling into the hands of these monsters! The horror of friends turning on one another was bad enough, but now I had both Otto and Lady Pelanot to somehow get up the trail—and at any moment, one of them might turn on me! As for Steed, he never moved. I could see the strangely carved hilt protruding from his back.

It often works out that when things seem about as bad as they can get, something worse happens, and this time was no exception. Three of the Risshe bore down on me, accompanied by one of Maureen's

Hithians. I snatched up a club and swung wildly, but I knew there was no escape.

Even now, with their faces blackened by the fire that had destroyed the village, their women and children scattered or killed, the Risshe showed no more emotion than their slaves. They just kept coming. The only good thing about it was that this time, I didn't think I'd have to worry about being taken prisoner.

I swung my weapon in a half-hearted way and the Hithian, who was a bit clumsy, fell at once, impeding the rest. They swarmed over him and seized me. I was held fast and disarmed.

Still, no one spoke, the very absence of a common tongue adding to the horror of my plight. I expected to die at once as someone raised a club. But he only threatened me as they dragged me back into the village. I saw in a moment, they were going to throw me into the fire.

So the Risshe did have feelings after all! It didn't make them any more winsome, but it was something, at least.

We paused before a burning hut, the heat of it searing my face as I struggled in the grip of the villagers. And then I spotted a familiar face among them—two faces!

Otto had regained his feet and he had someone else with him, a thin woman, her eyes wide and haunted. Maureen!

I made a lunge toward her and for one moment it seemed that they both knew me, she and Otto. He reached out one hand as though asking for help. And then, as I watched helplessly, one of the Risshe brought a club down with smashing force on the back of his head. He looked at me once—I'd swear he did—with full recognition in his eyes. And then he fell. This time I was sure there would be no rising.

I glimpsed Maureen's shocked face, saw the pitiful thinness of her, the alternations of madness and grief and horror that fled across her features. And then I saw the Risshe raise his club again, all covered with Otto's blood at which point the battle madness of the Lost Rythans came over me.

"Maureen!" I cried, wrenching free of the Risshe, actually shoving one of my captors against the burning wall. With a groaning crack, the roof beam fell in and a great gout of flame shot outward, singeing those nearest. I realized my jacket was aflame and shucked it off, not once taking my eyes from Otto's killer. I never felt my burns as I threw myself on top of him and dragged him to the pyre. I think he was already dead when I thrust him into the flames—I think so anyway.

Maureen had watched all this and now she turned to run. I don't know if she was aware of herself or whether she was still no more than a tool of the Risshe, but I darted after her, shoving aside the Risshe as they milled in confusion beating out sparks in their own hair and clothing. Someone loomed beside me then—Heth Andrew Wolfbane—and together, we broke free of the crowd.

"Maureen," I panted to him. "She went that way!"

"Eduardo, wait."

I ran and he ran after me, down one burning lane and around a corner. I saw a woman's form ahead and plunged after it. There were no more Risshe. There was nothing now but flame and smoke and a madness on me that was not of any god but pure yearning to see once more her own tormented soul looking out of her eyes.

I rounded another corner and leaped over the burning remains of a fallen porch, the veranda of the cookhouse in the central square. At last she turned at bay, for there was nowhere else to go. Behind her roared a wall of flame.

My eyes smarted and my throat was raw as I called her name. I wanted to ask if she had killed Susanna—and I wanted to forgive her. But her eyes were dark and flat. She gasped as she breathed and reached up one hand to shove unruly hair from her face. Her fevered glance flicked over my face and then settled on Heth Andrew who had come up behind me.

"Maureen," I husked. "Come away from the fire."

Her look grew puzzled. A little line formed between her eyes. She took one tentative step toward us. "Eduardo?" she said. "Eduardo?"

"That's right," I told her. "I'm going to take you somewhere else, Maureen. Away from here."

She held up one slender wrist and I saw the firelight reflected on the slave band. "There is nowhere else," she said sadly. "Not for us."

Suddenly a smile transformed her ravaged features and she tried to sweeten her hoarse voice. "Come to me, Eduardo," she said. "If you want to be free, come to me!"

I did not understand her at first. Then, as I groped for her hand, I realized too late what she meant to do.

Seizing my arm, she tried to drag me into the flames. We struggled for one moment on the edge of the inferno and then she was gone. I saw her hair alight, her slim outline haloed in the flames like the salamander of the ancients, as she ran, oblivious to the burning.

Then mercifully, she fell and I saw her no more.

CHAPTER THIRTEEN

A sudden chill wracked me and I found myself suddenly longing for the flames. How crystal clear seemed the smoke burdened air! I knew even before it happened that Heth Andrew was going to slug me and I ducked away effortlessly and tried to follow Maureen.

Here, I said to myself in the cool deliberation of that place beyond madness, is the antithesis of the tomb. Here is my answer to Feullier and Tokot—and to Net Central and to every Quele who ever cursed a heathen!

"But not to me."

I turned without surprise to see the old man beside me. How true it is that when faith dies, its revenant often remains.

"I have no answer for you," I told him. "For you are a liar."

"Not a liar," he said, taking my arm in a grip I could not break. "I lived in the morning, Eduardo. The dawn time of the Earth."

"Liar! Liar!" Somehow we were moving away from the place where Maureen had died.

"And when I looked up at the stars, I did not say, 'these are the suns of Sachsen, these the suns of Quele, these Lost Rythar'."

"Go to hell."

"I saw that all was set in order and I called that order nature. The hand of Zeus."

We had left the huts now and the cliff wall lay before us. There was the thorn patch—and a body or two.

Above us, the Risshe were on the ledge. A rock fell past my head and another struck nearby. We turned back and there was the fire.

"It is still better, that fire," I muttered, "than the tomb. And she is there already in the great heart of it."

"What do you know of death, you poor child? You peel away the layers of servitude, and when you are half done, you cast aside what lies in your hand."

"But we are going to die," I said reasonably. "By fire or Risshe, there is no way out."

"Poor boy. My foolish son."

"I am not your son, Epictetus!"

But the old philosopher was tugging me away along the cliff base until, quite suddenly, a face appeared, flat and brown, amber eyes reflecting the firelight. White teeth showed in a savage smile. "Climb," it said. I thought it must be the god of the underworld.

Still, I set foot on the rock and climbed. Suddenly the fire was gone—and the enemy and the stars. A great quiet descended. In the sudden cessation of heat, I felt for the first time my burns, and they were many. I shivered in the chill.

"Keep going," someone said. "Hurry."

"You saw the fliers?" That was Heth Andrew's voice.

"Yes. The fire brought them just like we thought it would." Was that Steed? But wasn't he dead? I tried to puzzle this out, then remembered his synthetic body. I tried to concentrate on his words.

"And they'll drop a bomb, Godcountry or not," he was saying.

"Keep going!"

We kept going. There was water after a time and we splashed in it as we ran. Ahead, someone's torch led the way. After a time, I recognized Heth Andrew beside me, helping me along.

I remembered many things during that passage. Otto. I had not even had time to mourn for him. Another image came to mind—the savage face I had confronted at the base of the cliff. "Who was that man I saw," I asked, "before we came in here?"

"Qitsork—the pilot. Jenn found him and brought him in another way—this way."

"Another way out of the valley?"

"We may not make it, Eduardo."

"Pray for me, Heth Andrew," I said. "I'm pretty sure there are devils in my head."

"Yes."

We did not make it. When the thunder rolled, it was like the approach of some great, relentless machine, roaring, crushing everything in its path. The ground bucked beneath us.

Things fell and someone—the pilot, I think—screamed just before the light went out. A moment later, it came on again, illuminating veil upon veil of shining dust. I thought a nebula had come to visit.

"Everyone alright?" Steed's voice called. His words made a very flat sound.

"Over here." Heth Andrew had left me and was crouching above a pile of stones somewhere to my left. One of the stones moved.

A whistling, gasping sound came from the mound. I saw Lady Pelanot standing there as well, both hands covering the lower part of her face.

"Oh kill it," she moaned in a voice that was unlike her own. "End its suffering!"

Though he could not have understood her, I saw Jenn lay one hand on the knife at his belt.

"Be still, woman," Heth Andrew told her sternly as he began removing rocks from the pilot. "It is unseemly to urge an innocent man's death as though you were God!"

That remark struck me as odd, I remember, since Wolfbane had been urging a full-scale massacre of the Risshe just a few hours earlier. But I did not say anything.

As he freed the pilot's upper body, I saw that things were hopeless. His legs were crushed beneath a great chunk of rock that we could not shift without dumping a good many more down on him. And there were other injuries as well.

Steed shone the light down onto the pilot's face, but now the eyes were closed. "Let's do what we can," he said.

Wordlessly Heth Andrew slipped something from about his own neck and laid it in one of the pilot's hands—the right, since the left was crushed. I saw the fingers close.

I looked up and the Lost Rythan shrugged. "Scapular. Who knows, Eduardo? It may do him good."

Meanwhile Steed had given the light to me. I tried to hold it steady while he searched his belt pouch for a painkiller. There wasn't anything else to give the pilot.

"You're next, Sabat. You look like the main attraction at a barbecue."

"Steed," I said, trying not to let the light dip and waver as I spoke.

"Behind the pilot. The rock—"

"That's right, Sabat. There's no way back to the valley."

My old fear came back to me redoubled. Feeling the weight of the mountain above us, I swung the light about, flashing it on the tunnel ahead which was also blocked.

Lady Pelanot's eyes widened.

"I wish you hadn't done that," Steed told me. "Not just yet."

I sat down. Whatever had sustained me was ebbing fast. I relinquished the light to Heth Andrew and let Steed minister to me, spraying my burns and shooting me up with whatever he thought appropriate.

"Do a stim," I told him. "We've got some digging to do." If he heard the fear in my voice, he did not say anything. Wordlessly he complied and, after an initial bout of nausea, I started to feel better. As my mind cleared, the dawn of reason was like being kicked out of a warm bed on a winter morning.

A lot had been happening lately. I set in order the cold facts and tried not to flinch. Maureen was dead. She had chosen the flames rather than my arms—and I could not blame her. She was broken beyond repair and knew it. What could I have done for her save to prolong her suffering?

That was the first fact and I swallowed it. And Otto's death. Then, not far from me, Hermradon's pilot, Qitsork, was dying. And up ahead, the rest of the tunnel lay on the floor, blocked up solid. We were buried alive. Otherwise, everything was fine.

I forced myself to go on counting. "The apprentice? Leon whatever his name was?"

"I'm here," the Quele said, hearing his name. He had been with Steed up front when the shock wave hit. He had a bruise on one side of his face.

I added us up. Me, Heth Andrew, Steed. Lady Pelanot, apparently herself again, or so I hoped. Jenn and the apprentice.

I got up. It was not, I told myself, as though I had never been buried alive before. Sure, I suffered from claustrophobia and, if I chose, I might even now succumb to the panic that lay in wait. But that fact didn't matter as much anymore so I let it slip away.

I looked down at the pilot, up at the others waiting for me to lead them and I knew that if I bid my fear be still, it would. It was still my fear, but it no longer had the power to rule me.

And so, with a certain amount of gratitude, I ticked off another fact: I had mastered my claustrophobia.

Anything more?

Oh yes. We still hadn't rescued Hermradon. And we were buried alive and my best friend was dead. And I'd lost Maureen. That about covered it.

"Let's see what we can do," I said. "Up there at the front end of the tunnel."

Lady Pelanot stayed by the pilot while the rest of us began pulling away the blockage, the light propped safely behind us. It threw grotesque shadows as we worked. After a while, Heth Andrew and I together dragged free what must have been the coping stone and we were rewarded by a groaning crack. Another bit of the top fell into our part of the tunnel. Steed was knocked down but no one else was injured.

I heard a cry behind me as the stones fell and turned quickly. Lady Pelanot moved away from the pilot, a scarf in her hand, a look of terror on her face.

"What were you doing?" I asked as something prickly inched its way up my spine. It was the way she held herself, I suppose. Beneath the fear, she had a furtive look.

"He—he was coming to."

And you wanted to make sure he didn't, I almost said, but that was absurd. The poor woman must be beside herself with terror. And those things she had said—probably it was the custom where she came from to hasten along the moribund. It was a custom she would have to give up if she took on Otto's religion.

"Well," Steed said abruptly, "I guess that's that. We don't dare move any more of that stone."

"Let's look at the other end," Heth Andrew suggested. We did so. Things were more stable there but it was going to be a long job and before we could begin, we would have to move the pilot.

"We can't get that stone off his legs without killing him," Steed decided. "Look how the rest are balanced."

"We can wait," I told him. "It won't be long until it doesn't matter anymore."

In the meantime, we settled ourselves for a much-needed rest. Our little stream had ceased to flow, dammed at both ends, but there was still plenty of water. All we would need, anyway. As to food, no one was hungry.

"The light," Steed said to me softly. "I'd better cut it down a bit to save power."

I nodded and he adjusted the power torch until it gave no more illumination than a candle. Afterwards, the dark came in to drape itself about the curves and hollows of our tomb—and it was well. Lady Pelanot drew closer to my side.

This too was fine with me. I wanted to talk to her and I was not without sympathy for her plight. Also, it seemed like a good idea to keep an eye on her.

A dark bruise along the right side of her jaw gave witness to the blow Steed had struck her back in the valley when she stabbed him. Certainly, he was none the worse for the experience. From his seat beside the pilot, he nodded ever so slightly in my direction, his face as usual giving me no clue as to the meaning of that nod.

Ah well. Steed would have his secrets. It was not for me to ask him just how much flesh he retained and how much of something else. No more than I could ask Lady Pelanot how it had felt to be brainwashed by aliens. I wondered, though, if she would tell me.

Instead, to my surprise, she spoke about Otto.

"I am sorry, Sabat," she said without preamble. "About Mr. Zeller."

"Not half as much as I am. I saw him die."

"He was very competent, your friend."

I nodded, watching the pilot's face. I thought I saw one eyelid flutter and I felt a great sadness come over me. It was a distant, mellow sort of grief, as though all these things had happened to someone else, long ago.

On the other side of the cave, Jenn squatted on his heels against the tunnel wall, head down on his knees, bowed within the shelter of his crossed arms. It was the pose of the dead.

"That Wolfbane brought you in?" Lady Pelanot asked.

"Yes." I wondered if I was responsible for Otto's death. If I hadn't run off after Maureen, might we have yet saved him? After all, Lady Pelanot had recovered. There might have been hope for Otto. "You were talking as you came down the tunnel. I heard you."

I looked up at her. At that moment I could almost believe she had seen the shade of the ancient stoic pacing along beside me. Did she believe in ghosts? Probably she did. Probably I should too since we would all fall into that category soon enough.

The pilot opened his eyes.

"Excuse me," I said and got up.

Lady Pelanot rose too and did not leave my side as I came over to crouch beside Steed. I looked into the pilot's face. "Water?" I asked him.

He licked his lips and I dipped him up some from the stream. He choked a little down, grimaced and suddenly stretched his lips into a smile.

"In the net," he whispered. "So beautiful the things I have seen."

I nodded. "You have certainly seen what I have not."

"Stiffs, that's what we call you normals. When we take you along the ways between the stars, you are no more than cargo."

"I'm grateful," I said, "that you do it." I saw that he still clutched the bit of brown wool Heth Andrew had given him.

Suddenly he looked beyond me, his glance tightening. I turned and there was Lady Pelanot.

"He is suffering, Sabat," she said.

"Since when—" I cut off what I was going to say about her capacity for pity and turned back to the pilot. "Should Steed give you something more?"

There came a ghost of a chuckle. "Lady—Death. Your long, long fingers—between the stars—"

"He's delirious!"

"He's mad," I corrected her. "He can't help it."

"You really should do something," she said to me. "He cannot live."

"He will have peace," Heth Andrew said from where he sat against one wall, "when it is God's will."

Lady Pelanot looked away. "As you wish," she said.

I decided to ask about the Risshe after all. I took the plunge, starting with her abduction.

"Yes," she said in answer to my question. "They had a network of tunnels beneath the village. They came on us and—"

"You cut one. I found your knife." "I cut one. He didn't seem to feel it much." "What are they?" I asked.

She shrugged. "Who knows?"

"We have yet to discover a race," Heth Andrew told her, "that does not descend from human stock."

"Then these have made a very long descent," Lady Pelanot said tartly.

"What did they do to you and Otto?" I asked. "Can you remember?"

At this she looked down. "I don't know what they did to him, but for me it was like an argument," she said. "Only it was in another language—in my mind."

I pondered her words but they made no sense. "Tell on," I said.

"That was all. Sometimes I won and sometimes I lost. I never understood the words, but the whole thing made me angry. The presumption of it!"

I hid a grin. Now she was sounding more like herself.

"But you attacked Steed," I said.

She started. "I could hardly help myself," she said quickly. "After all, Mr. Zeller attacked you."

I nodded, not wanting to remember that blow I had given Otto. I had sworn the Risshe would pay, but it was not I who made them, and that thought saddened me.

"In the end," Lady Pelanot said, "when we got to the cliff and they were on the ledge above, I told them to go to hell."

"You won the last argument?"

"I generally do."

"But not everyone wins." I thought of Maureen and glanced at the pilot. The Risshe would have had a hopeless job of it, arguing with him.

She was silent after that, and I thought that the darkness and the low ceiling above us were bothering her. Now I know it was something else, but I didn't know then.

A long time later, the pilot roused again. This time, Lady Pelanot beat me to his side. We watched him together and by the look of things, I was pretty sure we'd be pulling out rocks soon enough. The apprentice came over too.

"Get him some water," Lady Pelanot suggested. "He wants another drink, Sabat."

I don't know what made me hesitate. Was it something in her voice? Some oddness in the line she made silhouetted there against the light? I turned to Qitsork.

"Lady Death—" His voice was a lot weaker. "Webs and shadows all around—he said—"

"Don't let him talk," she whispered. "Look! There is blood on his mouth."

"Lungs," I told her.

"Blood," the faint voice said dreamily. "He knew—what you are."

She leaned over. "Get him a drink, Sabat."

The ranger, who did not speak Basic, was watching her. Suddenly his hand darted out, seized her wrist as a drift of white powder descended onto the pilot's face.

I blinked, trying to understand what I saw—the others frozen in place, three people in a meaningless tableau.

Then things happened. With a scream, the autarch's sister tore herself free. "How dare you touch me!" she cried. Producing one of her seemingly endless supply of knives, she swung wildly at the ranger.

I ignored this figuring he could take care of himself. Shoving my way past the two, I leaned over to blow upon the pilot's face.

He was coughing, great, tearing, blood-bringing coughs, his dark eyes meeting mine in silent agony. I touched one finger to a bit of the dust and brought it cautiously to my nose. Nothing.

Behind me, the struggle ended as Steed upped the light and helped the ranger to disarm his attacker. She spat at him and then, fixing her eyes on me, grinned nastily.

"Qitsork," I said with gentle urgency, "tell me about Lady Death."

The pilot went on coughing, but I thought I saw intelligence in his eyes.

"Who told you? Hermradon?"

The eyes narrowed. His good hand flexed, fingers spread, the cord of Heth Andrew's scapular running among them like life's blood.

"She hired us to rescue him, Qitsork. Tell us what we need to know. Was she playing a double game?" Bloody lips smiled broadly.

"Or," I went on recklessly, as new ideas came to me, "was it to make sure that no one else hired me?" I stared hard into his eyes. "There were so few of us who knew the ways of Godcountry. Maureen and her party—me, Steed, Boris."

He coughed a little more, grimaced, and shaped a word or two. I bent down to listen. "Autarch—tell her—he no good son. Must—die—Hermradon knew—"

His eyes closed. He drew one last breath, shuddered, and stopped. I looked up at Steed. In his grip, Lady Pelanot remained still, her face a mask, aged and frozen. She too might have been one of the dead.

"So," I whispered, "Hermradon knew about you." I thought of this for a moment or two. "But of course he never thought he'd need rescuing."

She shrugged. "We did not want you to come at all, Sabat," she said. "But it was necessary to hire you for appearance' sake. So we decided to make use of the fact that you were mentally unstable, after a certain experience with your slave band. We had already taken on that Kavanaugh woman to make sure no one rescued my nephew and it was easy to act on what she told us about you."

A new conviction took hold of me and I trembled with it. "It was you! Wasn't it? You sent Boris to the studio that night. It wasn't Maureen at all!"

"That's right," she agreed, "slave."

I did not rise to the bait. "So you were going to sabotage things—at the end."

She shrugged.

"Even at the cost of your own life?"

"It was a risk. I serve the autarch."

Something else came to me then and I glanced at Steed. "That so-called argument you had with the Risshe. You won, didn't you? Right from the beginning, you won."

She gave me a deep smile and I wondered that I had not seen before that this woman was at least as mad as Maureen—a veritable psychopath. "That's right, slave. The Risshe may have suspected, but they kept me as one of their creatures anyway."

"And when you attacked Steed, you were really acting on your own."

She smiled again.

"But the Star Brothers," I said, my head spinning as I unraveled skein after skein of deceit. "Your brother got their help!"

"They were stupider than we thought."

At this, Heth Andrew rose and came to her. "No," he said quietly, "they weren't."

For a long moment, they looked at each other, he in his knowing innocence and she in complete surprise. Then she wilted. "But—"

Heth Andrew's mouth thinned in distaste. "Your brother's bargain, which he never expected to keep, was formalized as an interstellar treaty while we were still on Sachsen."

"What!?"

"If he breaks it," Heth Andrew added, "he will face a Net Central court."

I smiled grimly at this. To think of Net Central enforcing the Star Brothers' right to evangelize Hithia Colony!

But Lady Pelanot was shaking her head. "The Star Brothers cannot make a treaty. Not even their Church can do that. The autarch told me so."

"But Lost Rythar can."

I whistled. "Do the Star Brothers have as much influence as all that, Heth Andrew?"

He did not answer. He didn't need to.

"But you don't have him," Lady Pelanot said. "Hermradon. We'll all die here and what you know now is worthless."

"Maybe," I said. "But I'm glad you confided in us." I turned to Steed. "Tie her up," I said. "If we get out alive, I'll see that she's charged with murder."

I turned to her again when Steed had placed her propped against the wall. "What did you use on Qitsork?" I demanded. "What was that stuff?"

She laughed contemptuously. "Rock dust, Sabat. That's all. He was simply trying to sneeze."

I winced, staring at how the light caught on my slave band. Why, I wondered, did I have no desire to kill Lady Pelanot as I had killed Boris? She was a monster, far more than Maureen had ever been. Maybe it was this new thing in me—this freedom that did not depend on my own will. Maybe I was even free to pity her a little after all.

I caught Steed watching me. "Let's get out of here," I said.

We set to work, carefully freeing Qitsork's body now that we couldn't hurt him anymore. The tunnel itself appeared stable and, within a few hours, we had cleared our way into another section pretty much like our own.

"But there's another block," Steed said. "We have a long way to go."

Later, we rested, and then again, later still. No new openings appeared as we cleared our way, meter by agonizing meter. The air began to go bad.

"This is it," Steed said quietly to Heth Andrew and me. "We use a lot of oxygen when we work."

"What choice do we have?" I asked. "Lay down and die?"

I looked around at the others. Lady Pelanot, now reclining in the new cavelet, the ranger hiding his fear as well as he could. Jenn, once more in burial position. He hadn't been much help.

"We could vote," Steed suggested.

I laughed and even Heth Andrew managed a grim smile. "I vote we don't," I said. "Vote, I mean." We went back to work.

The stones grew heavier, or so it seemed to me, and besides, a lot of me hurt. My burns were covered with spray, my cuts likewise. But the stim had long worn off and Steed didn't have any more. It was very hard to breathe.

My body worked like a machine and, like a machine, its movements grew slower and slower in the absence of oxygen. A dark rhythm took hold of us all—bend, lift, turn and release. Sometimes we worked together to get something bigger out.

Part of the time, I remembered where we were, but mostly not. All I knew was that I had to lift stones. It was my task.

"And you may count yourself lucky," the old man told me as we labored together. "For it was said in my time that the dead in Hades had lost their strength. That they knew not their friends again." "You never believed that crap," I told him.

"What did I know?"

"Virtue. You knew virtue, remember?"

"But not much else." He glanced around at our dimly lighted prison. "Ah, my poor son—that we should come to this!"

I wanted to tell him again that I was not his son, that our home on old Earth had been a dream. But I could not do it. After all, if I said that, I might find out that the rest of my life had been a dream too. And if he wasn't my father, then I was a bastard indeed. A fatherless slave.

"Virtue," I said instead, "is everything. It is the only power we have."

"I taught you well."

"Yes," I agreed. "And so we may endure this place because we choose to do so and because—because I forgive you for the things you did not know."

"You are not afraid?"

I thought about that. "I don't know," I said hesitantly. "But I do not think it matters anymore—at least not to me."

"But surely you are sad?"

Again I had to think. "Yes," I said. "I am very sad."

"But did I not teach you that things like fear and grief must be seen and studied as they really are? That when you understood them, they would cease to trouble you?"

"If these things did not trouble me," I said, smiling a little, "I would not be a man."

"But it demeans you to suffer base feelings!"

I laughed out loud, dragging at the stone of my tomb. "Poor old man! Poor old Stoic who thinks he's a god and tries to act like a machine!"

He reddened at this, but true to his own philosophy, he did not rebuke me. "Sometimes," he said mildly, "when I behold the folly of my race, I wonder if of all the emotions, sadness might not be permitted to rule us after all."

I took up another stone, cast it aside, and there in the crevice where it had been, lay a bulb. Who knows what might have grown from it? Not I, for I pulled it apart as I spoke.

"Fear," I said and cast aside the skin. "Anger. Grief." Two more layers fell to the rock floor of Hades. "Sadness."

"The universe must be grounded in sadness," Epictetus insisted. "But it is a less noble thing, even than grief."

"Look." I held up the core and it was joy. Glory shown like flame in my hands and I held it aloft. "Explain that away if you can, you old fathead!"

But he would not be defeated. I had at last rubbed him on the quick and his normally serene face showed it.

"Why you young fool! If I weren't dead, I'd show you a thing or two!"

"Ha! What do you know?" I gathered up my peelings and began to reassemble the bulb.

"Now look again," I said, pulling off the top layer once more. "This is Lady Death! She tried to kill her own nephew. I thought she was beautiful." I cast away the layer and somewhere, I heard a soft curse.

"Slave!" she muttered. "You are nothing but a slave!"

I chuckled. "And this," I told Epictetus, pulling off the next layer, "is my wife. She thought she hated me, but she painted the sunshine and I will not forget her."

"Nonsense! Self-indulgent nonsense."

"Not at all! It was she I indulged, not myself." I pulled off the next layer.

"Maureen," I told him more gently. "The love of my heart."

"Now I know you are an utter fool!"

"Yes," I agreed. "But look!"

I held up the diminished bulb and once again that bright glow shone through my fingers, turning the rocks I had lifted aside to so many gems—diamonds, emeralds, rubies.

"Pretty, aren't they?" I said and they were.

At this, he left in disgust. I sat down then, for I was pretty tired.

Beside me, Heth Andrew leaned against the stone, head bowed. I think he was praying.

Steed must have worked the longest, because he was the one who shook me when the noise started. It sounded like an animal trying to get in.

I did not want to wake up. My head was splitting and only the whisper of air blowing from a little, dark tube directly into my face kept me from falling back into the tangle of my dreams. How easy it would have been, I thought muzzily, to remain in that place of uncaring, the Hades of the ancients.

But after a time, my head cleared. I drank air as a thirsty man drinks water. Then Steed shoved the tube into my hand and began to work on Heth Andrew. There was another tube for him. They were growing from the rock pile in the tunnel.

I sat up. My head still ached. So did Heth Andrew's. I could tell.

"Lady Pelanot," Steed said loudly. "Lady Pelanot!"

I did not care about Lady Pelanot. I wished he would be quiet.

Outside, the animal scratched and dug. I had a feeling I wasn't going to like it when it finally got in.

"How is she?" Heth Andrew called to Steed and the latter shook his head.

"And the others?"

"The apprentice is reviving. But that other one—"

"Jenn," I said distinctly, leaving my tube to crawl over to where the guide still maintained his dead man's crouch. "His name was Jenn."

I touched his arm and then left him as he was. In all my years as a tomb robber, I had never altered the posture of a dead man.

Our rocks had begun to tremble as the noise increased. We all moved back from the tunnel mouth. Mechanical arms snaked inward, clearing away the last of the rubble. Someone turned on the lights and a couple of rangers came in.

I cannot honestly say I wasn't glad to see them—after all they had saved my life—but I cannot say I was glad either. My truce with the apprentice had probably expired.

So the rangers came in, weapons ready, which was hardly necessary. None of us except Steed could even stand up.

"Eduardo Sabat," one of them said and I gave him my attention.

"Escaped slave—"

Something ominous in that.

"I arrest you on behalf of Tokot Limited."

CHAPTER FOURTEEN

The hospital room was exactly what I had expected. The bed was hard and so were the staff; the gods of Quele glared at me from the walls, and a never-ending line of quotations from the Book of Quele passed across a screen in front of me. There were bars on the windows.

"The defiler of the tomb will rot forever, gnawed by the worms of the nether caverns—"

I closed my eyes but it was no better. As I gained strength, so did my memories—and they were very bad.

Otto. Maureen. Susanna. Even Lady Pelanot. I had been used—used by the Hithians, used by the Star Brothers, used and abandoned among those who held me now. Left to await an even worse fate.

Once more I was buried alive, but this time there was no slightest hope that any effort of mine would clear the way to freedom. Wherever I went, the slave bracelet would go with me.

The slave bracelet. I owed my life—all of our lives—to the thing, for by it, we had been tracked and found. Tokot had broken the first of the codes.

This much the Quele told me when I was arrested. I knew also that I was in Quele City and so were the others. So was Hermradon.

I cracked one eyelid. "—and of the unbelievers' hell there is no bottom—"

Heth Andrew, I thought, regretting that I was not physically strong enough to get up and relieve myself on the gods of Quele, will have his wish. He will die for his faith as surely as I will live.

"—no certainty is given even to the Quele, for the gods grow angry and they despise the race of men—"

I closed both eyes. No sense calling for a nurse. The Quele did not use robots, and no human would come except at the scheduled times. There was a monitor to tell them if I died.

I thought of Tokot and in my weakened state, my vision of that vast corporation became confused with the gods of Quele.

"—for Tokot grows angry. They despise the race of slaves—"

No one would have gone to the trouble of tracking me and bargaining with the Quele if they didn't want me very badly. What for? My services? Punishment?

I turned my head aside on the thin pillow. There was only one thing they could want and that was my memories. There were enough memories stored in my head to indict any number of people, if someone were petty enough to dredge it out.

And that had to mean Net Central was involved.

Why, I asked myself, could I not just die? Heth Andrew Wolfbane would die. Almost certainly Steed would die, unless Net Central had found a way to buy him too.

I had days to think of these things, eyes closed, my only comfort being that I did not have to cover my ears as well. An audio rendition of the Book of Quele was a refinement of torture my captors had not yet thought of.

A doctor came in from time to time. Or maybe he was a veterinarian? Certainly he treated me as though I were an animal. We did not speak to one another.

Nurses appeared and did menial things, grey-faced women who flinched as they touched me. I saw one of them staring at the slave band.

Sometimes I stared at it too, the words of the Book of Quele running like disjointed ravings somewhere at the corner of my eye.

"—to kill enemies and curse them, these things abate the anger of the gods—"

I fondled the band, its dry smoothness growing damp at my touch. Almost I could feel it yielding, like flesh. So long had I worn it, year upon year, that it seemed as though the band might be fusing into some new hybrid of flesh and metalplast.

At last the doctor spoke to me. "You can get up," he said coldly and I did so, hanging onto the bedrail as he regarded me with unconcealed distaste.

"You shall dress," he instructed, "in prison clothing and seat yourself in that." He indicated a plain, metal chair. "Your interview is scheduled for fourteen hundred hours."

I clutched the bedframe, feeling the cold from the floor seeping into my bare feet.

"Failure to comply promptly with orders or to answer questions improperly will result in immediate punishment."

"I take it I'm no longer on the sick list."

"Do not speak unless you are ordered to," the doctor snapped. "You are a prisoner of Quele, under sentence of death so long as you remain in this colony. Is that understood?" "I haven't had a trial," I protested.

Wordlessly my—former—doctor turned and pressed a switch on the wall behind him. A pair of uniformed guards entered the room at once. As one of them carried a nerve gun, I subsided.

"As a slave," the doctor continued, not quite curling his lip, "your value is such that your owners are willing to pay indemnity for your conduct. No doubt they will punish you suitably for running away when they have taken you offworld."

I glanced at the nerve gun and held my peace. No doubt they would.

"In the meantime you will be treated according to your current status. Is that understood?" I nodded.

"Escape is out of the question," he went on, "since your whereabouts can be traced at any time. Consequently, it will not be necessary to confine you to the temple cells."

I shrugged. What did I care where they put me? Though maybe I would have seen my friends in the holding cells.

He got up to go, turned, and fixed me with one last, dark look. "Remember," he said, "that I have terminated your invalid status. Full compliance will be expected from now on, for as long as you are in our custody."

The guards followed him from the room, but I was sure they hadn't gone far. I thought of them outside the door, probably watching my every move on the monitor.

"—no act of ours remains without its judgment. The gods will strike and strike again—"

Deliberately I walked over to the god-infested wall and spat, but nothing happened. Maybe the monitor didn't pick that up after all. My pitiful defiance gave me strength to dress, after which I sat, or rather slumped, onto the chair. I was still pretty tired and already I had a headache.

Perhaps I dozed a bit. When the door opened again, it took a moment before my eyes focused on the face of my visitor. It was plain from the look he gave me that I was expected to come to my feet and when I did not, his official scowl became more personal.

"Rise, slave," he said curtly and, since he too held a nerve gun, I did so.

For long moments, he looked me over. It was strange how my skin crawled with revulsion at this scrutiny, for I had often before dealt successfully with the officialdom of Quele.

But then I had been a slave.

Slowly I raised my eyes to the wall of gods and really looked at them, seeing them for the first time as they really were, pitiful constructs of a sick culture confined to a planet so poor they would sell away the right to kill their enemies. Beside the door, the hate-filled words of Quele's founder continued their dreary and unending passage from one side of the screen to the other.

"I'm not," I said in sudden wonder, "a slave." The nerve gun rose. "What did you say?" I looked at him and shrugged.

"Your name is Eduardo Sabat," he told me. "Contract slave of

Tokot Limited." Still I said nothing.

"But until your masters take possession," he said, aiming the nerve gun, "you are subject to the laws of Quele."

I shuddered and nearly fell as the beam caught me, shocking my muscles into a series of painful spasms.

I righted myself, kept my balance. "Tokot won't like it if I'm damaged," I gasped out and knew by the way he held back that I was right.

"Sit down," he ordered, pulling up the other chair for himself.

I was only too glad to comply.

He holstered the gun and reached inside his jacket for a sheaf of papers. "I am Under-Director Bator," he said, "acting for Quele in your extradition." He looked up at me then. "And that of your companions," he added.

I gaped at him.

"As condemned criminals, both Amid Steed and Heth Andrew Wolfbane are ours to dispose of as we see fit. We have seen fit to sell them."

At last I found words. "To—to Tokot? But why?"

"It is not my job to speculate about the motives of aliens. Probably they have information and skills Tokot can use."

I digested this and did not like the taste. Steed, I could understand. As a free contractor who had often worked for Feullier, he was at least as valuable a source of information as I was.

But why Heth Andrew?

And then I remembered that Wolfbane was a Faring Guard. Of course Tokot—or Net Central, as the case might be—would want him. They'd use the probe to drain him dry and in so doing, how many secrets of Lost Rythar and the Star Brothers might not lie revealed? He'd be better off dead!

I tried not to let these thoughts show as I shifted about to ease the lingering ache left over from the nerve gun. If I had had the strength, I would gladly have killed Under-Director Bator. But it would not have done any good.

"Oh yes," Bator said then. "Before I fill out these release forms, you must make submission to the gods."

I remained where I was, Bator fingering the nerve gun while I braced myself for what was probably going to happen. For I would no more submit to the gods of Quele than I would cooperate with Tokot. I knew that now—and the knowledge thrilled me with the nearest thing to happiness I was ever likely to know.

Then I saw him relax. Though he plainly wanted to shoot me, he dared not. Which could only mean that Tokot's representative was enroute.

"You," Bator said grimly, "deny that you are corporate property. Yet here is your contract and by all I've heard of Tokot, your defiance will be short-lived."

I glanced at the slave band. Had I imagined a twinge there? Probably.

"It isn't defiance," I said, no longer angry at him. "It is something else. Something I found in the caves of Godcountry. I think it is called hope."

He looked at me curiously. "You must be brain-damaged after all," he said. "But they will break you at Tokot."

I shrugged. "I've been broken before," I said. "That doesn't change what I am."

"Death will change you. The hell of the defilers—"

It was a funny feeling, sitting there opposite the Quele and knowing he would have tortured me to death if he had dared. Knowing that my slave band was nothing to the one that dictated his every move. Epictetus, I thought, you would be proud of me now.

If a tyrant threatens—

And then the door opened again and the representative of my new master came in. He was a man of medium height, dark-haired, oriental, brisk and dignified. He reminded me a little of Father Liu.

"Hideo Tokot," he said and actually bowed to the Quele. "I have taken the other two into custody and now I have come for this one."

I stood up, gripping the slave band as I faced Tokot. When a tyrant—

But he did not look like a tyrant. He looked like a cold-blooded businessman taking possession of his company's newest purchase. He bore me no malice—as the Quele most certainly did. But I knew I was no more to him than one of the components of a new shuttlecraft. A thing.

"If you are ready, ah, Sabat?"

I looked down at my feet which were manifestly bare.

The Quele, too, rose, rang for a guard and ordered that my boots be returned to me. After that, there was nothing to do but follow Tokot into the corridor where we were joined by his secretary and another man who might have been a bodyguard.

After a few more formalities—in which the gods had no part— we came out onto the roof. A large flier awaited us, already half full.

"Heth Andrew," I murmured as I seated myself. "Steed." Now at last, we were equals, we three—and the sudden love I felt for my comrades nearly overwhelmed me. I had never felt this way before about anyone.

The Lost Rythan leaned back, revealing another man who sat dwarfed in the far corner of the back seat. A Hithian.

"How do you do, Eduardo? May I present Prince Hermradon Pelanot?"

I almost didn't get in the flier. Tokot, impassive as ever, waited for a moment and then gestured politely for me to precede him. Glancing at the bodyguard, I did so.

From my seat beside the secretary—who was apparently to be our pilot—I twisted about to stare at Hermradon. For this man, Otto had died. And all the others. And everything else.

"Where are we going?" I asked Heth Andrew in a low voice, still staring into Hermradon's wild, dark face. He did indeed resemble Lady Pelanot. I wondered if I should hate him.

"Shuttleport. The Quele want us offworld as soon as possible."

I sighed and turned away. "That suits me," I said. As we spoke, I was aware of the Tokot functionaries, four in all, ignoring us. Either they did not think it worth their while to silence us or else they had decided our chastisement could wait until we were all aboard the company shuttle.

But the shuttle, when we boarded, was a plain one of the usual sort Ponia Complex employed. And when we arrive at the port, stepping high in the moon's lower gravity, there was no Tokot starship waiting to receive us. We were disgorged directly into the station complex.

We stood together in one of the processing chambers while Tokot's secretary presented our papers. It was refreshing to see no Quele, no gods.

"Mr. Sabat?"

It was Hermradon.

I looked at him silently.

"Whatever happens to us, I want to thank you. In a way, you saved my life."

"Circumstances saved your life," I told him, a mirthless smile twitching at the corners of my mouth. "A long string of them."

"They were going to bury me alive."

"They sometimes do that."

Tokot came back to us. "Mr. Sabat," he said, "you will accompany me—at once, please."

This was it, then. Formal relations with my new masters were about to begin.

I glanced at Heth Andrew and he nodded ever so slightly. I knew already what that nod meant. Pray for me, Heth Andrew, I thought, and knew that he would do so.

We passed along a slidewalk, up a lift and onto the level of suites. We were alone with no guard, not even the secretary. I could have attacked him then, but what would have been the use? I glanced down at the slave band and saw Tokot staring at it too. I could not read his expression.

"In here," he said. He fingered a lock and stood aside.

The small, functional sitting room contained only one person, tallish, dark-clad and completely immersed in setting out cups on a table. "Good to see you, Mr. Sabat," he said, looking up.

It was Father Liu.

I clutched the doorframe. There was nothing else to hold onto except Tokot, though he did come up on my other side. Maybe he thought I might need him.

"Please come in," the Star Brother told me. "I wanted to see you alone before the others are brought up. Though they are being told now."

I staggered inside. "Told what?" I croaked.

"You would like something stronger than tea." Father Liu produced the required beverage. After a moment, I felt better.

"Alright," I said. "Talk."

"Allow me to introduce my brother," the priest said with a small smile. "Anthony Liu."

The erstwhile Hideo Tokot gave me another little bow. "My pleasure, Mr. Sabat."

I shook my head. "I don't understand," I said, knowing full well that the words were inadequate.

"Of course." Father Liu seemed to be thinking over what he would say. "You have done and seen too much these past weeks," he said finally, "and now, perhaps I have been inconsiderate."

"Otto Zeller is dead."

"Yes. I suppose that is why I wanted to see you first. Because Mr. Zeller is dead." He took a seat, fiddled with his own cup, reached for the butter and then pushed everything aside. "He was a very close friend of mine, Mr. Sabat. I have already been in touch with his family."

I did not say anything.

"You think you've been used. That is not so." The explanation that followed was a bit complex. Otto's arrangements for our departure, he told me, had been thorough and, if he had lived, we would have eventually used them. But Otto had not lived—and the Star Brothers knew that.

"How?" I asked and then, "Oh, I see. You were monitoring Otto through his implants."

"Yes. And Andrew Wolfbane as well."

"But not me?"

He shook his head. "Not at that range—or through rock. There has been no new breakthrough on the codes."

"No new breakthrough?" I nearly shouted. "But then you—you tricked the Quele!"

"We did."

I stared at him. "You used me as an excuse to open negotiations—"

"It was providential. There you were—or at least we hoped you were—alive, and in the company of Andrew Wolfbane whom we could monitor."

"You've got a Machiavellian mind." I don't think I meant that as a compliment, no matter how he took it.

He finally laid a slice of butter in his tea and stirred. "I always did well in school," he said.

I wanted to hit him. He had saved my life and my freedom, and all I wanted was to knock him off that chair.

Instead I hid my face in my hands. We were both silent for some time after that.

"You've got what you wanted," I said at last. "Hermradon—and Hithia."

"Because of you, Mr. Sabat."

"But it must have cost you a lot of money."

"We could afford the credits. But Quele would never have negotiated with the Star Brothers. Surely you realize that."

"Of course." I thought of the Quele and what I had said to the under director—that I was free. And I had even spit on the gods. It was a small, mean thing to do and not at all like Heth Andrew heartily smashing idols right and left. Maybe that was because freedom was more than just not being a slave. Maybe I still had further to go.

I looked inside myself. The old philosopher was still there. I guess he had no place to go, but it was okay. No man could abandon his own father.

"Mr. Sabat—before the others come, I want to say one thing more." I saw Father Liu looking at me and it wasn't a Machiavellian look at all.

"Go ahead."

"I said we could afford the credits. But what we ended up paying..." He looked down at the table. "If I didn't know Otto Zeller as well as I do—hadn't known that he would have—"

"That he was a hero?" I finished for him. "That he did his job and he was not afraid to get killed for something he believed in?" "Yes, I would say that about covers it," he agreed.

We were silent again until Heth Andrew walked into the room, followed by Steed and Hermradon. The prince seemed much subdued as he thanked Father Liu. Maybe he wasn't looking forward to meeting his father—and who could blame him after all that had happened? His life on Hithia wouldn't be worth much, whether the colony became Christian or not.

And then I realized it would. Hithia, Father Liu was telling us, had made one hell of an agreement with Lost Rythar. The autarch's throne had been tottering for some time, not because of palace intrigues but because the nobles, Hithia's original rulers, didn't like the idea of centralized authority. Originally there had been a sort of canton system, slowly eroded by wars and plots and dynastic marriages, but looked back to now with a certain nostalgia by the citizens.

And Hermradon, more interested in his own concerns than in ruling the colony, would have gladly let things go back to the old way. In short, he had a fine sense of justice and no particular desire to be autarch.

No wonder his father and his aunt had decided he must die. And no wonder, to placate the nobles, they had to make elaborate arrangements for his rescue when he got into trouble. And then there was Lost Rythar, quietly offering a helping hand—as a special favor to the Star Brothers, of course. And such innocents they seemed, those overly pious giants. Such simple folk—

"It's pretty straightforward," Heth Andrew told me. "We back the nobles for an overthrow if anything happens to Hermradon. And if he outlives his father, things fall out as he decides."

"Heads, you win," I said. "And tails."

"But you forget, Eduardo," the Lost Rythan told me soberly. "If you hadn't been there in the cave with me—"

"He's right." Father Liu's brother had come over to us. "I would have had a hard time explaining things to the Quele if you hadn't been there for Tokot to claim."

I nodded slowly. "And you, I take it, work for the Star Brothers, too?"

"Sometimes. But I have responsibilities on my homeworld as well."

I moved over and gave him room on the settee. "I'm glad," I told him, "you didn't have to make those explanations."

"Imagine," he said, fishing about in his pockets for something to smoke, "not being able to tell a Nippon from an Asian National." "That's Quele," I said and caught him grinning at me.

"What will you do now, Mr. Sabat?" he asked. "After you have collected your fee?" I looked away.

"Will you go back to—Sachsen, isn't it?"

"I don't know."

"Eduardo," Heth Andrew said quietly, "there is something I think you should consider. About your status, I mean." He gestured toward the slave band.

I looked at him curiously. "No one's really cracked the codes yet. I'm probably safe enough."

"I know that. But they've done a lot of work back on earth in that place where your friend Mr. Steed was fixed up."

"What are you trying to say?" Something was twisting itself in my gut.

"He's saying they might be able to take that thing off," Steed told me. "The Africans are getting pretty good at stuff like that."

I had not seen him and Father Liu come up, but suddenly everyone seemed to be looking at me.

"We've been checking with them," the Star Brother said. "They owe us a favor or two—and we owe you far more than your fee could ever buy."

"But there is no guarantee," Heth Andrew added. "Only a very good chance."

My mouth went completely dry as one hand crept to the slave band. It didn't mean what it once would have, this purely physical freedom they offered me. I was already free—not because I could retreat to some inner citadel and certainly not because the door of death was always open. My freedom was of a different sort, not a denial but an affirmation. An affirmation of life, I think, and more.

But the thought that the band could never be activated was sweet to me. To have that hateful reminder gone forever from my flesh would still mean a lot even if it cost me an arm.

"It is a risk," Father Liu told me. "You might even die, though that is not very likely."

I nodded, running my fingers over the familiar smoothness.

"Perhaps you would like to think it over. To go away somewhere."

I looked at my hands. "I have a lot of things to think about," I said in a low voice. "I am just beginning to realize how many."

"I'd like to bring you to Lost Rythar," Heth Andrew said. "Someday. But I cannot return any time soon." He trailed off, slightly embarrassed.

"Someday," I said. "When things are better for you, I'd like to come."

"Meanwhile," Father Liu put in, "my brother was wondering if you would be willing to visit Temu Colony. Our family raises horses on a large estate. Who knows, you might even learn to ride one."

Beside me, Anthony Liu regarded me through a fragrant drift of smoke. "Plenty of space," he added. "I'll take you bear hunting if you like. Mr. Wolfbane too. But whenever you want to be alone—I mean really alone for as long as you like—well, the steppes go on just about forever."

I thought of that. Another world's sky, and the horses and the plains.

"Thank you," I said. "That would be fine."

ABOUT THE AUTHOR

Colleen Drippé has been producing fantasy and science fiction for quite a few years. Along with many short stories now being published as e-books, she is the author of six science fiction novels which can be found on Amazon.

OTHER BOOKS BY COLLEEN DRIPPÉ

Gelen
Sunrise on the Ice Wolf
Treelight
Vessel of Darkness
The Dawnstrikers
The Branded Ones
Sharan

House Avers
Recall

Frightliner & Other Tales of the Undead (with Karina Fabian)

Please leave a review on Amazon. Just 20 words about what you thought about the book helps readers who are considering the book and helps the author with Amazon ranking.

Made in the USA
Columbia, SC
28 October 2024

44894792R00126